A Jail with Feathers

Other Books by Virginia Castleman

Sara Lost and Found, Simon & Schuster
Strays, Archway Publishing
Erosion, Perfection Learning
Puppetbooks, Hearthsong
Mommi Watta—Spirit of the River, Heartland Publishing

A Jail with Feathers

VIRGINIA CASTLEMAN

ARCHWAY PUBLISHING

Archway Publishing books may be ordered through booksellers or by contacting:

Archway Publishing
1663 Liberty Drive
Bloomington, IN 47403
www.archwaypublishing.com
844-669-3957

Cover Design by Theodocia Swecker
teddy@teddyswecker.com

Interior Image Credit: Virginia Castleman

ISBN: 978-1-6657-0095-5 (sc)
ISBN: 978-1-6657-0096-2 (e)

Library of Congress Control Number: 2020925828

Print information available on the last page.

Archway Publishing rev. date: 6/25/2022

To my siblings, Glenda, Harv, and Eileen, my adoptive parents, Ken and Bebs, and my brother, Ken, who supported my need to find my roots. Ken is and always has been a pillar of strength. And to my precious sons, Michael, Adam, and Jon, who add a boundless depth of meaning to life, love, and joy.

A Jail with Feathers was not written alone, but with the patience and guidance of caring souls who diligently put up with reading, editing, letting me win at Scrabble, and encouraging me each step of the way, including Vicki Housel, Adrienne Tropp, Linda Peterson, Ph.D MN, Adam Johnson, *The Orphan Master's Son*, Jack Sevana, CEO, Sierra Tahoe Film Productions, Cheryl Carmado, Carol Purroy, Sharon St. George Owen, Tom Bakewell, Dottie Hansen, Mim Castleman, Deke Castleman, my Archway editors, and many other loving friends and family members who have so deeply touched my life.

Lastly, to J. Michael Nelson, MD. If you should ever by great fortune read this humble book, thank you, thank you, thank you from the center of my being for helping me and others find our voices.

1

SOMETIMES LIFE TAKES YOU PLACES YOU DON'T WANT TO GO. When that happens, things can get really confusing. Like today. It *feels* like a Wednesday draped over a shower rod, like a sheet waiting to dry. Turns out it's not just some Wednesday in September. It's not even Wednesday at all. Today is Monday. I only know that because it's the dreaded day our caseworker has picked my sister, Sara, and me up from Ben and Rachel Silverman's house to drag us to some other temporary foster home. No amount of hollering and crying can keep us there.

A blast of a horn brings me back to the car, Sara, Ruth Craig—our social worker—traffic, and the rain. Our social worker is still talking.

"It's out of my hands, Sara. The court's decision is final."

"You lied! You said you could talk to judges and tell them what was best for us."

Sara's got a right to be mad. Nobody likes being lied to, let alone tricked. It must be bad, whatever the news is, 'cause Sara hardly ever gets kicking mad, and right now she's kicking the caseworker's seat.

"You're right. I did say that, but it wasn't a lie, Sara. I've tried over and over to explain that what's good for one child might not be good for the other; we've talked about this."

I hear a long sigh and see her stretch her neck to look at Sara through the rearview mirror. Then she glances over at me. I wave my doll, Abby, back and forth in a fake plastic wave. Our caseworker's cheek rises up like one of Rachel Silverman's biscuits and cushions a forced smile. I can still smell the golden-brown biscuits in Abby's hair. I miss Rachel and Ben already. They were our favorite foster parents. Why did they have to be so old?

Sara crosses her arms tight against her chest. "The court might be out of your control, like you say, but you control the car, right?"

Our caseworker's smile collapses. "Yes, Sara. I control the car."

"And the turn signal, right?"

"Sara, please." Our caseworker changes lanes. I look out the window and up at the last exit I recognize and drift, dreamily, when my side of the car splits away and takes the exit that would have taken us back to Ben's—or, better yet, home. Sara and our caseworker talk on top of each other. Their voices grow muffled, like their mouths are full. I can still make out the words.

"If only it could be that easy, Sara, but where Anna is going is good for Anna. She needs help. What you're suggesting is called kidnapping, and I'm not about to break the law!"

"But I promised."

"Do you know how many promises I've made that I couldn't keep, not because I didn't want to but because I'm not the judge? You're only ten, Sara. These things are hard to understand, even for a grown-up."

Sara's voice rises to a high note. "I'm almost eleven. And you didn't just break a promise—you broke *my* promise that Anna and I would never get split up, and that's not fair!"

I look out through the drizzle of rain, at the trees whipping by, hoping to see a familiar sign or fence post or house, but I feel myself being sucked back into their side of the car. I grip the door handle to hold me and Abby back. I know some people find it strange that a girl my age clings to a doll, but Abby's all I could see to grab when we had to run away. Me, Sara, and Abby—we're like three lost sisters, or we were until the police found us.

The wind suddenly sucks in, instead of out, and I lose the battle of staying away from their horrible conversation.

"Anna, do you have anything you want to say?" Ruth Craig's voice takes a sharp left turn and drifts over the front seat toward me.

I twist my mind toward the front of the car, landing right back where I was not two minutes ago. I stare straight ahead, mouth clamped shut. Nothing I say changes anything, so why even say it? That's why I bite people, if you can call grown-ups people. Some of them are monsters.

I used to be able to talk as well as Sara. But that was before the thing I can't talk about happened. Now I'm too scared to talk about what I'm too scared to talk about, for fear of what would happen if I did. That includes telling Sara.

And yeah, I'm almost thirteen, but that doesn't stop me from sinking my teeth into someone when I can't get them to leave me alone. Sometimes, when I make a move to bite a grown-up, they jerk their arm away and say something stupid like, "Did someone forget to feed you?" as if my biting has anything to do with food. Get real. Oh, and by the way, someone *did* forget to feed me. Sara and I still eat pieces of paper towel when we get scared we won't have any food. I know people say stupid stuff like that because they're more scared of me than I am of them, and they're just trying to pretend they're not. But I'm two steps ahead of them. I could teach them a thing or two about being mean—if I wasn't so afraid to talk, that is.

I don't always bite. Only when I freeze, like that time my hands were tied, or when we had to escape from the cops and my feet grew cement shoes—which seems to happen a lot more often now that both Mama and Daddy are gone. I up and freeze when I think that a grown-up will grab at me, and when that happens, numbness takes over. Numb's that feeling that starts at my head and works down to my feet. Numb leaves me feeling trapped like a fly in a web, right before the spider races over, sinks its fangs into the prey, and wraps it up in a tight cocoon.

Daddy calls it a "cocoon of death" when a fly has met its taker. "No wings'll get 'em out of that mess," he'd say. Just thinking about Daddy gets me all choked up. It's been so long since I've seen him or heard him talk. He's right about the fly. Still, it seems kind of mean that something with wings can't get free, but a caterpillar who doesn't have wings gets to grow them in a cocoon and turn into a moth or beautiful butterfly. And it gets to not only fly away but also start all over again.

Sara's right. Life isn't fair.

I used to wish I had wings. Even now I'm wishing that very thing. If I had wings, I'd fly right out the window of this car and go anywhere but here. Well, almost anywhere. I would never go back to the place I can't talk about. But wishes are bubbles, and bubbles pop. Wishes aren't things with wings, and neither are people. Don't tell Mama that though. Just thinking about her brings stinging tears out of nowhere, and I brush them quickly so no one will see.

Mama says we have the makings of wings already on our backs. She calls them angel wings for angels in the making. When she first said it, we'd just raced back from the empty field that Mama calls a park, across from our house. She was bent against the wind and rain, walking toward home from the welfare office. We knew it was Mama by the plastic bag she had over her head to cover her hair. Plastic bags give a different sound to the rain, like what it must sound like when someone's typing a hundred words a minute on a keyboard.

I wish I could type a hundred words a minute. I wish I could type, period, but that would mean I'd have a computer and someone to teach me. Mama and Daddy don't type. Daddy says Mama doesn't type because computers don't have a font for sarcasm. I don't know what a font is, but I do know what sarcasm is, and Mama didn't like what he said. She told him he doesn't type because keyboards aren't drums. Some people measure time by clocks. Daddy measures time by the measured beats of a rhythm. Sometimes I find myself bobbing my head to Daddy's beats when he pounds invisible drumsticks against the air. Daddy can make anything seem real.

On that wet, wet Tuesday, when we got back in the house and dried off, Mama had Sara and me raise our elbows up shoulder high with one fist facing the other and then stretch our arms back, just like people do when they do those stretching exercises. When we did this,

Mama pinched the two bones that stuck out on our backs as proof that what she was saying about us having the makings of wings was true. She told us that the budding bumps would sprout into beautiful angel wings when we got to heaven. But when I asked her why bad people had budding wings too and not just angels in the making, her eyes went blank and rivers of black eye makeup from being out in the rain rolled down her cheeks, turning her face into a big, ugly spiderweb. I couldn't look at her. Don't get me wrong. Mama can be pretty. But that day, she looked scarier than a circus clown. I hate clowns. She rolled her eyes to the sky, like the answer was floating around somewhere up there.

Mama never did come up with an answer. Sara told me later that when she looks up like that, she's looking to God for answers. Sara also said she thinks bad people have the start of wings like everyone else, but because they do bad things, their wings never grow. "Like Pinocchio's nose, only different," she explained. Sara's answers make total sense, but sometimes they make me afraid.

I do bad things. Does that mean my wings won't grow? And even if they do, what if I'm like a butterfly in the rain? What good are wings if you can't fly? Chickens have wings and can only fly four feet, if even that. That's probably why we eat so many of them. They can't get away. Mama once said freedom has wings, but I'm starting to think it doesn't. Just ask that fly.

Oh, wait.

You can't.

It's dead.

Right now, I'm the one wrapped up, only I'm not in a spider's web, and I'm no mummy. I am, however, being held down by a stupid seat belt. I don't like being held down, especially after that thing that happened that I can't talk about. We've been driving for*ever*, but when Sara complains, Ruth Craig, our caseworker, says forever isn't on any clocks she has ever seen and it's been only forty-five minutes.

"Come back to us, Anna!" the caseworker calls out. "Anna!" She slaps her hand on the dashboard, and the snap of it makes me jump, cinching the seat belt even tighter around my stomach and chest. Alarmed, I look to see what all the noise is about.

"There you are! Welcome back." Ruth again grins at the mirror, turning it slightly toward me. "Where'd you go this time, Anna?"

I want to say that I turned where we were supposed to turn, but when I open my mouth to talk, nothing comes out.

"I'm not done being mad," Sara snaps, kicking the back of the seat. "I might never be done being mad. I might be mad at you for the rest of my life!"

"It's a temporary arrangement, Sara."

"Yeah, well *we* aren't temporary, are we, Anna?" She looks at me, eyes wild, bumping her chin up against the air a couple of times like she wants me to shout something, too, then looking all mad at me when I don't.

The car swerves sharply into the right lane, rolls off a new exit I haven't seen before, and within minutes, heads toward a parking area. I have my first real clue that something's very wrong when our social worker yanks up on the parking brake like it's a weed that won't let go of the ground. I glance at Sara, who rips off her seat belt and wildly kicks at the door, yelling something to me I can't make out. That right there is the second clue that something really awful is about to happen. I try to think of a good next move, but I'm still frozen in that numb place, unable to think, or kick, or talk. Our caseworker jumps out into the rain and grabs my sister's arm, blocking her door so she can't up and run away again. The cold wind hits me full force, and a whole heap of whys bounce back and forth in my head.

Why are we stopping? Why is Sara so mad? *And why is our caseworker kidnapping my sister?*

Sara reaches back into the car with her free hand and grips my arm. I lean toward her with my ear pressed against my arm as I stretch. Her hand slides down to my fingers and then pops off at the ends, making the very same *thoop, thoop, thoop* I hear when I pull off my doll's arms and legs.

I want to scream like Sara's screaming. I want to run, like she's trying to do. But I can't scream. I can't run. I can't even move. Numb won't let me. Numb takes every feeling in me and turns it into something squishy like dough. But numb isn't just a sticky trap for feelings.

Numb's that other place where yells aren't so loud anymore. That dazed place where pounding rain can suddenly feel like a million feather-light caterpillars crawling all over my skin. Numb is that white, absent-of-color space where brittle cold turns into rippling chills.

Numb is that crossroads place where fear meets who cares, no matter which way I turn. And it's a holding place, where feelings inside and out push and tug at each other in slow motion, not wanting to come or go, until I finally just give in and float to somewhere in my head that makes me feels less afraid—or at least safer than this place is feeling.

Today didn't start out numb, but I learned long ago that a day can go from bear hug goodbyes to complete chaos in a click of a turn signal.

"This the one?" a man shouts, and our caseworker nods her head wildly like a bee got in her hair. A gust of wind slaps the cold rain against my arm when my side of the car is opened. A hand reaches in and grips my shoulder. Then the other hand grips my arm and starts pulling me out into the storm, scarin' me more'n I've ever been scared, except on that day I can't talk about.

Sara's voice cuts through the buzz of people who have appeared from nowhere. They block my view.

"Sara!" I reach for her.

"Run, Anna! *Run!*"

2

PANIC OOZES THROUGH EVERY PORE OF MY SCARED SELF, and I freeze. Sara's warnings get harder and harder to hear. Through the side of my eye, I can see her mouth open and close like a fish. Mrs. Craig clamps her arms around Sara's shoulders, gripping her hands so tight around her own wrists that her knuckles turn white. I don't get it. *Why is our caseworker stealing my sister?*

Run, Anna! Run! Her last words race through my mind. But right now, my thoughts are glued to the hairy, wet wrist my mouth is wrapped around. His salty, coconutty skin doesn't taste like anyone I know. I don't like the feel of the hair on his arms poking my lips, but I still hold on. Whoever it is, he's wearing rubber gloves. They smell thick and pasty, like wet baby powder.

I bite when I'm scared or mad or cornered. Right now, I'm all three. I'm scared of the person connected to the arm and afraid to hear why he has grabbed me. I'm mad at Ruth Craig for holding Sara so tight that she can't break free to help me, and I'm cornered by Numb, who's taken me over and won't let me move, just like—

I push the thought away.

"Run, Anna!"

Let go of her! I shout in my head.

What is this place? I try to look around, but it's hard to turn your head to look at something when your teeth are locked onto an arm. I grip Abby and search as far as my eyes will roll for Sara.

Sara Rose Olson.

She's being torn away, like a flower being ripped from the dirt it was so loosely planted in, and I can't do anything to stop them, leaving a hole in my heart so big I feel sure it, too, will rip into two.

Think, Anna. Think.

Mama pops into my thoughts, maybe because Sara's face is red like Mama's name: Rose. The word is like a release, and just like the flower's name says, I lift and float away from this place, looking down on all of us, searching for Mama in the rain. I can see rows of flowers along the wall surrounding the place.

"Every girl on my side of the family is named after a flower," Mama once told me, including Aunt Daisy, cousin Dahlia, cousin Violet, Grandma Camellia, Great-Aunt Juniper, Aunt Lily … I can't remember all of them. Most live somewhere in the Midwest, and we live here in Nevada, so it's not like I ever see them. I'm the only one without a flower in my name.

I float up and up, till Sara looks like a button on Mama's dress—the one she was wearing when she left and never came back. Mama should have named us after Nevada flowers, like sage, desert marigold, or bearpaw poppy. Ben says there's even a flower that's a weird kind a dandelion called a hairy cat's ear. I guess I should be glad Mama didn't know about that one.

Ben told us that Native American tribes give their babies names related to a greater whole—he called them "us" names, not the "me" kind we're all stuck with. They do that to teach and remind kids to help others and "make the world a nice place for *their* children—like payink love forward," he had added, saying *k* instead of *g* like he always did.

I float higher.

He also told us that some Native Americans were named after things like animals or flowers or were given names like Running Bull and Flying Eagle. I wonder what the Native Americans would have named me. Right now, Scared Rabbit fits, but who would want that name?

My name's just plain Anna. Anna Olson. Which is—

Run!

Like our caseworker clapping her hand on the dash, Sara's scream slams me back to earth. "I can't!" I want to yell, but since my teeth are still sunken into the hairy-armed man, what comes out of me is more like an angry growl. I press harder and feel a sudden give—like my teeth have broken through the skin of a grape. Everything is happening so fast. A weird sound comes out of the man. I stare down my nose. The lip of the white rubber glove turns pink.

Another arm appears out of nowhere, and the hand connected to it reaches under my chin and grabs hold of my cheeks, way back by my ears, and presses hard against my back teeth, forcing them open. I freeze. Someone else once grabbed me like that.

When my mouth opens, Hairy-Arm pulls free. He races toward the door of the building and disappears. The guy pinching my cheeks stops pinching and grabs my arm before I can take off running.

Numb creeps over my face. It hurts to breathe. A familiar pounding inside me lets me know The Inside Girl is trying to get out again. She showed up right after that thing I can't talk about happened. Doesn't she get it? *They'll hurt her. It's not safe!*

Wrapping my free arm tightly around my stomach, I try to tell her, *Don't worry. They won't harm you. I won't let them.* I roll my head around, looking over my shoulder for Sara. The numbness spreads toward my feet again. Sara fades into a cloud of white. I fight and fight, trying to get my eyes to focus, but just like that, my world turns into a blanket of wet white cotton.

"Breathe!" shouts a faraway voice. It must be The Inside Girl.

"Anna!" Sara's last cry cuts through the wall of fog before getting chopped off by the slam of a car door. I know that sound well. I know it because of all the times Sara and I have ridden in Ruth Craig's car, moving from one temporary home to another. It's the sound that final must feel like. I don't like that sound. I don't like it one bit.

Squinting, I can see Sara's face through the glass. Everything starts to blur. She gets the car window down and stretches her arms toward me. I try to reach out to her, but an octopus of arms grabs at me. Everyone is talking at once.

The numbness starts to wear off. I fight, kicking and clawing as hard and angry as Tig is kicking and clawing inside me. People all around shout orders. "Grab!" "Go!" "Hold!" "Watch out!"

A hand grips my arm, and I turn my head toward it to bite, but then something pulls my attention away. Someone is rubbing my other arm with something colder and wetter than the rain. What follows is a sharp pinch.

"Ow!" A bee stings me. Can bees fly in the rain?

My head falls back. My bones start to melt. And just like that, I go limp.

The last thing I see through a rip in the fog is my arm dangling at my side. My head bumps loosely back and forth against someone's arms. I try but can't move to bite it.

There's only one thing that could have happened. They didn't kidnap Sara.

They kidnapped me. Only I'm not me anymore.

I'm stiff.

Empty-headed.

Oh, no!

Am I Abby?

Did I turn into my doll?

"That's silly!" I hear Tig say through the fog. "People don't turn into toys."

It's a relief to hear Tig's voice. It means she's okay. She made it through whatever this is, but that doesn't mean I don't feel stiff, like Abby must feel. Or empty. Or totally out of control.

I WATCH AS THE FAT-CHEEKED FOG PARTS ITS THICK LIPS AND swallows Sara's screams. The relentless rain that at first pricked at my skin now taps lightly against it like those feather-light caterpillars crawling over my arms, letting me know I'm slipping further away. Everything moves sluggishly slowly, and muffled voices sound like burbling water. I'm in that middle place between here and wherever the new there ends up being.

My legs flop this way and that. I have no control. I try to stiffen my knees, but instead they buckle, and I land on something rigid, hard, and unbending, forcing my stiff legs to crack at the knees. My eyelids barely open. A roll of thunder rumbles under me. The rumble travels up my legs and jiggles my butt. My head bobs up and down. Shapes and fleeting voices flit past. I try to focus, but nothing works right.

Suddenly everything stops, and I rise up, like Mama once said Jesus did. A white cloud drifts above, then floats down over my face, and while *I* might have risen, *my body* is suddenly flat, and my eyelids snap shut, just like Abby's do, lying down, and just as quickly, white spots dot the ink-black sky.

It's in the darkness you see the light.

Ben told us that. He said the dark he was talking about "doesn't have to mean somethink bad." He said it could just be something we didn't know or understand. And right now, it's both. I don't know what's happening, and I don't understand why Sara and I can't be with Ben and Rachel and not here. Not separated either. *Where—Sara—why—why—*

I can't think of answers because right now I'm falling—

down,

down,

down …

a long, dark hole and can't stop. I try to fight it, but finally just let go and

float …

like a feather

down …

I try to force my eyes to open, but they won't.

Help! Can't see!

Down.

Can't move.

Down—

Can't—

Where do you land when there is no bottom?

AND WHAT IS THAT HORRIBLE TAPPING ON MY FOOT? *Stop! Go away! Don't touch me!*

My mouth twitches, and I shiver. My skin grows warmer and warmer as hot blood rushes through my veins. I know I'm turning back to the old me, because I want to bite whatever keeps tapping my foot, but my mouth isn't working. Since that bee sting, nothing moves as fast as I want it to.

Stop tapping me!

"Anna. Anna. Wake up! Wake up, sweetheart. Wake up!"

The woman's voice won't stop yapping. I don't recognize it. How does she know my name? Who is she? Where am I?

"Wake up, Anna. That's it. Open your eyes."

I try to focus. The shadows around me slowly take shape. The box they've buried me in is not only fog white but cold and deep. My face is at least a whole person's length away from the lid. They've stuffed me in a big, empty milk carton.

"Anna. You're going to feel a little drowsy. We had to give you a sedative, honey, to calm you down."

Sedative?

Suddenly, I don't feel numb or stiff anymore, but I don't feel all back to me either. I'm stuck in that in between place where everything just kind of mixes together—that swirly place where the ceiling goes round and round. I close my eyes and open them again to see if anything changes. It doesn't.

I still can't get my mouth to work. My tongue feels even thicker and lazier than before. The sound coming out of me is muffled and bubbly, like I'm under water. Maybe the carton they've put me in isn't empty after all. I flap my arms and try to swim to the surface.

Sara and I used to talk underwater in the bathtub at Ben and Rachel's. Maybe this white carton is full of milk!

Let me out! I can't breathe. I can't breathe. My lungs burn from holding my breath.

"Hey, hey, hey. Easy there. Deep breaths, Anna. You're going to be okay," a woman's soothing voice says close to my ear, but nothing about what's happening right now feels soothing.

An arm comes toward me. Is it mine? I bite it to see if I feel any pain. A shriek fills the room, scaring away any thoughts I try to hold on to. I screeched like that once before when I fell into another nightmare. Only, it turned out not to be a nightmare but a real, happening thing. I fight the memory, not wanting to go back to that horrid pink house, but this time, even kicking and thrashing, I can't keep the memory away. My fuzzy mind won't let me hold back any more thoughts—even the horrible ones.

"Go away!" I shout, but the memory keeps coming back, again and again, like a fly bobbing against a window. I kick and thrash, trying to get it—trying to get him—away.

His breath reeks of stale cigarette smoke and sour beer. His bony knee digs into my chest, pinning me against the couch. I can't move. I can't breathe. When I try to shout for Sara, a sick sneer sweeps across his face.

"She can't help you. 'Member? She ain't here. It's just you 'n' me." He eases up on my chest.

I breathe so hard I almost pass out. He's right. Sara's not here. I try to remember where the caseworker took her and why she didn't take me too.

"You're hurting me." I kick and fight him.

He sucks hard on his cigarette and sends a new puff of smoke in my face with each raspy laugh, making me cough, scaring any and every word right out of me.

Before I can do anything, he grabs my right arm and forces it over my head and presses the burning end of the cigarette into my skin. A thread of my hair catches fire and twizzles to ash. The smell of burned skin and hair reaches my nose, forcing me to hold my breath. He touches the burning end of the cigarette to my skin again.

I turn my head toward the pain. The skin on my arm bubbles, making tiny sizzling noises close to my ear. My screams turn to a razor-sharp wheeze. Starting from my head and working down to my feet, I go numb, until I can't feel anything anymore. Not even his boney knee pressing into me.

"You want to wet the bed?" he seethes. "How 'bout I burn a little reminder or two into you every time you pee where you ain't sposed to pee? Will that jar your memory on where you're supposed to go?"

I thrash my head side to side, listening to the frantic sound of it rubbing against the cushion, stare at the ceiling, and float up and away—from me. From him. From the pain.

His last words still linger in my ears. "You say anything 'bout this to anyone, and I'll burn more than your arm. You hear me?" He pinches my cheeks, forcing my mouth open. I can feel the heat of the cigarette close to my lips. "I'll burn that tongue right out of you so you can't talk no more. You want that?"

I shake my head as hard as I can with his hand still pinching my cheeks, all the while whimpering. A yelp leaps out of me when a piece of ash floats down and settles on my bottom lip.

The pinprick of pain was enough of a reminder of what would happen if I talked. He didn't need to worry. I wasn't going to say a word. No way was I going to let him burn out my tongue.

5

I wasn't a bed wetter before I had to go to that horrible pink house with that awful man, but I am now. I don't know why I just can't hold it when I'm having a bad dream, or when I'm sad or scared, or when I get nervous. But even when he burned me over and over to make me stop, I couldn't. Burning me made it worse. By the time I was taken out of that temporary home, he had burned me nine times, branding the letter P into my arm, leaving an even deeper burn mark inside of me.

I shake the memory away and focus on the new nightmare I've landed in. It turns out the cry I'm hearing is not coming from me after all. It's coming out of the lady who was thumping on my foot.

"Kurt! Help!" Her voice turns thin and shaky.

The fog lifts a little. I start to make out the fuzzy outline of a person at the other end of the arm stretched toward me. She's wearing a white smock. I turn my eyes down and see that her arm is in my mouth. I quickly let go. She tastes the way flowers smell.

"What the—" A big man comes up behind her, scaring me. It's the same man who pulled me out of the car. I kick against the tight sheets, trying to get away from him. Together, they hold me down. He stays at my head. She goes to my feet. I whip my head back and forth, but my teeth can't reach either of them.

"Let go!" I snarl, but my words sound more like a growl. When that awful man burned me, he took my words away. The few I had left grew teeth.

The big man shifts his position to better grip my other arm. I start feeling dizzy, then light-headed. The room won't stop turning. I roll my eyes down and see his hand gripping my arm.

"Look, you …" The big man snarls.

I saw a dog cornering a cat once that looked like he does right now—the same drawn-up lips, same wild look in his eyes.

"Her name is Anna," another lady in a white smock says firmly, coming up behind the mean man.

"I don't care if her name is Miss Looney Tunes," he lashes out. "You don't bite; you hear me?"

"I do hear you!" I want to shout. But all I can manage is to roll my eyes to one side, searching the big white box they've put me in for some sign of Sara.

"Sis," I finally manage to get out, surprising myself.

"Your sister's not here," the big man snaps. The lady who's been holding my feet down lets them go and pats his arm. She quickly wraps a bandage around her arm. It's white and airy, just like the one the big man has around his wrist.

My head is still all cottony, but I can see them just fine.

"We better get shots. For all we know, she has rabies," the mean man tells the lady.

"Kurt! Careful. She can *hear* you," she scolds under her breath.

"I'm not so sure of that," he answers, heading for the door. "What is she? Autistic?"

"I don't think so." She forms a word with her lips, without saying it out loud, but I have eyes. I can read her lips. She follows it with "is the word I got when they called about bringing her in."

"*Disturbed?* Ha! Damaged is more like it." Clearly Kurt can't keep secrets, so mouthing stuff to him is useless.

"Kurt, please. I'm telling you, *she can hear you*," she whispers hoarsely, pointing to her own ears.

The mean man takes another look at me, rolls both his eyes from one shoulder to the other, and then leaves in an exaggerated show of disgust.

"Sorry," I try to tell the lady, but she's busy writing on a piece of paper clipped onto a board. I'm not sure what I'm sorry for, but grown-ups usually act nicer when you say it.

I listen to the pen scratching out words. The sound reminds me of rats scratching on the hardwood floor at our old house.

A hot tear rolls down my cheek and disappears into the pillow. I don't know where it came from, but I do know that right before it rolled down my face, I was thinking of home and Hope, the rat that Sara and I buried just a few days ago, before the police found us.

Now I'm in a box, and like Hope, I'm being buried.

Only unlike Hope ...

I'm still alive.

6

Another hand touches me. I snap my head around, lips drawn tight, with my teeth fully prepared to do what they do best. Even though the words that are attached to the person gripping me sound friendly, I don't like being touched. And I especially don't like when someone grabs me and holds me down. I fight and fight, pulling and tugging, like an animal in one of Ben Silverman's stories, but no amount of trying gets me free.

Exhausted, I fall back on the pillow. The Inside Girl cries and cries. I wet the bed. It doesn't take long for the smell to reach the surface.

What would Sara do? She'd talk to me, that's what. That's what I have to do. Talk to The Inside Girl. *It's going to be okay,* I think-talk to her, saying what Sara always used to tell me, but I know words can break. Sara promised that we would never get split up, but we did, and when we did, Terrible Ted burned me. I know it's not Sara's fault. She meant her words and thought that was enough.

I don't like this place, wherever it is. It's colder than I am, and I was pretty cold to start. The noises in here are hollow and far off. I should have listened when Sara was yelling at our social worker. I bet this is what she was shouting about. She knew they were going to take me and stuff me in here. I wipe my nose on the sheet. Sara just has to be here. She just has to be. She probably waited until the car stopped at a stop sign and jumped out. She's fast, so there's no way Ruth Craig would have caught her. She's probably hiding in another room, waiting for the perfect time to run in and get me. She's planning our escape. I just know it.

Thinking about Sara hiding someplace close makes me feel better. I already miss her, just like I miss Ben and Rachel Silverman. Sara and I went to the Silvermans' when everything turned upside down at home, and their house smelled good, and the beds were soft, and there were two people who liked both of us.

Sara's easy to like. She got picked over me at the orphanage before they closed the thing down and opened these new places, called cottages. But now I'm locked up in this stupid milk carton with no way out.

I try to remember what day it is, but days have mashed together like thunderclouds, leaving one giant clash of awfulness hanging over me.

"Where'm I?" I blurt to a woman still standing in the room. I roll my head around, look at the bare walls, and try to sit up.

"Well, good morning, Anna. I'm Emily, one of the staff here at Maple View Center. We are a residential treatment center, or you can call it RTC like most of the residents do. You came in yesterday afternoon. Wow! What a night you've had."

I try to wrap my foggy thoughts around her words, but the one that gets my heart beating faster is "residential."

"Don't live here," I snap, attempting again to sit up, but the sheets around me are tucked in tight, holding me down. The bottom sheet is icy wet. I move my legs to try to get away from the cold pee soaking it.

Why am I in residential treatment center? I'm not the only one terrified. My thoughts are scared too. Daddy had to go to a treatment center once for his drinking, but he called it rehab. He said rehab was "a jail with feathers." Is a residential treatment center like rehab? I look around. I don't see even one feather.

"Anna, relax. A residential treatment center isn't just about getting people a place to stay. You're safe here."

"Safe?" Is she crazy? I look down at the sheet wrapping me up like some giant spider cocooned me and back at her.

Her hazel eyes widen. "Are the sheets too tight? I can loosen them. Do you remember that you bit me?"

She loosens the sheet, and a new wave of pee smell escapes from under them. She crinkles her nose, then holds up her arms, fingers spread, like she's getting arrested. I stare at the bloodstain on the bandage. It has turned brown. I frown, confused. Why is the bloodstain shaped like Sneaker?

"Cat." I pull my arms out from under the sheets and narrow my eyes at her questioning face. But to my surprise, her eyebrows suddenly shoot up, and a quick smile crinkles the skin around her eyes.

"Well, well! What a small world we live in! You know Kat? Is she from your neighborhood? She's in group right now, but if you want, I can let her know you're here."

I frown. Wait a minute. They have cats here? *They put cats in groups?* I look around. Where did they *really* take me? What if this place isn't a residential treatment center at all but some freaky shelter for crazy people and animals they conduct experiments on? I hold up my hand and stare at it, trying to focus, since my head is still fuzzy from the medicine they gave me. I look to see if even one finger has started to change shape, grow hair, or do anything even slightly weird. But no matter how hard I stare, my hand doesn't change.

Relieved that I'm still human, I turn my attention back to her. I look around to see if they've trapped Sara in here too, hoping deep down that they have. I don't want to be in here alone. My head throbs something fierce.

The wall to my right suddenly lets out a raspy, low, humming sound, like a saw cutting through wood. I jump and grab at the sheets. Is someone sawing the wall down? My mind flashes to the time Daddy had to ax a door down to get to me and Sara before Mama could send us to Jesus. But this noise is different. The hum is followed by a loud click. I snap my head and lock eyes on the door. My breath comes out short and fast, like I've just run a race. I clutch the sheet tighter under my chin.

7

"It's okay, Anna. You're hearing the door unlock," the Emily lady assures me. "This place has a lot of noises to get used to, but you will. Don't worry."

Something heavy clanks and pushes against the door. A man appears. I recognize him as the mean one who grabbed me out of the car and grip the sheet tighter. Turns out he's not coming in to grab me this time. He's bringing food.

Careful, Anna. I hear Daddy's voice in my head. Daddy says people who are mean, then nice can turn back to being mean as fast as a woman can change her mind. "You can't trust them," Daddy warned us. I wasn't sure if he meant women or mean people but decided he meant everyone. And actually, not trusting anyone is easier than all this trying to sort out who you can and can't trust.

The mean one sets the tray on a side table, never saying a word, then turns and leaves, rolling the cart out with him. My mouth comes alive at the smell of food and fills up with spit. I swallow.

"Oh, good. Breakfast!" the Emily lady chirps.

"Not hungry!" I lie. "They'll trick you with food," Daddy once told us. *They*, he reminded us, could be anyone.

Emily pulls a metal lid off a plate and sets it aside with a *thunk*.

I stare at the toast, eggs, sausage patty, and juice, and a new waterfall of spit slides down my throat.

"Haven't you ever heard the saying, 'Don't look a gift horse in the mouth'?" she says, smiling slightly.

"No," I answer quickly, and anyway, who says that? Don't look a gift horse in the mouth? What does that even mean?

"It's a proverb—" She stops and stares at me, like she's looking for that hidden mark on my body. I pull the sheet up tighter around my chin, hiding as much of me as I can.

What's a proverb? I wonder.

"A proverb is a story with a lesson," she says, jumping in my head and reading my thoughts.

Now I'm the one doing the staring. How can she read what I'm thinking?

I hurriedly look away, all the while trying not to think of anything so she can't read any more thoughts. But it's hard not to think of anything. Mama always said her mind could go blank in the blink of an eye, so she must have learned how to tune out thoughts, but not me. My mind is never blank.

"Long ago, people gave horses as gifts," the Emily lady continues, "and it was rude to look in the horse's mouth to check its teeth to see if the horse was healthy as a way of determining if the gift was acceptable."

Even with an explanation, it still seems like a strange saying. For one, I didn't get a horse for a gift, and I wouldn't look it in the mouth even if I did, but I don't say anything. Instead, I focus on the food. Her little proverb did remind me of a story Ben once told me and Sara about a different kind of gift horse. He said the story took place a long, long time ago in an ancient city called Troy that was off the coast of Turkey.

I remember liking that it was going to be a story about horses and turkeys, but it turned out that while the story had to do with a horse, there wasn't one turkey in it. Turkey is a country. Who names a country after a bird? Who names a country, period? I forgot to ask Ben after he told the story, so I never did find out the answers.

Ben said Troy was a small city, but the Trojan people—that's the people from Troy—had built high walls around it. "Twenty feet up, the walls went!" Ben exclaimed, pointing to a wall in our room. "That's like three of your walls up, up, up—" He arched his fingers and pressed them against the air, one after the other as if he were climbing something.

Sara and I had tipped our heads all the way back to imagine such a wall.

Ben said the walls had tall gates and that the city of Troy was also protected by Trojan warriors who fired arrows down at any Greeks who tried to break through.

"For ten years, the Greeks tried to bring down the wall," he said, "but through the gates they couldn't get."

He then shared how some Greek general named Odysseus got the idea to build a big horse and leave it by the front gate to the city, figuring something like that would be hard to ignore.

"The Trojans, they saw the Greeks wheel to the gate this big horse and then scurry off, as if they had no fight in them left. And when the Trojans were sure the Greeks were gone, they opened the gates, cheerink and admirink the great horse, which into their little city they wheeled. To them it was from the Greeks an apology gift for all those years of attackink them."

I smile, remembering how Ben's accent got thicker the more excited he got, and how he mixed up his words even more than usual.

"And what do you suppose happened next?" he'd asked.

Sara guessed that they gave the horse a name and took turns riding it.

I didn't have a good guess, other than they might have started fighting over it, but Ben said, "To bed they went."

"They went to bed?" Sara and I looked at each other, both wondering how anyone could go to sleep with a giant present like a horse right there waiting for them.

"Yes, but while they slept, men inside the wooden horse hidink climbed out, opened the gate, and let the Greek army in. And that is how they overtook Troy!"

Guess they should have looked that *gift horse in the mouth*, I think, feeling smug at using the Emily lady's weird expression to finish my thought about Ben's story. Could I do something like that? Could I find a box that they take in and out of here and climb into it and escape? A coffin pops into my head, and I push the thought of it away, not that I'm not dying to get out of here. Daddy once said some prisoners escaped from the jail he was in by hiding in a big laundry bin.

"The laundry services wheeled them out, threw the bin in the truck, and drove off, never knowing they were freeing prisoners!"

I turn my attention back to the Emily lady, wondering if this place has laundry bins. She leans closer, which makes me press my head harder into my pillow. "Tell you what, Anna. If you eat your breakfast, I'll round up some books for you," she whispers, smiling secretly, like she can read my wants, too, and not just my thoughts.

My breathing comes faster, no matter how hard I try to keep it slow. How does she know I like books? Could Ben have called and told them? Is that how she knew? That would mean Ben knows I'm here.

8

MY THOUGHTS BRIGHTEN AT THE THOUGHT OF BEN SHOWing up, sending a wave of warm through me. If that's all true, it would mean that Ben might come and save me!

"What kind of books do you like?"

At the mention of the word *books*, my teeth start to quiver and drop open like a drawbridge, as if the very word *books* was the key to unlocking my resistance. I know Daddy wouldn't be happy with me right now because I let her bribe me with food *and* a favorite word to get me to eat the food. But I can't help it. I have no pieces of paper towels left to trick my stomach into feeling like it's been fed. I'm hungry.

My lips close around the warm, spicy breakfast sausage. It tastes much better than any salty arm I've ever bit into.

"Ben's," I answer through the food I'm chewing, remembering his Magic Journey book with its blank pages, and all the nights he read to us from it.

"Bends?" She frowns. Then her face brightens. "You must mean twists and bends in the road? I get it! You like adventures! I'll see what I can come up with."

I frown, wondering what Ben had to do with twisted roads, but I'm learning in life that sometimes it's better not to question someone's answers but just to nod, so I do just that.

"In the meantime," she chirps, "we weren't able to check you in yesterday. So, after you eat, grab a shower and—" While she's talking, the wall hums, and the door clicks again. I jump at the sounds.

"You can meet me up front," she finishes.

"Whoa, whoa, whoa!" a voice interjects. The mean guy Kurt pokes his head around the door. "Em, Em, Em!" He lowers his voice with each "Em," landing on a gruff whisper. "Hotheaded vampires stay in cool-down rooms." He mouths the word *vampires*, but I can still tell what he's saying. I'm guessing *vampires* is his code word for me. Oh, wait. I get it. Biting. Blood. Vampires.

"I think that particular cool-down-room order was lifted," Emily challenges, shooting him a look that even I know means "Stuff a sock in it!" But that doesn't stop him.

"Look, she'd be in lockdown, not cool-down, if it wasn't already occupied."

"That might be true, but for now, she's in cool-down, and she'll need to get started on the program so she doesn't fall behind."

The mean Kurt shakes his head. "No, no, no. She bit two people, Emily. You and me. She needs to be transferred to lockdown as soon as it's available. We can't have her going around biting the residents; plus, if we give her a free pass, it gives the wrong message to the others."

"Yes, boss."

The Kurt guy's face turns red at Emily's words. I can't tell if it's from being embarrassed or being furious.

"Can you go check to be sure while I get her situated? She needs to shower and get dressed."

Hello! I wave my arms and shout, *She-as-in-me is right here,* but my mouth doesn't work, and it comes out sounding more like "Sheeee. Meeeee. Heeeee."

The Kurt guy looks at me, cheeks pinched up like he's in pain or he thinks I'm a germ he could catch, then spins around quickly to leave.

"Sorry, Anna, but he's probably right. You would have been put in lockdown if it had been available, and it's a lot worse than this. At least you have some furniture in here, and it's not just a cot and no windows.

"My point is we might have to keep you in the cool-down room until you show that you won't go around biting people."

I want to say, "How can I show anyone anything if I'm being locked up?" But I can't get the words out, and anyway, being in here by myself might be better than getting stuck in an empty room or put in a room full of people I don't even know—if they even *are* people. I eat the rest of my breakfast not saying another word, wondering about this new milk carton I'm now trapped in, where animals and people are caged together. And what about when they move me to a different area? Will people come into the building and up to where they've caged me? Will the sticker with my picture on it that they've attached to the door read:

Female. Almost thirteen.
Not good around kids.
Bite is worse than her
bark. Is not completely
housebroken.

The only good thing about that horrible thought is that maybe Ben would come in looking for a new kid to temporarily foster, and maybe he'd recognize me and take me home. Or maybe Sara would talk her new temporary foster parents into getting a pet, and they would take her here, and she would find me mixed in with whatever is out there. I try to picture what they're planning to turn me into in this experimental lab. I hope it's not a skunk, or a pig, or some mouse eater like a snake. Hopefully, it will be something in the cat family, maybe even a lioness cub or a leopard. Leopards are cool, though I'm sure I won't get a choice in the matter.

"Go ahead and shower. Put a fresh robe on, and we'll go across to the front and officially check you in and get you some different clothes."

While she talks, I look down at the robe. I wasn't wearing it when they locked me in this carton, so how did it get on me?

"I put the robe you're wearing on you last night, as the clothes you had on were rain soaked," the Emily lady says, reading my thoughts again.

I pull myself up to sitting position and wrap the robe I woke up in tighter around me, trying to make some sense of this place. It creeps me out that someone changed my clothes. I mean, did she see the burns? Did she guess what happened? Will Terrible Ted find me and burn my tongue out like he promised? I tremble at the thought.

"Once we get you processed and settled, you can start in the program. The sooner you start, the sooner you can get out of here," she adds.

Processed and settled? That's how cheese gets made. Ben Silverman taught us that. He said that ten gallons of milk make one pound of cheese. I'm ninety-eight pounds. How much milk would it take to make me into cheese? It's something to think about later. I tuck the thought away.

A loud voice comes in through the walls right as an alarm sounds. I jump.

"Code red. All staff. Code red. West wing. Two fourteen."

Emily leaps around to face me. "Oh, no. Not again. Hurry! We have to go outside, Anna. Make sure your robe is buttoned and follow me."

"Why?" As I start to get out of bed, I see that I peed on the robe, too, and try to cover up the yellow stain.

"Code red means fire, Anna. We have to leave—quickly."

"Fire?" I freeze.

"This is no time to stand still, Anna. We have to get out now just in case there really is a fire!"

But just the mention of fire chases the run right out of me, and I stay rooted to the spot. She presses a button on the wall and yells in a box for a wheelchair.

Seconds later, the big, mean Kurt guy wheels one into the room.

"She's panicking. We have to wheel her out."

"Why am I not surprised?" He lifts my stiff self up off the floor and plunks me onto the chair, while the Emily lady holds the door open. "She's wet!" he groans.

"I know, I know. We'll deal with that later." Emily grabs the blanket off the top of the bed and spreads it over my legs, tucking in the sides.

Mean Kurt then rolls me down a hallway, racing toward a ramp that leads down to the outside door. I look around, surprised to see that the others rushing out with us aren't wild animals at all. They're actual people—most of them older kids like me.

I'm also surprised to see something else: some of them are boys!

9

I sniff the air but don't smell smoke. Outside, I sniff again. I still don't smell smoke. Part of me is relieved. Thanks to Terrible Ted, just the thought of fire terrifies me, but part of me feels tricked. What's going on? Who did this and why?

It's chilly out, but the sun is shining so brightly that I squeeze my eyes shut. When I do, I can see the shapes of the trees behind my lids. I open them and blink a few times to get them used to the light. The ground is still damp. The air smells and feels clean, like it always does after a good rain. The fresh breeze clears my head.

In my mind, I picture Ben parked at the curb, waiting anxiously to get me, but when I open my eyes and scan the parking lot, Ben is nowhere to be found. If he was here, he would be shocked to see me in a stupid wheelchair. The thought reminds me of the time he was fixing a broken chair at his house.

"The leg you cut too short," Rachel tells him in her thick Russian accent. "It rocks."

"So, it is now a rockink chair," Ben tells her.

I throw my head back and laugh, just like Sara and I laughed that day. It feels good to laugh. Ben is so funny!

"This is not a joke!" Mean Kurt barks.

I tilt my head back and glare at him. A big, fake smile takes over his face, not for me but for all the people staring at him for snapping at me.

From where I sit, he looks like a clown. I hate clowns. They lie. They have great big smiles painted on their faces, but they aren't happy. I know because their eyes aren't smiling, and neither are Mean Kurt's eyes.

"This is not something to laugh about," he says again through clenched, fake-smiling teeth, like that look is going to fool anyone.

You don't know Ben, I want to tell him, because if he did, he would know that what Ben said was definitely something to laugh about.

"False alarm!" someone in the crowd shouts. By now, what looks like the whole residential treatment center has filled up the grassy area beside the parking area. I search the bushes and along the edges of the building for some sign of Sara. She's good at hiding, though, which might be why even I don't see her.

"Let me guess!" Mean Kurt calls out. "Justin pulled the alarm again."

The person he is calling out to nods.

"Someone needs to burn a message into that kid's brain before he really sets a fire," Mean Kurt mutters.

I stiffen. How can he say that? How could he even think that? Nobody should get anything burned into them. I'm scared to even look up at him again. What if he tries to burn a message into me? I've got to get out of here! I think hard and fast, but my brain just won't help me out. Why isn't Tig giving me the answer? What would Sara do? Maybe thinking like Sara will work better than trying to think on my own or wait for Tig.

She would run; that's what she would do. I pretend she's with me and bolt from the chair, dragging the blanket along with me, but Mean Kurt is on me before I can even reach the parking lot.

"I should just let you go," he seethes, close to my ear so no one will hear. "Oh, wait. You don't have anywhere to go, do you?" He drags me back and plunks me into the chair. His words sting. He's right. Where would I go?

"I'll take it from here, Kurt," Emily says, rushing over and gripping the handles on the wheelchair till her knuckles turn white. I look up at her. She frowns deeply, shaking her head at him.

He stomps off, and I look the other way and again search the area. The parked cars are impossible to see through, and I slump in the chair when I see no sign of Sara or Ben. Before long, a buzzer sounds, and everyone slowly heads back inside—everyone but the one kid called Justin. He's in the parking lot, surrounded by cops and a few staff members.

I turn my head just in time to catch his eye. His hair is a burnt orange with black tips. Could he have burned his own hair? Long arms dangle at his sides. They're an even match for his long legs. I catch his eye again and try to look away but can't. It's like he has some kind of hold on me.

A slow smile curls the edges of his mouth, but his stare is cold enough to send a shiver chasing through me. His eyes look like two dark holes stuck into his doughy, pale, freckled skin. Creepy doesn't even come close to describing him. It's like he sees right through me—like my fear of getting burned again is somehow written all over my face and he's spelling out my terror, one burnt letter at a time.

I wrap my arms tightly around my stomach. *He can't hurt you,* I assure Tig. *I will protect you. I won't let him, or anyone mean like him, near you.* It's the same thing I said to her when Terrible Ted burned my arm. Maybe I couldn't keep me safe, but I kept The Inside Girl safe so that she wouldn't have any scars burned into her.

I look back right as they pack Justin into the police car and haul him away, probably to a new "safe" place.

Jails. Crazy houses. Residential treatment centers. This town seems to be full of them—that and crazy people.

10

"GLAD IT WAS JUST A FALSE ALARM," THE EMILY LADY says. I tilt my head back but can't see her.

For a second, I think about just getting up and walking instead of being in the wheelchair, but then I remember that the robe has pee on it and change my mind.

Other kids stare at me as they pass. They drop their voices, but I still hear bits and pieces. "New kid." "Handicapped." "Freak job." "Mental case."

I want to shout at them that I can walk just fine and that I'm not a mental case, and even if I was, to stop staring at me and talking behind my back. Ben says some of the deafest people in life are the ones who can hear.

I take a moment to look around and take in the place I've been sentenced to—the jail with feathers. The walls are the color of celery. The floors are large white tiles covered with blue specks. When you look down the hall, it looks like a million bugs are crawling on the floor. That right there gives me the creeps. Every now and again, there are different colored tiles stuck in the mix. Red. Yellow. Green. Blue. Like someone laid them down to see if they would look good but then forgot to pick them up.

Quickly, I scan the place looking for some sign of Sara. My heart beats faster when a girl rounds the corner who kind of looks like her, and I even open my mouth to shout and get her attention, before realizing that it is not Sara. I flash on the time Sara and I were with our temporary foster mother, shopping for clothes, and Sara thought she saw Mama. She ran over to the lady and even hugged on her before it became clear that the woman she was hugging wasn't Mama but some total stranger.

I swallow hard just thinking about how sad Sara had been and force my own tears back. The Emily lady pushes me up behind two women. I can tell by their matching white shirts that they're staff members.

The talk in the halls is all about false alarm guy. The tall one reads from her cell phone: "About one in every four fires is purposefully set—and almost half of those are set by kids under eighteen."

"Arson is the last thing we need around here. I read somewhere that it's connected to animal cruelty and bedwetting," the shorter one, walking beside her, says.

I suck in my breath and cross my ankles under the damp robe. My breathing quickly turns to panting before I can stop it. But I can't be a fire starter. I'm not mean to animals.

So what if I wet the bed? That doesn't mean I'm going to go start fires. Does it? I don't want to set fires. But I don't want to wet the bed either. I can't seem to help that. Am I going to wake up one day and suddenly start setting fires and acting mean toward animals?

The panting makes me light-headed again. Heat creeps up my neck. I pull Abby apart. But that can't count. She's not even real. She's a doll.

Is this where it starts? Am I going to set fires next? I choke back the memory of almost suffocating that boy to death at a park near the last foster home we went to. He was making fun of me because I had a doll, and I got so mad. I just wanted him to stop making fun. Choking him is not something I'm proud of.

I try to make room for a happier thought, but instead, another bad one slips in.

Ben says humans are animals, so is what I did to that boy the same as being cruel to animals?

"Wonder if he'll end up in juvie," the taller staff person says, more like a statement than a question. She's still talking about that Justin kid who pulled the fire alarm.

"I don't care how old he is; they should put him behind bars. Arson is a serious crime. I hope nobody else in here is an arsonist." She glances over her shoulder at me and back to the other lady, and some kind of secret communication passes between them.

Arson. Arsonist. Arson. Arsonist. I say the words over and over in my head, shaping them in my mouth without parting my lips.

"Fortunately, it's males that generally start fires—not females—so I don't think we need to worry," the shorter one assures her, smiling thinly.

Ar-son. Our son. Mostly boys set fires. I feel a little better hearing that. And that the word is Ar-*son*. She clearly said Ar-*son*.

"So, what's the word on this one?" The taller lady has lowered her voice and makes a back-rocking motion with her thumb toward me.

The other staff member glances over her shoulder and sighs, casting Emily a sympathetic smile. In an equally low voice I can still hear, because there is nothing wrong with my hearing, she whispers, "It's hard to say just yet. They're going to run some tests to see if she's autistic, but that's usually detected long before a kid is twelve. She's almost thirteen. I hear she's a biter, though, so keep your arms and hands away from her."

"Really? Almost a teenager and she *bites*?"

"Welcome to the zoo." The tall one looks down at the shorter one. I see her raise her eyebrows and draw back her lips, showing her teeth, making a fake scared face.

Emily clears her throat loudly. They both straighten up, stifle their laughs, and turn down another hall.

"Anna, I'm sorry if you heard any of that," Emily says quietly. "We just hired some new staff, and they're not fully trained yet. Just ignore it and focus on getting better." She leads me to a room that has a table with paper on it—the kind they have in doctor's offices, and hands me a fresh, dry robe, then turns to close the door.

I think about what she said. "Not fully trained." Maybe *they* should be in RTC. Not me.

"Not my room," I remind her uneasily, unbuttoning the stained robe and grabbing the fresh one she's holding out for me.

"You are so right," Emily says, smiling warmly. "It's not your room; it's the clinic."

I turn around and put the fresh robe over my shoulders, then take my arms out of the soiled one and slip them in the new one, letting the soiled one fall to the floor, then button up the new robe.

"You can put the soiled robe in there. She points to a plastic container in the corner. We need to officially get you admitted, and step one is to check you over so we can check you in."

She faces me. "I need to get your vitals, then look at your skin for any piercings or tattoos. Okay?"

"No tatts," I say, gripping the robe tighter around me. I don't have any piercings either but keep my mouth shut. I don't like where this is going.

"It's just SPP, Anna. Standard processing procedure," she adds, like she's answering a question, even though I didn't ask one. There she goes again, getting in my head.

"Every boy and girl in RTC goes through this. You haven't been singled out. For starters, I'm going to take your blood pressure."

She wraps a wide cloth band around my arm and presses what must be sticky cloth to another patch of sticky cloth to hold it on, then squeezes a ball hanging from a tube. The band gets tighter and tighter.

"Ow!"

"I know, I know. Sorry. It'll be over in a sec."

She turns a nob by the ball, and the band slowly breathes out all the air it has been holding. She then rips it off my arm and grins.

"Well, there's definitely one thing very normal about you! Your blood pressure!"

I rub my arm.

"Oh, come on! That's a good thing." She has me stand down on the floor, pulls the robe away from my back, and then lets it fall onto my shoulders. "Okay, take out one arm, and after I've looked at it, put it back in the sleeve and take out the other arm." She pats the table, and I climb up onto it again. When I pull out my right arm, she turns it over. I try to twist it back, but I know she has already seen the P branded into it. She hesitates and lightly touches one of the marks. I jerk my arm away.

"So, where did this *d* come from? What does it stand for? Did you do this to yourself?"

Burn myself? Is she crazy?

11

I LOOK DOWN AT MY ARM AND REALIZE THAT FROM WHERE she's standing, it must look like a *d* and not a capital *P*. Something about that makes me feel better. I flash on words beginning with *d*: daffy, dancer, dasher, dizzy, dumpy, like I'm rattling off Santa's reindeer. All the *d* words thrown together are better than the P word.

"Some people harm themselves. They cut their own skin, pull out their hair, and bang their heads on walls—all different things to hide a deeper pain inside them.

"Do you want to tell me who did this to you?"

I shake my head, which suddenly feels heavy and drops down till my chin touches my chest. Hiding a secret about someone you love is one thing, but hiding one about someone you can't stand to even think about is a whole other.

"Was it someone in your family?"

I shake my head faster.

Sighing loudly, she makes a note in her chart. I stare at the chart and watch her draw an arm, adding dots to it, before she continues with the body search. First one leg then the other, and finally my feet, until she seems fully convinced that I was telling the truth all along. No piercings. No tattoos.

"Well, those marks certainly might explain the bedwetting."

How can marks on my arm explain bedwetting? I wonder but don't ask.

"Look, I'm sorry I couldn't take your word for it on the tatts and piercings, Anna. Believe me, I wanted to, but too many kids that come in here say they don't have markings on them, and then we discover that they lied to us, or they use unsafe methods to try and tattoo themselves while they're in here, using anything they can find that will cut their skin. You understand, don't you?"

I nod, even though I don't really understand why someone would do that to themselves.

"Okay, step on the scale. Then let's go get your workbook and some clothes."

"Workbook?"

I could have told her I was ninety-eight pounds without standing on the stupid scale, but she probably had to see it for herself. I get it. Kids lie. Like adults don't?

"Yes. For the forty-or-so days you're here, you won't be able to leave the building like some of the kids until you've had some anger-management therapy and such. We'll work with you on completing your workbook so you can get out of here faster.

"You'll have a schedule that includes meeting with group, individual therapy, and keeping up with your workbook, and there will be workshops that you may attend, if you've kept up with your work. We also have tutors who can help you keep up with math, English, science—"

I stopped listening when she said, "get you out of here faster."

And go where? Then a more troubling thought hits like a hammer to a thumb. "Forty days?" It comes out loud and clear, surprising even me. I may not be the best at math, but even I know forty days is very long time when you have somewhere else you'd rather be.

She studies my face. "Are you worried that you'll be locked up the whole time you're here? Well, as soon as you show you won't bite when you get mad, they'll place you in a room that doesn't stay locked; I promise."

Promises break. Anyway, that's not what I'm worried about. I'm worried that I'll be stuck here till I age out, with no place to go, and that Sara won't find a way to get here and help me escape. I have to think of a way out. I just have to.

"I know promises made to you in the past have been broken," she says, and I press my hands to my ears. *Stop reading my thoughts!*

"Ninety-seven pounds; that's a little light for your height."

I can hear her through my fingers. "Ninety-eight," I correct, dropping my hands to my sides.

She looks again at the scale. "No, it's definitely ninety-seven. Let's keep an eye on that. With all that's happened to you recently, it's no wonder you've burned off a pound."

A shiver races through me at the word *burned.*

"One last thing. You're almost thirteen. Have you started your period?"

Heat creeps up my neck. I clinch my arms to my sides and clasp my hands together in front of me. A school nurse once talked to our class about periods. She said that a period was when a girl started her monthly cycle. The only cycle I knew about was a bicycle, so it didn't make much sense. Then she said the girl starts bleeding once a month. It sounded awful. I did not want to have the kind of period she was talking about. Ever!

I was happy to just say no to the Emily lady.

"Well, don't be frightened if you do. Just let me know, and I can get you some pads. We also have machines in the bathrooms. In the meantime, let's leave the wheelchair here, shall we, and go get you some fresh clothes." She folds up the wheelchair and rolls it into a corner.

I walk out in the hall and fall into place behind her, listening to how different from mine her footsteps sound on the tile. The soft padded beat of her step reminds me of Pablo, a temporary foster brother we lived with for a while who walked softly and taught us how to make it rain. Not to really make it rain but to tap out different beats on a table to make it sound like it was raining.

He taught us three different beats: On Wisconsin. Mississippi go! And—

"Anna? Anna!"

It takes me a second to realize the Emily lady was not adding the last beat Pablo had given to the mix, which was my name. "You went somewhere in your thoughts! Where'd you go?"

"Wisconsin," I tell her. *Or was it Mississippi?*

"Wisconsin! Well, I certainly wasn't expecting you to say that!" She stops by a counter and grabs a thick spiral notebook and a small, clear plastic bag. Inside the bag is a toothbrush, a small tube of toothpaste, and a red plastic cup.

"What's in Wisconsin?"

"Cheese."

She looks at me and smiles, shaking her head. "Cheese. Yes. You're right. There is definitely cheese in Wisconsin."

She hands me the small plastic bag. "Hold onto the cup. We try to conserve around here and not waste things. Let's go to the closet, get you some clothes and shoes, then get you back to the room."

While we walk, I try to add in my head how much milk it would take to make me into cheese if I'm ninety-seven pounds. Ben said ten gallons of milk makes one pound of cheese, so ten times ninety-seven—

"When you multiply times ten, just to the number you are multiplyink add a zero," Ben once told us. If that's all true, then the answer would be 970 gallons.

Wow! It would take 970 gallons of milk to make me if I was cheese. That's a lot of milk. If a gallon of milk weighs a pound, that would be 970 pounds of milk! I can't even picture 970 pounds of anything. A baby elephant, maybe. I wish Ben were here to ask. How can 970 pounds of anything make something that's only 97 pounds?

I look up at the Emily lady while we walk. I try to ask her what a baby elephant weighs, but the words come out all wrong. I think really hard about baby elephants, so she can read my thoughts, but her thought radar must be turned off. Instead, she starts talking about "the closet."

Turns out the closet is a big room packed with new and "gently used," as she calls them, clothes. She explains that all the stuff in the closet has been donated to the RTC by people in the community. Tops, underwear, shoes, coats, sweaters—all girl's clothes and all marked by size. Some are brand-new, with the labels still on, and some are used.

"When you find something you like, put it in this bag. Choose only a week's worth of clothing, and you can select more next week." She starts to hand me a bigger plastic bag but then switches it out for a paper sack with handles, after putting the smaller bag with the toothpaste and stuff into the paper bag. She glances at her watch.

"Sorry, in cool-down, you can only have paper bags."

"Why?"

"It's a safety issue."

I frown but don't have time to figure out what she means. I grab a week's worth of underwear, a couple pairs of sweatpants, three sweatshirts, and some sneakers, stuff them in the bigger bag, and sling it over my shoulder.

Heading back to the room, we pass a window, and I can't help but notice my reflection. I look like a hunched-over Santa carrying a sad sack of toys. I quickly look away, not wanting to plant another sad memory in my head about how lonely the holidays can be, but it's too late. I do remember having to write a holiday poem at one school we went to. If chosen, our poem would appear in the school journal. A girl in my class wrote how she was thinking of all the Christmas joys, like getting clothes and candy and toys, and how she wanted people to think about all the happiness Christmas brings.

The teacher had given us three words that had to appear in our poem that didn't even sound Christmassy to me. The words were *grit*, *gloom*, and *windswept*. My poem didn't get picked. But I still remember it. It went like this:

Santa's Beard

Christmas is a ghost in white
that creeps from room to room.
Its beard of snow sweeps 'cross the floor,
removing grit and gloom.
The gift that Santa leaves behind has no wrap or bow,
for it's the windswept patterns of
our footprints in the snow.

It didn't win, but I recited it to Sara every Christmas after, especially when we were the only ones home, looking out at our footprints in the snow.

"I like your poem, Anna," she always told me, before saying how sorry she was that she only had a button game she made for me out of a button she had found and string. She didn't know it, but that right there, what she said about liking my poem? That was the best gift she could have ever given me and might even be the reason I like writing poems even today. Terrible Ted stole the voice out of me but not the poems.

12

I LOOK AWAY FROM MY REFLECTION AND TRY TO SHAKE THE lonely thoughts free, hoping I won't have to feel the ache that comes with them. But thinking of my sister brings a new load of tears, prompting the Emily lady to ask if I need a hug.

I shake my head, brushing off my cheeks, furious at myself for letting my feelings show. It's just that sometimes, like pee, you just can't hold tears in. The Emily lady glances at her watch again and looks back up, her eyes darting this way and that, as if a new set of dots needs to be connected.

The halls are empty, but I can hear a hum of activity in some nearby rooms.

Back in the cool-down room, I sling the paper bag onto the bed, wondering why foster kids can't have regular old suitcases. The bag rips and spills the clothes over the bed and floor.

"That's why plastic works better than paper," she says. "I know kids in transition are sensitive to having their things stuffed in anything that looks like a trash bag, and in cool-down, like I say, we must use paper bags, but we're working on getting suitcases donated. For now, though, it is what it is."

"What is, is," I say, relieved to see that lunch is waiting. It's lukewarm, but I eat it anyway. *Yum.* My favorite: hot dogs and baked beans.

"Normally, you'd go to the cafeteria and eat with the others," the Emily lady says, pointing to the dresser where I'm to put the clothes. I nod, letting her know I understand her point, and chow down the food.

"But again, until you get out of cool-down room, you're pretty much stuck here for seventy-two hours. You've already used up one day, so you're down to forty-eight hours. It will go by fast." She checks her watch again and, if she's like our caseworker, probably still doesn't know what time it is.

"You did really well today, Anna. I have to get to an appointment, but I'll check in with you in about an hour. Go ahead and start reading through your workbook. And feel free to make up the bed with fresh sheets."

"Okay, uh—" I stop and stare at her, feeling suddenly oversized and awkward. What do we call people in this place?

"It's okay. You can call me Emily," she says, answering my thought again. "Around here, we go on a first-name basis." She smiles and turns to leave, then stops. "You'll be seeing a therapist while you're here, Anna. Dr. Kitanovski is a psychiatrist."

"Psy-chi-a-trist." I say it slowly out loud, sounding out each syllable. Saying it turns my tongue into an acrobat, leaping this way and that.

Funny how people can scare stuff out of you—make you say stuff you don't want to say, and others, like Terrible Ted, can scare you so bad you can't talk for fear of what will happen if you do. When you stop talking on the outside, you do a lot more talking on the in.

"A psychiatrist studies the brain."

"Brain," I repeat.

"Yes. The brain. Behavior. All sorts of things," Emily adds, smiling like she means it.

I narrow my eyes. *Just try and mess with my brain and see what happens!*

"I think you'll like her," she says, not even scared of what my eyes are shouting. "Our goal, while you're here, is twofold. We want you to talk again in complete sentences. And then to help you work on some other more effective communication skills. Whoever burned that *d* on your arm was not a kind person," she adds quietly.

It's a P! Tig shouts. *Terrible Ted burned her! Terrible Ted burned her!* But I swallow hard and squeeze my arms to my sides to shush her. Just the mention of that awful man's name, even if it's in my head, puts a horrible, ashy taste in my mouth, and hot tears force me to turn away.

"Dr. Kitanovski will help you find your voice again," Emily tells me, before moving to write something in her folder of papers. "Okay, I think that's enough settling in for today." She snaps the folder closed. "We don't have call buttons in every room, but we do have them in the clinic and the cool-down room, so just press the button in the bathroom if you need anything."

"Sister," I say, hoping she can call Ben and have him bring Sara right over, if she's not already here.

She opens the folder quickly and flips to a new page. "I did see in your chart that you have a sister and that you've been asking for her. The problem is that the court has ordered that you complete the program here before you can be reunited with her. That's unusual, since they normally encourage family visits, but they must have their reasons, Anna. I know forty days sounds like an awfully long time, but if you try really hard to do well in the program, you should be able to see your sister right after you complete the requirements."

That's not fair!

I throw myself on the bed and grab Abby, yanking off her arm and hurling it to the tile floor.

Emily sighs and picks it up, setting it on the table beside the workbook.

"Give us a chance to help you, okay, Anna? It's your only ticket out of here. We'll work this week on anger management and talking in complete sentences, but the hard and cold fact is you have to participate in your own success."

Whatever that means. I stare at her hotly.

She turns and walks back to the table. "It means that one can lead a person to knowledge, but they can't force them to think. That they must do on their own. Before I leave, I want you to look at this." She pats the cover of a workbook.

At first, I just stay put. What's she going to do? Drag me over there? But she doesn't move, and after a while, the air around me starts to feel heavy and uncomfortable. I slide off the bed, tromp over to the table, and stare at the upside-down cover, still mad about the court's decision to keep Sara away.

Emily turns the workbook around so I can see it right side up. The cover has a funny-looking cartoon person climbing a colorful ladder. A red heart floats in the corner of the cover. Beside it in big red letters, it says THE MASTER PROGRAM in all caps.

"In your record, it says that even though you pretend you can't read, you're perfectly capable of it. Is that true? Can you read what this says?" She points to the title of the book, but I stay silent, wondering what else is written in her folder that I don't know about. And who found out I could read and ratted me out? Even Sara doesn't know.

"This workbook is part of what's called the MASTER Program we practice here. MASTER stands for Mindful Acquired Skillsets Targeting Effective Rehabilitation." As she says the words, she uses her index finger as a pointer, jumping from one brightly colored letter to another and filling in the word it stands for.

"The program teaches, in carefully thought-out steps, how to, one, master emotions, and two, identify what's truly important. It helps you to figure out what you want to stand for in life and helps you learn to make sound decisions you can be proud of. Ultimately, the program teaches you how to handle challenging situations by developing solid communication skills, building trust, and setting both short- and long-term goals for yourself."

Blah, blah, blah. I look around the room for any hope of an escape, but the only vent I see is too small to squeeze through. She can talk, talk, talk till she turns into a parrot for all I care about what the program does, but where does it say, "You can get to be with your sister?" Where does it say that?

"All our residents go through the program, but we also add things individually to help each person learn, grow, and excel in his and her own unique way. Part of that process is to write in your journal daily, which you'll take to group to share."

Blah, blah, blah.

She pauses. "I know it's a lot to take in, and I guess that's why we have to stretch it over forty days. Still, like I've been saying, it will go quickly. You'll see. A staff member has been assigned to you. Mr. Jackson will meet with you tomorrow. The handbook covers important rules and policies, as well as Nevada's Foster Youth Bill of Rights, which he will go over with you. I know it says that you have the right to call a family member, and because of the judge's decision, we will have to hold off on that, but you're smart, Anna. Also, the handbook comes with a workbook, which has exercises for you to think about and write about. You can do this.

"See here. The first one is to tell something about your life."

I suddenly feel too tired to think or even care. Emily does that creepy thing and reads my thoughts again, then pats my arm before telling me to get some much-needed rest.

"You know what?" She unlocks a cabinet and pulls out a plastic bag with handles. "How about if I help you change the bed before I leave?"

She pulls the bag open, and I yank the sheets off the bed. If Sara was here, she would find a place to hide them, but since she isn't, I guess it's up to me to take care of them now. I look around, but there's no place to hide anything in this room. I'm hoping the Emily lady won't tell any of the others that I'm a bedwetter.

"Your secret is safe with me," she says quietly, totally freaking me out again. *Stop that!* I want to shout. *Can't a person have some private thoughts?* Still, I'm relieved to hear she's not going to tell anyone that I wet the bed.

Before leaving, she digs in a cloth bag hanging from her shoulder and pulls out another book—a blank one, it turns out—and sets it on the desk. "You can use this for journaling. Writing is part of the healing process, but sometimes it can also help time fly."

"Thanks."

"You are very welcome, Anna." She turns, then turns back. "Just one more thing." She again reaches into her bag and this time pulls out a folder and walks back over to the table. "Let's go ahead and get some of the paperwork out of the way while I'm not being called to go somewhere else."

She pulls out a document and has me sign it. At first, I hesitate, and she explains it's part of their policy to document everything, and it helps to get things moving forward and speeds up my getting to leave.

Works for me. The sooner I can get out of here, the better, so I sign.

"You're exhausted, so we can go over these other documents later. How does that sound?"

"Good."

After the door closes and locks behind her, I look around, feeling like I don't belong. I also feel silenced, as if even if I could talk, nobody would want to hear what I have to say. So much stuff just went on that I didn't have time to feel how alone being alone could feel. I try to distance myself from it, like I did in the car with Sara and our caseworker, and will myself away from this place, but no amount of staring into space lifts me out of this mess. As the seconds pass, I realize I can't pretend this isn't real anymore. I can't control my breathing, which is so fast I go dizzy.

Glancing around, I try to find something that can take the awful, dreaded lost and lonely feeling away, but without Sara here, that's like trying to find a hanger in a big, empty closet to hang your fears on.

I say that because hanging up our fears and worries is what Ben would have us try on nights that we couldn't sleep. He'd tell us to picture our fears as a shirt or coat that we put on a hanger and hang them in the closet, so we could sleep fear-free. It worked most of the time. Some fears, though, don't want to let go. Like the one I'm having right now. Hang it up? I can't even shake it loose.

13

About the only thing I can see that can make me feel a little less alone is a tree outside the window. We had a tree just like it outside our window at home, so this tree is like a sister tree. Sara and I both know that a tree can be a comfort when everything else is in shambles. The tree isn't going anywhere. I can go to sleep looking at it, and it will be right there when I wake up the next day, unless someone cuts it down, but I don't want to think about that happening. Still, it's a reminder to not get too attached, since things can change, or even disappear, in a heartbeat.

I walk over to the window to be closer to the sister tree, and after just a short time, my breathing slows. I can't help but wonder what you hold on to when everything has been taken away. I wrap my arms around myself, making my arms like a butterfly. When I do, I don't feel so dizzy anymore. Looking down, I can see the backyard of the building. I do notice a few scattered picnic tables chained to stakes in the ground, like anyone would steal a picnic table. Still, I guess they could drag one over to the concrete wall and try to climb over it. Some girls are sitting around one of the tables, but they don't look up.

I turn around and scan the room, trying to figure out which things feel okay and which don't. The table, chairs, desk, and bed don't bother me. They're just there. The bars on the window overlooking the yard scream, "Trapped!" I pull at them to see if I can rip them loose, but there's no getting out the window, and even if I did get out, it's a long way down.

I walk back and sit on the bed as a chilled silence wraps around me. Then I pay extra close attention to the noises. I don't like the sound of the door, or the wall when it hums, before making that loud *click.* I squint but don't see anything I can break that might make those sounds go away.

And I don't actually feel time flying either, like the Emily lady said it would. If anything, it's dragging "like a stubborn pack mule," which is how Daddy would describe it before telling us of the mule he had as a pet when he was a kid that wouldn't budge unless he said, "Alfalfa." Me and Sara didn't know what alfalfa was, but just hearing the word, especially when Daddy said it, made us laugh so hard. Sometimes when we were scared, we'd whisper it to each other just to lesson our fears. I sink down on the bed.

"Alfalfa," I whisper, but without Sara here to whisper it with, it doesn't do anything except make me want to cry.

I try again. "Alfalfa."

Nothing.

"Alfalfa!"

Still nothing.

"Alfalfa!" I shout, jumping up and down before storming around the room, kicking the walls and screaming the word over and over, hoping it will start to turn funny, but there's nothing funny about this place.

In a rage, I try to turn the desk over, but it's bolted to the floor and no amount of pulling at it does any good. I about pull my shoulder out trying. I try the chair next, but even it is bolted down, so I grab a pillow, half expecting it to be bolted down too, but when it isn't, I hurl it across the room before flopping on the bed.

It takes a while for the heaving to stop. Being alone with your thoughts when others are around isn't too bad, unless your thoughts are being listened to, like they seem to be in this place. But being all alone with just your thoughts as company can be scary as all get-out.

Like right now, being locked in with no one to talk to, not that I would even be able to talk if someone were here, is awful.

"Not as awful as—" Tig starts to say, but I stop her cold before she says his name. What if the monster can read thoughts, too, from wherever his sorry self is, and follows them to where I am?

After that horrible thought, I think I might have passed out, or maybe I just fell asleep, because when I next open my eyes, shadows dance on the floor and walls. Birds chatter in the tree outside the window. I look over by the door, and shapes suddenly pop up all around me. The shadowy branches on the wall are plump with birds that look round and full like ripened plums. One by one, the fruit starts to lift.

But I know fruit doesn't fly, and when I look back out the window at the tree, I can see that the birds have now all flown away, and a few more leaves have dropped to the ground. Some yellow. Some orange. Fall is moving in, as if time has no boundaries.

If Ben were here, he'd tell me that shadows are like illusions.

"An illusion is when your eyes somethink tricks," he once told me and Sara. I knew he was trying to say, "When something tricks your eyes," and just got his words mixed up. "A mirage," he added, "is for instance an illusion."

Sara and I didn't know what a mirage was, so he took us on a walk. "Look down the hill. See how it looks like there is somethink on the road? Some water, perhaps?" He points ahead.

We nod, both of us grinning.

"Well, now. Watch. Ah, ah! Keep watchink."

I remember how excited and then confused and disappointed I felt when it turned out that the water we thought we saw wasn't water at all; it was a trick. A mirage. The closer we got, the more we could see that the road was as dry as Sara's side of the bed always is.

I wonder how many tricks are actually out there that we think are real that really aren't. Ben says some stars that we see have died long, long ago, but that light hasn't caught up to that fact yet, which is why some of the stars we think are still alive have actually already died. I think about Daddy's rock stars smashing together. I once asked Mama if we could be dead and not know it, like some of the stars are.

But Mama said no, "Because living things aren't dead, and stars aren't living things."

Daddy disagreed, saying, "Stars are light, and light is energy—and energy's the very thing that makes us living things."

Then he started singing a song that went something like "Starlight, not so bright—don't know that it died tonight. Knows not wrong, knows not right, just knows it glows more dim tonight," and Mama left the room.

Daddy's song makes me sad. Sara always wishes on stars. Right this very minute, she is probably wishing so hard that we could be together again, just like the wish I'm wishing, but if the stars we're wishing on are dead, does that mean our wishes will die too?

"Wishes are like spit in the ocean," Daddy said that day. "No different than all them stars up in the sky. You think yours is the wish that will come true? Well, so does everybody else that wished a wish. Spit, I tell you. Spit in the ocean." He might have been working on a song for all I know.

Right now, though, I feel a lump in my throat. I swallow around it and try to make the thoughts about Sara's and my wishes getting mixed up with everyone else's disappear. The wall suddenly hums, and the door clicks loudly. I jump and clutch at the blankets. When the door swings open, I see Mean Kurt bringing in a tray with dinner and a stack of folded sheets. I stiffen when I see him glaring.

"The bottom one's rubber. Put that on first," he orders, like he's the new boss of me, and then sets the food down on the table. "This servant stuff is going to end soon. I'm not your waiter. You're in the warehouse, not the Waldorf."

Nothing he is saying makes any sense. He lifts the lid off the plate. I roll over. It looks and smells a lot like spaghetti.

"Also, here's the lowdown on how things work around here. I may be new, but that don't mean I don't know what goes down. My shift ends in"—he checks his phone—"ten minutes, so I get to bust out of here. But you're in cool-down for forty-eight hours—which means you might get out tomorrow, if you don't bite anyone or throw any temper fits, that is. If you do, you'll stay locked in longer."

I don't look at him and stare instead out the barred window, watching another awful day dip into night.

He snatches the workbook off the desk. "I see Emily got you the book already. Just so you know, you're in DBT, so 'we can help you develop a life worth living.'" He says that last part in a fake high voice and snorts. Ben says people change their voices when they read to make the story more interesting, but if that's what Mean Kurt is trying to do, it's not working. Maybe it's a staff-in-training lesson he hasn't mastered yet. Maybe *he* should be taking the MASTER Program.

"You'll be assigned a case manager. Not me, thank Gee," he adds and glances up at the ceiling. "The other guy's not on yet, but he'll be here tomorrow. He'll go over all the rules, schedules, and let you in on how everything else works around here. Got that?"

"I know!" I say pointedly because Emily has already told me all this. I look away, wondering if Sara is already back at Ben and Rachel's and Ben is reading her a bedtime story right now. My throat tightens. I stare at the empty space next to me and try to make my own mirage of Sara appear, but I can't get my eyes to trick me. All I see is an empty space growing blurrier by the second.

"Well, why didn't you say so?" He snaps the workbook shut.

I just did. I roll my head back toward him and quickly brush tears off my cheek just as he checks his phone—again. Constantly checking the time must be part of his job. I wonder what happens when his phone doesn't work. Does he stop working too?

"So, any questions? You got about ten seconds."

"DBT?" I blurt.

"Yeah. Uh ... DBT is—well, it stands for—" The next noise that comes out of him is halfway between a rasp and a growl. He flips the workbook back open and runs a long, thin, freckled finger down the page, stopping about midway. "Dialectical behavior therapy," he blurts.

"Di-a-lec-ti-cal." I repeat the word slowly, letting the syllables flicker over the front part of my mouth before leaping to the back of my throat, tongue curling, then leaping forward, then back, curling my tongue again.

"Yeah, dialectical." He throws me a "this-girl's-gone-crazy" look before thumbing to another page in the workbook, again making that weird raspy noise.

"Here it is. 'A dialectic is a conversation between things that seem like opposites ...'" He pauses and looks around, scrunching up his cheeks like he's trying to remember something, then says, "In other words, it's like putting two unlike things together to create something new.

"For example. We take you and your rotten behavior and put it with us and our tools for making you less rotten—and bingo! You get better.

"In a nutshell," he adds, "it's treatment for people with something called borderline personality disorder." He pauses. "That would be you, though on second thought, maybe you're not supposed to know that part yet.

"Oh, well. You do now. Anyway—" He puts a finger in the book to save the page and adds, "It's designed to keep you from developing antisocial behavior. A little late for that, I'd say, but then I'm not the one with the problem." He suddenly laughs. "Did I say in a nutshell? Ha, ha! Good one."

He raises his eyebrows expectantly at me before breathing in deep and letting out a long breath in one giant huff. "Just to be clear, here, there's no need to tell anyone I said nutshell; let's just keep that between you and me. Deal?"

I just stare at him.

"Yep, yep, yep. Anyway—" He drops the workbook at the foot of the bed. "You're here to get help so you don't keep biting people. You bite; we bite back. That's how it works."

He turns to leave, then looks over his shoulder. "Oh, yeah. I'm s'posed to remind you that it's not all bad 'round here. Check out the chart on page twelve or so. It's on how to make money while you're locked up." He stops at the door. "Now, I'd *love* to stay here and chat all day, but"—he taps on his phone—"it's officially Kurt time. And that means I'm outta here!"

I'm glad when he's gone. The plastic fork is useless on the now-cold spaghetti, so I just grab it with my fingers and stuff it in my mouth. It's not like anyone's watching. And even though it's cold, it still tastes good.

When I'm done, I toss the plate and useless fork in the trash and tackle the bed. I unfold the sheets one by one and start with the rubber one. While I unfold it, I wonder about the new person—the case manager he and Emily talked about—Mr. Jackson, was it? I wonder what he's like. I'm hoping he's someone nice like the Emily lady, but something Mean Kurt said before taking off digs into my thoughts: "You bite; we bite back."

Nobody's ever bitten me back before. What if he really means that they'll bite me as punishment? What if the new staff person is a biter? I push the awful thought away. I know biting people is bad. I don't want to bite anymore. I never did. I thought it could be as easy as just saying, "Stop!" But it isn't. It isn't easy at all.

That's not all that's not easy. Making a bed is harder than it looks and becomes a battle. Every time I pull the sheet over a corner and go to another corner, the first corner pulls off. I finally get so mad I just spread the sheets out one on top of the other and "call it a day," as Daddy would say. When I finish making the bed, I sit on it and study the chart the Mean Kurt guy said to look at. I didn't know I'd get paid to do stuff. I've never gotten paid to do anything before. One column on the page says, "Points earned." The second says "Rank," and the third says, "Tokens earned." From looking at the chart, it looks like "residents," as they call us, can earn ninety-five or more points a day, plus certain freedoms, but they can also be docked points, including partial loss and total loss.

I quickly see that I can earn five dollars of tokens a week just by doing a journal page a day! On Token Friday, the tokens can be exchanged for cash. I wonder if poems count as journaling. I keep reading. I can also earn points and money for completing the workbook pages on time, doing chores, whatever those might be, participating in all their therapy programs, and going to whatever classes they make me go to.

I want to rip the pages out of their stupid workbook. The cartoons on the pages look happy, but they aren't the ones stuck in here for forty days. Well, actually, I guess they are, but they don't have to do anything or answer to anyone. I set the book down hard and look around the room, taking everything in again. I keep a mental list. It could all change by morning.

Suddenly, I'm too tired to think and lie down and roll onto my side. Staring at a sea of patterns on the wall, it turns out I can't do anything *but* think.

What's keeping Sara?

More troubling thoughts slip in. I try to force them away, but they're too strong to ignore. What if Sara never comes back? What if Daddy can't find where they hid me? What if Ben and Rachel have already moved on to other kids needing temporary homes? What if nobody even misses me? What if … what if …

Each thought rides on another tear rolling down my cheek, till my face and pillow are soaked. It's so hard not being wanted. What if I'm someone that's easy to forget? I flop my pillow over and roll onto my back, fighting more tears, furious with myself for being so unlovable. I hurl Abby at the ceiling and try to catch her and miss. She thumps hard against my chest, stabbing me with her foot.

"Ow!" I yell.

But I don't mind the sharp pain. I even kind of like it. It gives me a good excuse to cry, not that I need one. Being locked up alone in this room gives me that. How could Mama leave us? I just don't get it. Aren't parents an automatic thing kids get by being born? Don't you get two so that if something happens to one, you at least have one left over? Wasn't that God's plan, like Mama always used to talk about? Why do I have to be the kid with no family? Weren't my parents supposed to hang around and teach me stuff I need to know in life?

And why did I get stuck with you?

Tig's words cut so deep that my breath turns to short sniffs before the burning-hot tears cloud everything up. Now *she's* going to be mean to me too? That is so not fair.

I kick the air and scream, but all that comes out is a wheezy noise. "Where are you, Sara? Where, where, where?" Grabbing Abby by the legs, I slam her, one, two, three times against the covers, clenching my teeth with each blow and growling before ripping off Abby's arm and legs and launching them across the room. They bounce against the wall and fall like hollow sticks onto the tile floor, and I don't make one move to pick them up. Let them break. Let them get lost. I don't care. I don't care if I'm all alone. I don't care if Sara's not coming.

"You hear?" I shout to the walls. "Don't care!" Who cares if my words are mixed up? Who cares if everyone hates me? "Not me!" I shout.

Liar, Tig taunts, but I pretend not to hear her. The room grows even darker when a light flicks on. Where did that light come from? Is someone here? Who turned it on?

"Who's there?" My throat's raw from yelling. All this time, I thought I was alone, but someone must have slipped in and turned the light on. I didn't hear the wall hum or the door open, but I was making a lot of noise in my head. Did Mean Kurt come back?

An icy chill starts at my shoulders and creeps down to my feet. What if whoever it is has been in here the whole time? What if it's not Mean Kurt but that awful Justin guy who burns things up just for the fun of it?

"Who's there?" I call out a little louder, gripping the sheet tighter around my shoulders before pulling it over my head. My arms and legs stiffen.

I lie there for what feels like hours in a stiff, frozen silence, waiting for something awful to come out of the shadows, but nothing does. Slowly, heat comes back to my cheeks and neck. It moves down my body, leaving me no longer stiff.

Just terrified.

15

SLOW AND STEADY, I PULL THE SHEET OFF MY FACE. THE only things moving are my eyeballs, rolling from one side of the ceiling to the other, and my chest rising up and down from breathing. I still listen for the someone or something that has turned on the nightlight to step out from the shadows.

"Sara?" I can barely get her name out.

Except for the sound of air coming through the vents and my heartbeat pounding in my ears, the room keeps quiet, like even it is scared. Sara wouldn't hide from me. If she was here, she would let me know. Ever so slowly, I prop up on one elbow and look around but don't see anything out of the ordinary. I carefully put one foot then the other over the side of the bed and force myself to stand. My legs don't want to move, but I force them, no matter how straight and stiff they are, to walk across the room so I can look more closely at the little light.

I turn on the bathroom light, and the mystery light turns off. I flick the bathroom light off, and the mystery light turns on. Okay, so the light must be on some kind of sensor or timer. I start to relax back into me again and breathe more normally. The room gets even quieter when the drone of the air-conditioning coming through a vent cuts off. I shiver. September has already slipped into October. October is a cold month for air-conditioning. Maybe that should be on a sensor too. Thinking about it being October reminds me that it will be Sara's birthday soon.

I have to get out of here.

The walls suddenly belch and close in around me. I have to escape. I don't know how, but I do know I will not stop trying to find some way out.

A muffled thump jerks my attention toward the door, and my heart leaps to an even faster beat. I force myself to do like Sara would have done and cross the room cautiously, pressing my ear against the wood, but the noise is tricking me.

From across the room, it sounded like it was coming from behind the door, but when I listen at the door, it sounds like it's coming from somewhere else. The tapping stops, then starts up again. Maybe the pipes in the walls are making the noise. Daddy says pipes can sound like someone knocking, chains clanking, or even bones creaking. I shiver and back away.

What if it's not pipes? What if it's something else? Something horrible. October isn't just Sara's birthday month. It's Halloween, and Halloween always gave me the creeps. Sara likes it, but I just pretend to like it. The tapping starts up again. What if someone has died in this very room and now is a skeleton, living in the walls? Maybe this isn't some milk carton they've stuck me in. Maybe it's a coffin. Maybe I'm buried next to a restless box of bones, trying to get out, just like I want to get out, and like how Tig wants to get out of me.

I try and tell myself how silly that is, but is it? I try once more to ignore the eerie tapping by moving away from the wall and grabbing the journal Emily left for me. Daddy once said that the best writing is what you write when you're scared, drunk, or in dire pain. I don't know what dire is, and no way am I drunk, but I do know that I'm scared. Maybe if I pretend I'm Daddy writing a song, the scare will go away—anything to keep my mind full and free from hearing all the creepy noises in this place.

The glow from the light spreads across the blank page, turning it to a dirty, dusky yellow. The wall beside me clicks and taps out a beat.

I have to do something before all this noisy nothingness drives me crazy, But what? What can I do? I'm trapped in here with no way out.

Like me! Tig shouts hotly before I shush her, mad that she can't see I'm saving her. But it's starting to feel like there's nobody here saving me. There has to be a way out, but where? How?

The answer seems to find me, and I reach for a crayon, since in this place that's all they'll let you write or draw with, and since around here, getting out seems to mean writing your way out, and that's something I *can* do. I can write. I haven't had to in a long time, but now writing is more than just putting words on paper. As Emily said, it's my ticket out of here.

This time, I'll write about the walls. The light flickers but stays on.

The Coffin
Her wooden surface,
smooth and light,
hides bones that click
like sticks at night.
Her creaking pipes
leak secrets.
Shh …
    No voice,
    no words,
    no other sound
    can come around if
silence claims
this burial ground.

I read it back to myself and know deep inside that Tig probably wrote it, not me. Still, I wonder again if they'll let poems count for journal entries. It's not telling anyone about my life, like they wanted, but if writing poems does count, that would mean five bucks per day whether Tig wrote it or not. At least that's what I'm hoping. When they start paying me, I'm going to hide my money and save it up, so when I do get a chance to run away, I can get a taxi driver to take me to Ben's. He might know where Sara is, if she's not with him and Rachel. I wonder how much a taxi ride costs. Will the taxi driver be able to find her like Daddy used to find us? I let my thoughts drift to a less scary place, but the tapping on the wall starts up again and gets louder and more insistent: one, two—one, two, three. One, two—one, two, three.

16

I CLOSE THE JOURNAL AND CRAWL ACROSS THE COLD TILE TO the wall and tap the same beat I have been hearing. The beat on the other side suddenly gets louder and faster.

I try a different rhythm just to see what will happen. Whoa! No way! The wall answers and taps my beat back to me. I'm right! The wall is alive!

Wait! What if it's not the wall that's alive? What if it's a person? What if the tapper is Sara? My heart leaps with joy. It has to be her. It just has to be. Who else would it be? She found me! She found me! I knew she would. I just knew it!

"Sara!" I shout-whisper, pressing my ear so hard against the wall it burns the skin around the outside of it.

A muffled voice answers. "Hey! You in there. Whatcha in for?"

I hold in my breath, as the excitement I just felt drains out of me. I try to get my mind to trick me into believing Sara is the one who's really out there, like one of those mirages Ben showed us. But I know it's not Sara's voice I'm hearing. It's somebody else. A very short someone, by the sounds of it. I let out my breath, disappointed. I have to crouch down on my hands and knees, close to the floor, to hear the voice better.

"Don't know," I answer.

"You musta done *somethin'*," the voice huffs, sounding a little like

Mama sounds when she's "bent out of shape," as Daddy would say. The little person on the other side of the wall definitely sounds cranky. A question hasn't actually been asked, so I keep quiet.

"Ju do drugs?"

The sudden question throws me off. "No!"

"Ju kill anyone?"

Kill anyone? Do they let people in here who kill people?

"No!" I whisper harshly, trying to force my breathing to slow down. I don't want to pass out. Do I look like I could kill anyone? But then I remember that the little person can't see me, so how would they know?

"You run away?"

My eyebrows shoot up and stay there. The little person may have hit on something. Sara and I did run away, but then why isn't Sara here too? Or is she? The hope in me does a few flying leaps. Could they have stuffed her in another room, maybe on the other side of the building?

"That's it, ain't it?" the little person asks. The whisper turns raspy and rises to an excited wheeze.

"Yes," I finally admit.

"Well, then, why di'en'cha say so. You ran away. That's why you here."

Silence.

"Wha'chore name?"

"Anna."

"I'm Kat."

"Cat," I whisper. Wait. Cat? Is this the one Emily was talking about earlier?

Ben told us cats are nocturnal, choosing night to day, so that fits, since it's definitely nighttime. But no cat I know talks, unless—I freeze and let my eyes do the walking. What if this place really is some kind of experimental lab? What if they're going to turn me into a talking cat or mouse—or, I wince, "A bug," I whisper. Or maybe just shock my brain and turn me into some sort of zombie?

"What did you say?"

"What kind?" I quickly ask. She's definitely not a big cat, more like a little bobcat or a maybe a giant house cat. Her voice is about a foot off the floor, as close as I can measure. Ben read us a story about different kinds of cats once. She could be a minx.

"What kinda what?"

"Cat."

The silence that comes with waiting surrounds me, and I start to grow impatient.

"Oh, okay. I see how you are. Make fun all you want on your own time, jailbird. We done here." A shuffle and a soft thump follow. I quickly tap out a beat, but the cat has slinked off somewhere.

The long pause that follows is that lonely silence that happens when someone leaves and you're not done talking with them yet.

"No! Cat! Come back!" I call out and wait a few seconds to see if she actually does. I tap a new beat on the wall, but no taps answer. I get up and pace around the room. Before going to bed, I hobble to the bathroom and turn on the shower. The hot water feels good and gives me a chance to rinse off any bad thoughts before going to sleep. That was a Ben Rule. No bad thoughts before going to bed.

I quickly dry off, slip on jammies, brush my teeth, and crawl under the sheet, lying there, staring into space. Tired and confused, my mind spins. Mixed-up thoughts fill my head, crowding out any calming ones that could think me out of this place. I squint and gaze up at the vent to see if any giant eyes are staring back at me. Nothing moves. I press my hands tightly over my face, not wanting to see any more shadows or hear any more cats talking—not wanting to think or be scared or—

The wall creaks. I spread my fingers and roll my eyes over to the new place the noise is coming from—then freeze. A squished face stares back at me, like a creature trying to break through the wall's skin. I squeeze my eyes shut and open them again, thinking that the face will surely disappear. The yelp that comes out of me scares me more than my thoughts! It scares me! *It's her! Cat-girl! It has to be! Who else could it be? I was right! She's not outside the wall; she's in it!*

My legs stiffen, and I shake them hard. No! No! No! I kick and kick, not wanting to turn stiff like Abby again. Think, Anna. Think! What would Sara do?

Sara would meet her face-to-face, or face to whatever that is. "Hey!" I jump up and go stand in front of her, still pretending I'm Sara, keeping a good foot back, just in case she breaks through. Her head seems bigger up close. It's hard to say what she would really look like if her face wasn't smooshed against the plaster. Right now, it's not the prettiest thing in the world, but when it's the only company you've got, you put judgments aside.

"You came back," I say, trying to keep my voice from shaking.

"She's not real!" Tig shouts, but I squeeze my arms tightly around my stomach, trying to quiet her. Usually she's right about things, but this time, she's not. And who better to know? The girl trapped inside me? Or me, the one staring right at the smashed face pressing against the inside of the wall, clearly trying to get out?

"She is real," I snap. *I know because I'm looking right at her.* It does seem strange, though, that the wall is flat even up close. From back there, it looked like she had started to push through, but up close, the wall is definitely flat. Is this another one of those illusions? This place is full of them.

The wall moans.

We have to do something. *We've got to get her out of there*, I tell Tig. I search the drawer of the desk for something sharp. The closest think I can find to stab with is the toothbrush, since the crayons I used to write the poem would break.

If Sara was here, she'd help her escape, I explain to a clearly agitated Tig. I try to get her to stop kicking my stomach.

Stop fighting me, Tig, and help, will you?

Tig finally calms down. I stab again and again and again at the wall, all around the trapped, smooshed face. Plaster chips fly off, hitting me on the arm before falling to the floor.

"She's not real," Tig repeats flatly.

Maybe you're the one that's not real. Ever consider that? I stab at the wall harder, and a big chip flies up and hits me in the face, startling me more than hurting me, but tears leap to my eyes. Tig grows so quiet that I stop stabbing the wall in a panic and try to get her to answer me.

"I didn't mean that last part about you not being real. I know you're real. You know you're real. And you know I know you're real. It's just that I got mad, because you wouldn't see that the girl in the wall is real too."

She still doesn't answer.

Sweat pours out of me. I start to choke and squeeze my chest to make it stop hurting. Did she leave me? Is The Inside Girl gone?

My body shakes out of control. Tossing the cracked toothbrush aside, I wring my hands, but they still turn numb, just like when Sara and I figured out Mama and Daddy were gone and not coming back.

What's happening to me? It feels like my insides have been ripped out. Am I going to die? I race into the bathroom, feeling like I'm going to puke, but nothing but gagging noises come out. I spit and wet a washcloth and wash off my face and arms and neck before staggering back to the room.

When I look over my shoulder at the wall, I see the shadows have shifted and I can't make out Cat-Girl's features anymore. Maybe the pounding of the toothbrush so close to her face scared her off. I turn and flop onto the bed. When everything starts to spin, I close my eyes and try to make it all go away.

I must have fallen asleep because a sudden hum and a loud click wake me. I force my eyes to stay closed but feel certain that my heart is beating loud enough for all of RTC to hear.

Emily slips in. I can tell it's her by the flowery scent and the sound her shoes make on the floor. I listen hard to hear if Sara has slipped in behind her. But only one set of footsteps crosses the room. Emily leans over me, like Rachel used to do when we stayed at the Silvermans'.

Before she leaves, she puts something on the desk.

I breathe a sigh of relief that she apparently didn't notice the chipped wall. If she had, for sure she would have made me get up and explain it. The second the door locks, I open my eyes and slip out of bed to see what the package is that she has left for me. I hope it's not more rubber sheets.

17

IT TURNS OUT IT'S NOT A PACKAGE AT ALL! AND IT'S NOT rubber sheets either. It's another book!

My heart races so fast I can't slow it down. A book is pretty much the closest thing to a friend I've ever had, next to Ben and Rachel, that is. At least I think it is. Besides my sister, I've never had a kid friend, so I can only guess what having a real friend must be like.

Ben once said that a friend is someone who has something in common with you, and when you think about it, I guess I'm kind of like a book. Words are trapped inside me. The Emily lady can read my thoughts like they're words on a page. Maybe I really am a book, only I was made to look human or to *think* human, tricking even me.

I wish Sara and Ben were here to talk this out with. What am I thinking? I can't talk.

I grab the journal Emily left for me earlier and slip into the bathroom. Turning on the light, I press my back against the wall and slide down to the floor. The tile is cold. I tuck the robe under my butt and legs and set the journal on the floor beside me, then run my hand over the new book's cover. It's old and worn in a soft kind of way, and it smells like I remember Daddy's cowboy hat smelling. I pull the book away from my nose and hug it to me, then drop it to my lap and read the title. *Poems by Emily Dickinson!* The pages open like butterfly wings. Words lift off them one by one. I settle on a page in the middle:

"Hope" is the thing with feathers …

I hold my breath, trying to imagine what this Emily Dickinson person was feeling when she wrote those words. Was she also alone? Was she scared? I slowly let my breath out and keep reading:

> "Hope" is the thing with feathers
> That perches in the soul - And sings the tune without
> the words - And never stops - at all - And sweetest -
> in the Gale - is heard And sore must be the storm -
> That could abash the little Bird That kept so many
> warm - I've heard it in the chilliest land - And on the
> strangest Sea - Yet - never - in Extremity - It asked a
> crumb - of me

I read the poem over and over, picturing the little bird fighting the wind, trying to keep the baby birds warm and safe, like me trying to keep Tig warm and safe, and look how that turned out. Emily's words blur on the page.

"Hope *is* like a bird," I whisper, even though Sara's and my Hope was a rat we buried in a shoebox. I gently close the book. I bet she wrote the poem while watching birds outside her window, just like those birds I saw earlier.

Maybe those birds outside her window showed her what being free looked like. Maybe freedom *does* have wings. Could Mama have been right?

And maybe poet Emily wished *she* was a bird. But then I think about that fly trapped in a web and how wings didn't help it get free.

But Hope is different. Maybe Hope can have wings. I decide right then and there to write a poem to Emily Dickinson to show her she's not alone and that I hear her words without her even having to say them. Will she hear mine? I fumble around the desk and finally find a crayon to write with. Writing with a worn-down crayon isn't easy. It keeps smudging, but if I hold it close to the end, maybe I can pinch out the words.

On a clean page in the journal, I scrawl:

A Song with No Words for Emily

My thoughts are Silent
Words with wings
That only I can Hear.

I keep them locked up
inside me because I'm
filled with Fear.

My words are Broken
bits of thought that
drop like crumbled Stones

And Scatter on
uneven ground
Like brittle, broken Bones.

One day I Hope
a bird will Sing
a song of Liberty,

and when I hear
her voice on high,
I'll know that Bird is me.

I put some of the words in capitals like Emily Dickenson did in her poem, not sure why I am capitalizing them but liking how they stand out. I rip the page out of the journal and close my poem in the book of poems, on the same page as Emily's poem of hope. It's like having two wings of the butterfly come together—her poem on one side, mine on the other. Maybe *that's* what friendship feels like. I start to choke up again but push the feeling away. Who am I trying to kid?

Tired and cold, I put the journal back on the desk but take the book of Emily Dickenson's poems back with me and crawl into bed, missing both Sara and Tig but glad to have Emily Dickinson with me. The bottom sheet is icy cold, and I shiver, wishing harder than ever that Sara was here and we could keep each other warm. The rubber sheet feels stiff, and every time I roll over, it makes a weird, crunchy noise. After a short time, I can feel heat crawling up my legs and around my shoulders, and for a flicker of a second, I almost feel safe. My thoughts drift.

I remember what the Emily lady said about the first exercise. Tell us something about your life. I grow sleepy. What's to tell? In my mind, a poem takes shape, *"like sand gives shape to wind,"* is how Tig would describe it, if she was still here. Can she really be gone?

"Sometimes I feel out of control," I whisper, surprised that maybe I can talk normally, to myself anyway. Staring at the shadows behind my eyelids that float like tiny clouds, I pat the blankets and feel for Abby. When I finally find her, I pull her stiff, skinny body, minus her arm and legs, close to me.

"It's like something takes over me, and I can't do anything but fight. Even now, I feel a roar building up inside me, scaring everyone away," I whisper. She still has an ear to whisper in. I've scared everyone away except Abby, not that she has a choice, and this empty room with its one way in and no way out, trapping me between what is and what could be.

When I open my eyes and look at Abby in the shadows, her plastic eyes are stuck open, which is kind of comforting. Like she's really listening to me.

"I'm not some bird pushed out of its nest to be taught how to fly," I whisper. "I'm the motherless weakling—the homeless weakling—the loveless weakling—with no nest to fall out of and no place safe to land. So, I'm going to have to take my chances and leap."

My next breath hurts to suck in, so I let it out, fighting back tears, and turn on my side, tightly hugging both Abby and the book of Emily Dickinson poems.

"I'm still falling, Abby," I whisper, using what's left of her shirt to dab my eyes. "The wind is out there screaming, 'Fly! Fly! Fly?' Only, we both know—" My voice cracks. "Broken wings can't fly."

18

I WAKE UP JUST BEFORE MORNING CREEPS IN. AT FIRST, I don't know where I am, and I still don't know what day it is. When I roll over, I hit a cold, damp spot and quickly move back to where it's dry. Not again!

The new area is still cold, but at least it's not wet. I quickly check the book of poems, relieved to find it's not wet either. Abby must have fallen on the floor.

I try to remember the poem I told her before falling asleep, in case I want to write it in my journal and make some tokens, but I can only remember something about the cold truth falling and how broken wings can't fly.

Frustrated, I stare out the window, searching for the moon, and try to picture where Sara is right now. Maybe if she can't sleep either, she'll look at the moon too. The moon could be our secret meeting place. I send thoughts to her, hoping she's as good a thought reader as the Emily lady is here.

Can the stars that dot the sky lead Sara here, like Mama said a star led wise men to Jesus? Can stars lead someone to an *ordinary* person? I picture my sister sitting by me, cross-legged in the chair, staring at the stars while planning her next move: our escape. But right now, the only company I have is Loneliness, with a capital L.

Lonely is different from feeling alone. Loneliness chokes me to where I almost can't breathe. It makes me think of things other kids have that I don't. It makes me envious, even about my own sister! Are Sara, Ben, and Rachel doing something fun together without me? Is Sara even at Ben's house? And where are Mama and Daddy? Do they even know we're not at home anymore? Do they know I've been stolen and locked up?

Lonely is what left out feels like. It's a sad feeling, and I don't like it, so before it can swallow me completely, I push it away. But when I shove Lonely aside, Alone is quick to take its place, and Alone makes me feel saddest of all. Alone makes me feel invisible—or worse, insignificant, unimportant, and unwanted—and that makes me feel afraid. I have to pretend to be brave to get past it. I wonder if anyone else feels like me. I curl up into a tight ball, wrapping my arms around my legs so I can hold myself together.

Alone is what being left behind feels like. What if I'm like one of those balloons that gets let go of and it just floats higher and farther away, and nobody can catch me before I pop and flat-out disappear?

Being a nobody sucks, especially when everybody knows you're a nobody. I move my cheek away from the wet spot growing on my pillow. What if I'm too mad to be nice? I'm mad at everybody and everything, which doesn't leave a whole lot of room for any other feelings. But mostly, I'm mad at me. Why can't I be different from myself? Why can't I be normal like Sara? Forget love. Why can't I be someone somebody can *like*?

I hurry and sit up, quickly twisting the sheet like Sara used to do, and curl it around me in a hug, hoping it can take some of these awful thoughts away before too much more hurt gets in, but the sheet-hug doesn't feel the same as when Sara made it. Maybe because when she did it, we were in the hug together. I wish I had the button game Sara made for me, so I could pull the strings and have the buttons spin my worries away. Sara always has good ideas for getting rid of bad thoughts. I try to picture what she would do if she was here, but hard as I try, nothing comes to mind.

I drop the twisted sheets back to the bed and watch it uncoil.

Hugging myself with my own two arms, I rock back and forth. Sara always made up stuff when things got really bad, so that whatever we were going through sounded like a parade by comparison.

"We could be packed in the bowels of a ship on rough seas," she once said. Neither of us knew what bowels were, but Ben had used it in a pirate story he once told us.

"Or abducted by aliens," she had added, saying another line Ben had used. We guessed that abducted was the scary word in that sentence and probably meant they wrapped us in duct tape or something. Whatever the case, it was scary then, and it's still shiver-scary to think about now.

"We could be in an avalanche," she once blurted. "What's an avalanche again?"

"When the snow on a mountain lets go and slides down on top of everyone and everything," I reminded her, back before my words got taken from me. I remembered, because when Ben told us *that* story, he said, "If you're ever in an avalanche, spit or pee."

"Spit or pee?" Sara and I couldn't believe our ears. "Why?"

"So you can see which way is up. Up is the way the pee is not goink."

His advice showed the way out of the snow, but it also showed that sometimes spitting and peeing can be used for a good cause, like maybe even saving a life!

As the old stories come back to me, I start to think about all the things in the world, other than me, that might feel worse or might feel left out or forgotten. Usually, it's things that there are a lot of, like people, stones, trees, leaves, birds, bugs, animals, fish, stars, and flowers. I fill my mind with them. Words. Images. Thoughts. And let them float around in my head.

If Mama was here, she'd say, "A flower doesn't feel lonely. To feel lonely, it would have to have a brain."

Thinking about that reminds me of how Ben once said, "A brain can't feel anything."

But if a brain can't feel anything, how could Mama be right? And how come a brain can't feel anything anyway?

Ben said that the brain had to be sent a message that something felt good or bad and that the brain itself could not feel joy or pain. If all that is true, maybe a flower can't feel lonely or happy or anything else, because it doesn't have a brain that can receive messages sent to it.

All that thinking gets me to wondering if God feels pain. I don't think he does. Think of all the hurt he would have to feel if he did. No. I think humans feel pain and send messages to God through prayers to tell him where they hurt, so he can ease their pain. But if all *that* is true, wouldn't that make *God* a brain? I saw a picture of a brain once in school. It wasn't pretty. Maybe people had to put a face to God, because brains aren't that great to look at. If all that is true, then God is wearing a mask to hide that he's really a giant, ugly brain.

The thoughts grind round and round in my head. Right now, my brain has a strong message being sent to it, and that message is that something in me hurts really, really bad. Only the hurt feels like it's coming from my chest. What if the message being sent is saying that my heart broke?

I un-hug myself and quickly reach up to squeeze the half a heart on my necklace that Mama gave me. She gave one to Sara that was the other half. Sara lost hers, but I still have mine. All the while, hot tears spill down my face.

I will, I promise the empty room, n*otice things that don't get noticed. And I will*, I add, *not take things for granted, and I will*—I stop. If I add too many "wills," maybe I won't be able to do all that willing I'm promising.

Still, just making the promise helps some of the hurt go away, like the promise gives me a purpose and puts wings on both Alone and Lonely and sends them away. Maybe that's the secret: have a plan, figure out the steps, and put the plan in motion, like Sara did. I'm pretty sure that's how Sara must do things to figure out stuff like she does.

I slip out from under the sheet, covering the wet spot on the bed with the blanket, and bend down and feel around the floor and table for Abby's arm and legs. It's hard, but I finally get all her parts snapped back in place. Clutching her, I head for the bathroom, wash off my face with my one free hand, then grab the robe. Back in bed, I lay Abby beside me on the blanket, pretending she's Sara, because sometimes pretending is the only way I can make things okay enough to get back to sleep.

19

A LITTLE LATER, I WAKE UP RELIEVED THAT I MADE IT TO A new day but disappointed that nothing has changed. Same room. Same stuff. Same humming wall. But then I realize something else is still the same that I wanted to be different. There's still no Sara. What's keeping her? Who cares if the court said she couldn't come? Sara can always find a way to break the rules.

The wall hums and clicks, and Emily comes into the room grinning. "Good news, Anna. You made it through forty-eight hours without biting anyone! You're not confined to the cool-down room anymore, so you can get dressed and come out for breakfast in the cafeter—" Her eyes travel from the broken plaster on the floor to the crumbled wall.

I freeze and hold my breath.

"What in land's name happened here?"

I don't know what land's name means, but I do know what the beginning of mad looks like.

"Trapped girl," I answer, slipping back into scared speech but surprised that I don't turn stiff this time.

"Anna, I know you're feeling trapped, but you can't dig your way out. You're destroying your room. This is going to cost money to repair." She sighs before staring back at the wall and running her fingers over the chipped area.

"Sadly, it's going to have to come off your tokens." She takes out a cell phone and clicks a picture of the damage.

"Trapped girl!" I shout. "I saw her!" I try to explain.

Emily presses a few more buttons on her phone, then opens up the folder of papers she brought with her and jots something down.

"Trapped girl!" I shout again.

"I hear you, Anna. No need to shout. And the shadows no doubt were playing tricks on you. Sometimes when we're alone with our thoughts, they can seem pretty darn real, and we see all sorts of things we *think* are real that aren't. I'll see if Kurt can spackle the wall, but you will have to help him repaint it. Offering to do that might mean your tokens won't be removed. Destroying property is a punishable offense, Anna. They could send you to juvie, and I don't think you want to go there, do you?"

I shake my head. I don't know what juvie is like, but just by how she says the word, it sounds worse than this place, and who'd want to go to a place worse than this one? Sara once said she'd heard Daddy call Juvie "kiddie jail."

"On a cheerier note, did you see what I left you?" She glances at the desk, doesn't see it, and her eyes travel around the room, settling on the table by the bed.

"Poems."

"Ah! So you *did* see the book. I thought you'd like it. And did you write in your journal?"

I nod.

"Good, good, good. You can earn points back quickly and start earning tokens, though unless I can get Kurt to fix this without broadcasting that you destroyed the room, money will be withheld from your account to pay back the expenses. Go ahead and sweep up the mess and put it in the trash." She opens my chart and puts a check by something. Probably telling whoever checks the charts that I did my workbook.

She then uses a key to open a cupboard, pulls out a broom and dustpan, and hands them to me. "It occurred to me on my way over that with all the trauma-drama and excitement, you probably were never officially given the schedule of how things work around here. Am I right?"

I nod, still stuck on maybe losing tokens because I gouged out the wall. I'm mad at the stupid cat-girl trapped in it. I was just trying to get her out of there. She just cost me money I wanted to save for a taxi. I haven't even got tokens yet to exchange for money, and here they might already be spent. I should have let the stupid cat-girl claw her own self out. I dump the plaster into the trash can and put the dust broom and pan on the desk. Emily looks at it and at me, then over at the cupboard.

I sigh, grab the broom and pan, and put them away.

"It's quite easy really. The schedule, I mean," she says, smiling, not about the schedule but because I did what she wanted me to do. I'm not stupid.

She starts talking, and my thoughts drift further and further away. Daddy once got a nail stuck in his tire, and it made a clicking sound on the road. *Click-CLICK. Click-CLICK. Click-CLICK.* Over and over.

Emily's voice slips into that sound that voices make when they are repeating something that's on a schedule. It's like our classrooms used to sound when all the kids stood to say the Pledge of Allegiance at once, all pausing in the same places, all speaking in the same tone. *Click-CLICK. Click-CLICK. Click-CLICK.*

She pulls out another piece of paper and reads. "On Mondays and Wednesdays, you'll get up and do your morning rituals, brush your teeth, shower, get dressed, and have breakfast—the usual."

The usual? I don't have a usual. For that to happen, I would have to have one place to be usual in, but I decide to keep those thoughts to myself.

"Then you'll go to the rec room and do some group games and activities. Then you'll have quiet time to work on your workbook, read, or relax, followed by lunch. I'll show you where the rec room is after breakfast," she adds, pausing like she's trying to figure out if she's forgotten anything.

While she's thinking, I'm guessing that today must be a Monday or a Wednesday, since she said she'd show me the rec room after breakfast. I have no idea what day it is. Sara used to keep track by putting marks on the wall. I won't dare do that or they'll take out more money and I'll never be able to get a taxi out of here.

"After lunch, you'll go to either group, therapy, or a special program, depending on your customized schedule. I'll pick that up later and bring it to you. Most residents take a bus to school during the week. You will have individualized tutoring for the forty days you're here. So, don't plan on leaving the premises. The special programs are scheduled when people from the community come in and either read, perform, or do an activity with the group. Group is boys and girls, so don't be surprised to see boys there. We have someone coming in today. How does that sound?"

"Busy," I answer.

She laughs. "I guess it does sound a bit busy. And that's only Mondays and Wednesdays. Tuesdays and Thursdays, you'll work throughout the day on your workbook, read the—"

I tune her out again. I don't like her version of usual. It's too crowded. I want a usual of my own. My usual would be simple. Sara would be here. We'd act like we're doing all the stuff they're making us do, but really, we'd be planning our escape. We'd somehow get to Ben and Rachel's. We'd make them somehow, someway, see that we *have* to stay there.

I pause. Suddenly my usual is starting to sound too busy, too, and full of a lot of what-ifs. Like, what if we couldn't fake it here? What if they caught on to us? What if there's no escape? What if Ben and Rachel still say no? What if …

I look around. The Emily lady is still talking. I shouldn't even be here. I know I bite. I know I wet the bed. I know I can't talk right. I know I ran away. But why did they have to split up me and Sara? They could have fixed me with Sara here. But nobody cares what we want—what I want. What if they fix me wrong and I turn out worse than I already am? I try to picture what a worse me would look like. Would anybody like *that* me any better?

"Anna, we care about you."

I freeze my thoughts. Clearly, she's listening to them again.

"Anna, are you listening? Go ahead and get dressed. After breakfast, we'll have just enough time to move you to your new room before you go to the rec room for morning activities. Isn't that exciting! Your own room! I have to go up front for just a minute, so wait here, and I'll come back and walk you down to the cafeteria.

"Oh, and before I forget, we went over the weekly schedule, so I need you to sign here." While I sign, she sniffs the air and crinkles her nose. "Do you need a new set of sheets?"

I look away.

"Okay, well put the soiled ones in the bag in the bathroom. I'll show you on the way to the cafeteria where the laundry room is. One more thing." She reaches into her pocket and pulls out a key looped with a small string and a cardboard tab with a number on it.

"This is a key to the locked drawer in your room, which is where you'll store your tokens. Fridays are payday, so every Friday at eleven thirty, meet up front by the closet and you can convert your tokens for cash to buy extra food, or whatnot, or to save. Keep tabs on it because it's your responsibility to keep track of your tokens. If they get stolen, that's your problem, and if you lose your key?" She raises her eyebrows and shoulders at the same time, as if one controls the other, but it doesn't take words to get her point.

I finger the key she has handed to me, feeling suddenly electrified, like it's the first thing I've touched around here that makes me feel like I have some real control over getting out of this place. And even though it's a key to a drawer and not the door out of here, it still feels like a secret door has been unlocked. I smile for the first time in a long time and see they've put my initials, A.O., on the tag.

While she puts papers back into her folder, I head for the bathroom, moaning when I see myself in the mirror. My hair, sticking this way and that, looks like a can of tomato soup exploded and froze in midsplat. I pat water on it, trying to get it to settle down, but it keeps poking up. I drag a comb through it and finally call it quits. It's going to do what it's going to do, plain and simple. I'm glad it's a browner red than the False-Alarm guy's orangey-red hair. I wouldn't want anybody to think we were somehow related. Picturing him as a brother or cousin gives me the creeps. I grab a fresh robe and slip my arms through the sleeves, still clutching the keys in one fist.

"Better grab two bags: one for the sheets and one for the clothes. Are these going to laundry?"

"Yes!" I call out, irritated that she keeps bringing up those stupid sheets.

When I come out of the bathroom, I see the door is propped open and Emily is gone. She wasn't kidding! *I'm not locked in!* This is it! My chance to escape!

I look around for my clothes but don't see them anywhere. Wait. Was that Emily's plan? To take my clothes, so I couldn't run away? Well, two can play that game.

I button the robe all the way up, drop the key in the side pocket, yank on some shoes, and peer out into the hall, making sure to look both ways. I can see people lining up at a doorway down the hall to the left. That must be the cafeteria, and since everyone is waiting there for breakfast, I turn the other way and race toward the door we went out of when that Justin guy pulled the fire alarm.

I pass two hallways and am just about to pass a third when something flies around the corner and slams into me, sending me sprawling to the floor. A grunting noise escapes me, and I slide a good three feet on the slick tile.

"Hey, Robe-Rage! Wha'chore malfunction?" A girl who looks to be about my age glares at me. I watch as she rubs her arm and I nurse my own stinging elbow.

"Uh, *hello-o-o.* Are you D-E-F?" She moves her head from side to side as she spells the letters out. "Wha'chore problem, anyway?" She sticks her hands behind her ears and pulls them forward. Does she even know how dumb she looks? And who spells *deaf* d-e-f?

I pull myself up from the floor and glare back at her, wishing she was just a little bit shorter than she turns out to be. "You!" I shout, just in case she's the one that's d-e-f.

"Me? Wha'chu smokin'?" She throws her hands to her hips. One hand comes loose and flies up so she can wag a finger sideways, like a windshield washer, at my face. "You the one actin' like there's a fire, not me."

My arms and legs stiffen at the word *fire*; my head cements to my neck, and I sway in small circles right before her weirded-out eyes. Then I remember to let out the breath I've been holding.

"There you are!" Emily's voice fills the hallway before the head-shaking-finger-wagging-name-calling girl can say anything more. "Oh, good! You found each other. What a surprise, huh?" She looks at the other girl and back at me.

I continue glaring at her, swaying, since nothing else on me seems able to move. It would have taken me five seconds max to reach the outside if she hadn't run me over. I could have escaped all by myself. Maybe even found Sara if this gnarly girl had gone to breakfast on time.

Emily looks at me sympathetically. "I just realized I took the bag with your clothes. I don't know what I was thinking. I am so sorry."

I keep staring at the girl.

"Hi, sweetheart." I don't even have to look at Emily to know she's smiling while talking to Miss Weirdo. "How are you?"

"I'd be much better if Robe-Rage here would watch where she was going."

"Ah-ah. No name calling. You know better. You don't want to lose points, do you? You're so close to reaching your goal and getting out. It's partly my fault. I haven't shown her around yet, and she probably got lost."

Even though I'm not looking at her, I can see Emily glance over at me before turning back to the girl. "You better get down to the cafeteria. You don't want to miss breakfast. Oh, and by the way—"

The girl bolts, calling, "Yeah, yeah. See you later, Miss Emily!" before Emily can say anything more, which is fine by me. I start to feel myself breathing easier again and slowly feel my limbs softening enough for me to move them. That was a close call. We both stare after her. I thought the girl was going to bust me for trying to run away, which I bet would have put me right back in cool-down, but she didn't, and for that I'm grateful, even though she's bossy and hotheaded.

"I'm really sorry for grabbing your bag of clothes, Anna. It's like an automatic reflex to grab bags of clothes that need to go to the laundry. Let's get some clothes from the closet and get you dressed and down to breakfast."

I nod. I'm both excited and scared about going to the cafeteria, hoping beyond hope that today is the day that I'll see Sara hiding somewhere. I picture her under a chair or table, motioning madly for me to join her when she feels it's safe. Knowing Sara, I bet she has a plan. I just hope that her plan can work and that we'll be out of here before anyone can notice I'm gone. But I've learned that hope doesn't always show up when you want it to.

20

AFTER PUTTING ON A SWEATSHIRT, JEANS, AND TENNIS shoes right there in the clothes closet, and even remembering to take the key out of the robe pocket and put it into the pocket of the jeans, while Emily guards the door, I then drop my dirty laundry off at the laundry room, which Emily and I pass on the way to the cafeteria. I make sure I bury the sheet and robe under other clothes, so no one will see I had an accident. A hum of noise from the cafeteria pours out into the hallway.

The big, hollow room is surprisingly quiet for all the kids lined up in it. There are two long rows of tables, tons of food, and at least twenty boys and girls, but hard as I look, the room does not have the one and only thing I want to see: my sister.

I fall into line, crushed. I just don't get what could have gone wrong. Sara always finds me. Always.

"Over here are the cereals," Emily says, pointing along a wall. "Along that wall over there is fruit, scrambled eggs, bacon, sausage, cheese, bread. Pick out whatever you want. Sit anywhere. You only have half an hour. I'll be back then to show you to your new room."

She disappears, and I stand there, unable to move, like my feet have suddenly grown roots. Some voices come up behind me and push past. There's lots of "Who's she?" coming at me. Two girls glance over their shoulders, look down at my legs and back at each other, then shrug. They were the same two who saw me in the hallway when I was in the wheelchair, coming back into the building after the false fire alarm. They're probably trying to figure out how I'm suddenly able to walk again.

"Hey! Robe-Rage!" shouts a familiar voice.

I wince at the name and look over to see the girl who almost bowled me over in the hallway, sitting alone at a long table, waving her arms wildly. I have never seen so many pigtails on one person's head.

When I don't answer, she does this weird gesture with her hands, flipping them forward toward the floor like she's saying, "And here's the floor," while raising her eyebrows, thrusting her chin out, and doing this strange shiver-like shaking of her head, making the beads on her pigtails click—all at the same time. I can sometimes read lips, but I don't read weird.

I do realize after a long silence, though, that it might be her very odd way of saying she's waiting to see if I'm going to sit by her. I grab a yogurt and an orange and look around for a different place to sit.

"Hello-o-o," the familiar voice calls out. Her hands are in front of her, flipped up, like what she's really saying is, "I don't know," but without the shrug this time.

I look around. There are no other places to sit, so I work my way over to her table.

"I was about to ask if a cat gotcher tongue," she says, swinging her leg over the bench to face her food.

"Don't you mean *your* tongue?" a boy who looks like he could have been a blown-up balloon—sitting a table over from her—calls out. The other boys laugh.

"Or maybe your nasty tongue, Toe-Moss," the girl answers, shifting her head back and forth with each word. I can't stop staring at her. Words spill out of her mouth, but that's not what I can't stop looking at. It's how she talks with her whole body that has me glued to her every move.

She suddenly stops talking and stares at me. I freeze, unsure of what to do next.

"Well, whaterya waitin' for? A written invite? Eat. We don't got all day to conversate. All this food they providin' us, and that's all you got? Yer gonna be one Starvin' Marvin in all caps later. Hey, wait a minute. I remember you. I thought I recognized you. You that girl that can't walk, only clearly seein' you now, I can see you was fakin' it, makin' 'em wheel you in that wheelchair when we had that false fire alarm. You be that new girl they locked up in cool-down. What'd you do? Grow new legs in the 'tween time?"

Tween time? I stare at her, not saying a word.

She leans over toward her plate to take a bite of food and suddenly stops and turns her tilted head toward me. I look down at her, watching her eyes grow big and round.

"Oh-my-you-know-who." Still bent over, she points with her free hand up to the ceiling. I look up but don't see the "you-know-who" she's talking about.

"It's *me*." She bolts upright, drops her fork, and does this scooping of the air thing with both hands and flips them toward herself, all five fingers pointing toward her face, then does that shiver-shaking thing with her head. A strand of cheese dangles from her chin.

I frown.

"Me!" she says again, flipping her hands back toward me—all while making a pained face that goes perfectly with the weird motions, only this time, the string of cheese is wagging back and forth on her chin like a mouse tail. "Kat-with-a-K. You know. The one that was talking at you—through the wall last night." She whispers that last part, looking around like she's making sure no one has heard her.

Wait! *She's* the "Cat" Emily told me about? Kat-with-a-K?

A humming noise, like she's chomping down on broken *m*'s in her mouth, suddenly comes out of her, and she looks at me like I'm in deep trouble, making me actually feel like I am.

"M-M-M! You was running away again, wasn't you? That's why you 'bout bowled me over in the hall. You was tryin' to escape this place. Ha, ha, haaa."

Her last ha rises to a high note as she throws her head back. If she had frozen in that position, I could have counted all her teeth.

She looks at me, green eyes dancing. Her cocoa-colored face glows bright as a full August moon. She turns back to her stack of waffles and cheese-smothered eggs, still snickering, then wipes the cheese off her chin.

She's bent over her food again and curls her head around and looks up at me.

"Now let me get this straight. You get stuck in this snake pit for running away, and then the first thing you do when you get outta cool-down is to try to run away? I'm sorry, but in my book, that's the D-E-F of *stoo-oo-pid*."

Def? And what's with this place that everyone breaks words, no matter how many syllables they are, into threes? I stare at my yogurt and don't say anything. *Sara was the one who was always smart at running away. Not me.*

"Not that I'm calling you stupid," she quickly adds, looking around like one of those snakes she was yammering about earlier was going to come out of the pit and sink its fangs into her. "Look, don't go tellin' nobody I said you was stupid. Seriously. I'm this close"—she puts her thumb and index finger about an inch apart—"to getting out of here and don't want no points took away. And who knows? Maybe you really smart, but you like hiding it for some reason."

She takes a big bite of waffle and grins before chewing, then points at my yogurt with her fork. "I get it. Everybody gotta do what dey gotta do. C'mon, eat," she adds between chews.

I just sit and search the room for Sara.

"That be your answer? Okay, I won't stop you, but I also not gonna let food just sit here and go to waste, unless it's goin' to *my* waist." She grins and gives herself two quick pats to the stomach, then laughs, adding in a hoarse whisper, "A girl's gotta watch out for herself. You dig?" She reaches over, grabs the unopened yogurt and orange, and starts to stuff them in her pockets. But when she reaches back over for more, her hand freezes in midair—then in slo-mo, staring past me, she does something really, *really* strange.

She slowly pulls the food back out of her pockets and sets the yogurt and fruit in front of me, right where they were before she took them, even turning them so I can see the labels. A strange smile seems to search around for her face before finding it, and it settles there, giving her more of a busted look than a smiley one. Clearly, she's entered some kind of weird Numb Zone. But why? Whatever the reason, this girl needs to be locked up. She's crazy. Or should I say crra-aaa-zy?

"Dad! You early!" she suddenly chirps, sitting up tall and clasping her hands in front of her like some church girl. I turn around and see a large brown man standing just behind us, staring hard at her. "Didn't see you come in."

"I can see that." He glances over at me, nods, and smiles in what I've come to know as a brief hello gesture people give around here when they don't know you. He turns his attention back to her. When he does, his eyes, which are such a dark brown they look blue, harden to big, glassy marbles. I can't look.

"I was just trying to conversate with my new friend here, helpin' her—" A sharp kick under the table finds my foot, and I jump. "Save up some food for later. She not hungry right now. Ain't that right, Robe—uh—?" She stops herself from calling me the name and waves a thumb toward me just in case he can't figure out who the "she" is that she's talking about.

"Is that right." He doesn't say it like a question.

I glance up at him when I feel another swift kick from Kat-with-a-K. She is right about one thing. I'm not hungry.

"Right," I mumble, but he doesn't look like he's listening or believing either of us.

"You don't need to steal, Kat. Isn't that what got you in RTC in the first place?"

I stare at her. *Did he just say that Kat-with-a-K steals?* She first looks at me, then rolls her eyes back up at him, then rolls them back to me and ducks her neck down until it doesn't look like she even has one, making her look two inches shorter. And then she pulls her lips back into a new goofy grimace before shrugging her shoulders up but not letting them come down.

Stealing got her here, and she's stealing again? All the while making fun of me for trying to run away when running away is supposed to be what got me in here?

I look back at her dad, whose lips are drawn tight but just slightly curled. Never taking his eyes off Kat-with-a-K, he starts backing away. "Okay, then. I'll see you ladies later."

When he's a good distance away, Kat-with-a-K lets out a huge sigh and falls against the table like a balloon that has just deflated. "Man! That was close. I coulda lost points *and* money *and* been sent to cool-down. Sorry for the kicks, but you was jus' sittin' there not sayin' anything. Still, thanks for coverin' for me. You started your chart yet?" She reaches over and takes back my yogurt and orange and pockets them.

Frowning, I watch her and shake my head.

"Well, you will soon enough, and the only way to earn money in here is to get points and not lose them. That last part's the key and the hardest thing to do. First week I was here, I got so many points took away I was in the neg-a-tive." She laughs at the memory. "I built 'em back up quick enough. And I don't want to be losing them again because of no stupid runawa—uh, I mean because of some han-di-capper. That be you," she says, grinning.

"Not handicapped," I challenge.

"Yeah, tell that to the wheelchair, and why you talkin' funny?"

Why am *I* talking funny? I clam up. Better to let her think I *am* handicapped and that I talk funny than to find out I wet the bed and that Terrible Ted burned me and threatened to take away my voice if I talked, and that wetting myself was why I was in a wheelchair in the first place.

"By the way, next time you go to the closet and get clothes, make sure they be least two sizes bigger'n you would ever catch yourself dead in on the outside, so you can stuff food and supplies in the pockets. 'Specially if you plan on runnin' away. If nothin' else, you gots to have food. If I learned anything in here, it's that escapin' takes planning, but survivin' takes food!"

She jumps up, grabs her tray, and heads toward the door. "You comin' or what?"

I follow, not knowing what else to do.

"Dad?" I say, when we're out in the hall, turning the small word into a big, loaded question. It's not fair that Kat-with-a-K gets to be here with her dad. Why can't everyone have their dads here?

"Huh? Dad? Whatchu talkin' 'bout? Dad who?" She looks around when her expression suddenly changes. "Oh, oh, oh. Him? No, no. He ain't my daddy. Everybody jus call him 'Dad' around here. It's how it be. He be the closest thing to a dad some of these guys has ever seen. 'Cludin' me," she adds. "But then, my daddy's a magician." She looks over at me and grins.

I don't even try to hide my envy. Her dad does magic? Lucky her!

"He always be disappearing," she says, then does that weird hand-spilling, head-rattling, pained-looking face thing she does when I don't say anything. But then she busts up laughing.

"He *disappears.* Get it? He's a *magician?* 'Snot as funny when you got to 'splain it."

Suddenly, I get it and find myself laughing for the first time in I don't know how long. Guess by her description, my daddy's a magician too.

"How 'bout you. Wha'chore daddy do?"

"Sings."

"Really? Rap? Jazz? Blues?"

"Country rock."

Her shoulders drop. "Oh. Well, country's okay, I guess, 'specially with the rock in there." She nods her head like she's trying to convince herself. "Yeah, country's cool enough. Who he sing with? Damien? Keith? That ol' Willie dude?"

My eyebrows shoot up.

"Yeah, see there. Didn't think I knew nobody in country, but I do. 'Least you have a daddy. That's the main thing. And by the way, girl, we got to do something about that hair of yours." She stares at my head, and I look away. "I can fix it. Don't panic. We kin set up shop in the bafroom. You be lookin' fine in no time."

Emily catches up to us before I can say anything. "Oh, good. You found each other and made up. Small world, huh, Kat? Can I borrow Anna for a bit and help her move into her new room?"

"What number's she movin' to?"

"Two twenty-three."

"Hey, that be by me. I'm two twenty-two. Robe-Rage! We're almost roomies."

Emily gives her a kind of soft frown at calling me Robe-Rage but then smiles it off. I don't know what roomies are, but I do know that I'm happy for two reasons: Kat-with-a-K didn't give away my secret about trying to run away, and I'm not in the cool-down room anymore.

Make that three things: I get to have my own space. Funny, it used to be that if Sara wasn't in my room, I couldn't sleep, but being locked up all by myself, I guess I can sleep without someone in there. Still, that doesn't mean I don't miss my sister something fierce.

If nothing else, I'm learning that this place isn't a wild-animal farm or freaky shelter after all, and Kat isn't really a cat, and she's not stuck in a wall or growing fur or whiskers. That sedative they gave me must have really done a number on me. I'm embarrassed just thinking about it now.

Still, it's a residential treatment center, and a residential treatment center's not a home. It's a stopping place. What did Mean Kurt call it? A warehouse? More like a nowhere house, if you ask me, since Sara clearly isn't here.

I wonder if Kat-with-a-K has any ideas on how we could find her. She's good at stealing things, but is she good at finding things, too?

"I'll be in rec!" Kat calls over her shoulder. "See you there. Better watch out, Robe-Rage. Dodgeball's the game, and nobody, and I do mean nobody's, gettin' me out."

21

ON THE WAY TO MY NEW ROOM, EMILY GRINS, GLANCING AT me several times. "I thought earlier that you and Kat were strangers, but I see I was wrong. It must be nice to catch up with your friend again. How long have you and Kat known each other?

"Pretty long," I answer. About an hour is my guess. That's longer than I've known any kid in one sitting, except my sister, and Kat even seems to like me, which makes me wonder if she's just pretending, so she can steal my food. That last part makes more sense, and I accept it. Stealing isn't just a skill. It's survival.

It turns out the new room isn't half-bad either. It's a lot like the cool-down room. The walls are a lighter celery green than the walls in the hall. The floor is still white tile with a smattering of colored tiles mixed in. It has more furniture than the cool-down room. There's a bolted down twin bed, a bookcase that already has some books on it, a small table by the bed, a bigger table under the barred window, two table chairs, and a dresser.

"I put some clothes for you over there." Emily points to two bags by the dresser. "From now on, you can grab what you need from the closet each week. Someone from the front desk can open the closet for you."

I nod and look around. The bathroom has two doors, one to my room and one to—

"You and Kat will share a bathroom," Emily explains, reading my thoughts again. "Kat already has her toiletries over here, so why don't you put yours on the shelf on the other side."

I don't know exactly what toiletries are, but since the word has toilet in it, my guess is it's stuff you use in the bathroom. I empty out the bags and put what few clothes I have in the dresser and stick my toothpaste and toothbrush in the plastic cup and put them in the bathroom.

"Okay, time for recreation," Emily chirps, checking her watch. "I'll walk you over there. After rec, you can go to the great room and check the community board to see if there are any activities you'd like to attend. Also, I've scheduled for you to start Behavioral Mod later this afternoon. You'll meet with Dr. Kitanovski in that office over there, the second from the end. Group," she adds, "is in the room next to Dr. Kitanovski's office." She points out my door toward the front offices, and I nod.

"Tomorrow, Thursday, you'll officially start on your workbook, but go ahead and start reading it later today if you want. As you've no doubt figured out, there's no school this week, as teachers are doing their in-service, getting continuing-ed credits—"

I watch her lips move, not really understanding what she's trying to tell me, but I do get that today is Wednesday and nobody's going to school. The week's only half-over. It feels like I've been here forever. I know only one other kid: Kat-with-a-K. Well, and Justin, if him staring at me from the parking lot counts as knowing.

"After this week, I won't be taking you everywhere, and you'll be expected to know where you need to be and get there on time. Tomorrow, you'll probably notice other residents reading and filling in their workbooks throughout the day. Feel free to bounce thoughts off of them. You'll get to know them better in group."

If Mama was here, she'd tell Emily, "Thoughts don't bounce," but right now, I'm not so sure about that. Mine are bouncing all over the place.

"Here's the drawer for your tokens," she adds, tapping on the desk. "Most of the residents keep their key with them at all times."

When we reach the rec room, I can hear that's not all that's bouncing. I see Kat is already active in the game.

"Run over and join in." Emily steps to the side for me to pass. I stare at the girls, not sure of what to do or where to go. I've never played this game before. It doesn't look fun.

"You're playing against the girls wearing vests." She raises a finger in the air and makes a counting motion. "Okay, you are shirts, the other team is vests," she adds, nudging me. "It's dodgeball, so try to dodge the ball and not get—"

Before she can finish her sentence, the ball whizzes through the air and hits me square in the stomach. You wouldn't think something filled with air could hurt so bad, but it's like being hit with a cannon ball.

I buckle over, then try to stand but only get partway. *The Inside Girl! Did she get hurt? Is she okay?* Then I remember The Inside Girl escaped.

I stagger forward.

Emily bends down and looks up into my face. "Are you all right? Come sit over here. That must have hurt."

I stand as upright as I can, still gripping my stomach, and shuffle in her direction.

"Everyone. Back up. Give Anna some space. She wasn't even officially in the game." Emily puts her arms out and motions with her hands for everyone to move back.

I growl, because all the girls start to circle and close in around me in spite of Emily's attempts to keep them back. "She's out!" one of them shouts.

"Out of her mind is more like it," another adds, laughing. The more they circle, the louder I growl.

"That just cost you fifty points, Carla!" I hear Emily call out.

"Fifty? That's not fair. Fifteen, now that would be fair, but *fifty*? Come on, Miss E., that's extreme, don't you think? Give me a frickin' break!"

"Keep talking back, and I'll add another fifty," Emily calls out.

"That's enough, everyone." Emily puts her arms out toward them. "Go back to your game."

I turn in a small circle, one arm out, hand flat, trying to keep them back, while the other arm is wrapped around my stomach. Mean Kurt shows up and joins the inner circle. "Careful, girls. She a biter," he calls out, and the circle of girls fall back, erupting in whispers, leaving only the three staff members around me. Emily gets a call over the loudspeaker and shouts something over her shoulder to Mean Kurt before racing out of the room.

Kat breaks through the circle of staff members and comes right up to me.

"Wha'chore malfunction? I get that it hurts bein' hit in the gut, but growlin'?" She pushes on my shoulder.

"Back away from her, Kat," Mean Kurt orders. "I mean it. She bites."

Kat ignores Mean Kurt. "Stand up, girl. You one hot mess. Why you actin' like some crazy, wild animal? Stand up! You got to take the punches like a champ, you hear me?"

I feel myself turning stiff. Crazy, wild animal? She thinks *I'm* the crazy, wild animal?

"Look around!" I want to shout. "It's not me who's crazy."

But what if she's right? What if I'm the wild animal? What if that's why the judge says I can't see Sara? He's afraid I'll hurt her. He's afraid I'll hurt my own sister.

Hot tears spring up from nowhere, making me even madder. People should know I would never hurt my sister. Not on purpose. I hate this place. I hate dodgeball. I hate the judge that split up me and Sara. I hate our social worker for trapping me here. And I hate myself worse than I hate all of them put together.

"I hate you!" I shout, breaking free and turning on Mean Kurt, but it comes out sounding like, "Ah hay ya-a-a-a!"

Kurt stretches out an arm, circling, and by watching his devil eyes, I can tell he's looking for a good time to grab me. "You know what this means," he says, grinning like the evil clown he is. "You're going to end up right back in cool-down."

"Who died and made you zookeeper?" Kat snaps.

"Keep the attitude up, Kat, and you'll find yourself in cool-down room right alongside her. It could cost you getting out of here," Mean Kurt snaps back.

Kat clams up. Emily races in, trying to catch her breath. She pushes past him and shouts, "What's going on here?"

"Like I said, she's out," Kat answers. "Only, she don't seem to know it, and now she jus' actin' like some wildcat, hissin' and scratchin'."

Emily looks at me and nods like all this is suddenly making sense. "Are you okay, Anna? I know you were just getting ready to join the game, but when you're out in dodgeball, just go stand against the wall until one of *their* team members gets out, and then you get to go back in the game. Haven't you ever played dodgeball before?"

I shake my head, still gripping my stomach. A low growl follows every breath I let out.

"Seriously?" the one called Carla sneers. "Who doesn't know how to play dodgeball?"

"Tell you what. Let's switch to another game," Emily calls out. "I never did like dodgeball," she adds. "It's too rough and gets everyone all worked up."

Groans fill the room, drowning out my growls, till the whole place really does sound like some wild-animal farm.

"Thanks a lot," a lanky girl snaps.

"Yeah, thanks for nothing," the Carla girl who lost fifty points sneers. They pass me and head toward a net on the other side of the room.

"You know what?" Emily says, checking her watch. "It's almost time for community activities. Let's just go to your rooms and get cleaned up, and then go to your community group in thirty minutes."

Everyone shuffles past, still grumbling under their breath.

"We were ahead."

"Screw you. You weren't even close. Losers," Kat says.

"Watch your language, ladies. Break it up. Break it up." Even I can tell nobody's listening to Emily.

"Who you callin' a loser?" And on it goes.

Mean Kurt steps toward me, but Emily stops him. "I've got this, Kurt."

The grumblings grow weaker and weaker as the final girls file out of the room. It's like thunder fading, but that doesn't mean the storm is over. You can be sure someone's going to want to do something to make me pay for messing up their game.

When everyone is gone, Emily turns to me and sighs. "That was my fault for not preparing you a little better and introducing you to the others. Why don't you skip community activities today and get some rest, or start on your lessons in your workbook? I'll mark you as excused in your record. We've already fallen a little behind, and quite frankly, I think your time will be better spent catching up. What do you think?"

I don't really know what I think, so I don't say anything. I follow her, still a little bent over, out to the hall and across to my room. I'm not faking it either. My stomach hurts. That ball hit me hard.

"Did you get enough breakfast?" Emily asks, and I nod, even though my stomach is screaming at me. Right now, all I want to do is get to my room and crawl into bed.

Can the day get any worse?

22

Emily stops at the door of my new room, all the while telling me not to worry, that I won't lose points because it was a misunderstanding. She is about to say more when we hear her name over the intercom and she again gets called to the office.

"You sure you're okay?" she says, lightly touching my arm and looking me in the eyes. I don't pull away. She isn't scared of me. She's not afraid I will bite. She and Kat are the first two people outside of Sara and Ben and Rachel who treat me like I'm normal and don't act scared around me.

I nod and debate inside myself whether to try and run away again when she leaves or to just go "get settled in," as they like to say around here.

For now, I decide to settle.

I wave to Emily and almost walk into the wall, missing the doorway by half a step. Shaking it off, I step into the room, but a strange clicking sound jerks me back outside. I poke my head through the door and listen hard to try to figure out what the sound could be. A small hiss comes just before each click.

I know I've heard that sound before, but where? Something about the noise chokes me, turning scared into downright fearful. What is it? It seems to be coming from the bathroom.

Ffft click. Ffft click.

The sound abruptly changes and now sounds like one long *Fffftthhhhh*

Suddenly, it's all too clear what's making the sound, and I freeze. *It's a cigarette lighter.* Daddy has one. And so did Terrible Ted, the mean man who burned that P in my arm with his cigarette, because I couldn't stop wetting the bed.

Blood drains out of my head. My legs grow stiff. Then my arms won't move.

Don't freeze up! Run! I tell myself.

But it's too late. I'm already stiff as Abby and am frozen to the spot, staring straight ahead like a zombie.

I hear a hoarse whisper-laugh. *Someone is in the bathroom.* Seconds later, Justin pokes his head around the bathroom door, looks up surprised, and grins.

"Well, well, well. Handicap-Girl is walking. Whadaya know?"

"I'm not handicapped," I want to shout, but I just stare at his lanky self.

"Bet you don't know where I just got back from."

I keep staring straight ahead, not at him, but I can still see him.

"I just got back from attending a fire-safety course." He says "a fire-safety course" in a mocking tone and removes his thumb from the lighter before flicking it on again. My eyes drop to the flame that's now in front of him, casting a dim yellow light onto his eerily calm, deeply pitted face. His brown, close-set eyes droop down at the sides, giving him a tired, almost puppy-dog look. I wonder, does he really start fires? Or does he just pull fire alarms and play with lighters to make people think that he does?

"And guess what? I learned all about how fire burns things up, because dumb me doesn't know that, right? Did *you* know fire burns things up, Handicap Girl?"

I glare at him. *How dare he keep calling me that.*

"I got a question for you, or should I say a riddle."

I frown, and my breath comes quickly. What will he do if I don't guess it?

"Here it is: Tear it off, scratch its head, what now is black once was red. What am I?"

I don't want to play his riddle game, but my mind is already searching for the answer.

"You like fire?" He walks in a wide circle around me, like a wildcat circling its prey.

His question throws me off. I slowly turn as he circles, so he's never behind me. *Do I like fire?* Fire isn't something you like or don't like. It's something you need or don't need. But right when I'm thinking that, my thoughts leap to Terrible Ted. *He* certainly liked fire. From the look in his eyes when he lit the match to when he lit the cigarette, to when he sucked in the smoke, making the end of the cigarette good and hot, to then burning me—all that probably made him feel powerful.

Is that what's going on with this Justin guy? Does starting fires make him feel powerful? I get my answer by the look on his face. It's like his blank eyes are shouting, "You guessed it. You win the prize." Yet no fire is left in those eyes.

I don't want to win any prize, unless the prize is getting out of here. I look away. Ben always said to never look an animal in the eye, or it will feel threatened and want to attack.

"A match," I blurt. Of course. That's what his stupid riddle is about, because that's what he's about. Lighting fires.

Is that disappointment I see crossing his face? He didn't think I could figure out the answer.

"Good guess," he says flatly. "Great hair, by the way." He throws me off again. "Fire red. Isn't that what they call hair that color?"

Suddenly, I want to hide my hair. I want to hide, period, but he keeps on circling and flicking the lighter on and off. On and off.

"I'm not trying to scare you." His softer tone makes my throat tighten. I don't know what's worse, him sounding mean or nice. But for someone who's not trying to scare me, he's doing a super job of doing what he says he's not trying to do. Silence crawls between us.

"Not much of a talker, I see." He steps toward me, and I step back.

"Oh, don't worry. I like that about you. People who talk too much get me fidgety, and you don't want guys like me to get fidgety." He flicks the lighter upright between his thumb and index finger and rocks it back and forth. If it was a sign, it would be blinking.

"Like that chatty friend of yours. Kat, is it? Someone needs to shut that girl up. And talk about fidgety."

He takes another step forward, and I take another step back, putting me fully out into the hallway. I feel safer out here in the hall, as there's more room to run, if only I could get myself to do just that.

"This Kat's room?" He steps out into the hall, throwing his head back as a pointer. "Tell her I left her a surprise."

I keep inching away, giving him plenty of room to pass. Thankfully, he does, and walks backward down the hall toward the boys' wing, grinning at me the whole time. "I'm impressed you got the riddle!" he calls out, slipping the lighter into his pocket. "Not too many people do." He turns, rounding another corner. I clasp my hands in front of me, trying to stop the shaking. Last time I shook like this, I was pinned under Terrible Ted's bony knee, staring up at his burning cigarette.

Emily comes up from behind, and I jump when she touches my shoulder. "Anna! Why are you still in the hall? Your room doesn't bite—

"Oh, I am so sorry. I can't believe I just said that. Seriously, it's just an expression. I didn't mean anything by it." She stands a minute, staring at me. "Hey, what's going on with you? Come in here and sit down. You look like you're going to pass out."

"Justin." I force his name to come out and look to make sure he's not on his way back.

She frowns before speaking, looking first in the doorway of my room and then down the hall. "Wait. You saw Justin here?" She looks back to me. "On this wing?"

I nod.

She wraps an arm loosely around my shoulder and looks up and down the hallway. "Kurt is supposed to be keeping tabs on him. I am so, so sorry, Anna. Did Justin scare you?" She pulls her arm back and starts punching numbers on her cell phone.

I don't answer, but she reads my thoughts.

"Of course he did. I'll talk to Kurt and the other staff, and we'll make sure you're never alone with him again, okay?"

"Okay."

"Is Kat in community?"

I shrug.

"Okay, well do you want to walk with me on my rounds before going to group and then Behavioral Modification? You have a little over an hour. We'll just stay on this wing." She turns her attention to the phone.

"Hi, Emily here. Can you alert security that Justin was just seen on the girls' wing? Two twenty-three. Yes. Thanks."

I follow her down another hall. In the distance, a sound rolls toward us, like a wave racing toward the shore. The closer we get to one classroom, the louder the sound grows.

"Ah, I can see you are drawn to the chanting," Emily whispers, smiling her approval.

She's right. I am drawn to the sound, and I don't even know why. I've never heard it or anything like it before, but it feels like it's drawing the fear right out of me. I peer through the window in the door at the group activity.

"It's one of our community programs," Emily says quietly. "Did you see it on today's schedule?"

I shake my head.

"This particular program is called Healing through Music and Chant. I've not done it before, but it looks interesting. You want to go in and try? They just started, so you'll have time to take it in before group and B-Mod."

I hesitate, see Kat's red shoes, then nod before slipping into the room. The lady leading the group smiles, hands me a mat, and points to an open spot on the floor. I roll out the rubber pad and sit, crossing my legs like the other girls around me. I recognize some of them. I put my hands palm up on my knees like they're doing. Kat-with-a-K is across the room. She grins at me, and I nod, showing I see her. I search the room for Sara and let out a deep breath.

"Eeeeee-wahhhhhh," the leader says, and everyone repeats after her, holding onto the wah until they run out of breath. A recorded drum beat plays behind her.

"Eeeeee-wahhhhhh," she chants again, and they repeat the chant.

I join in, not loud enough for anyone to hear, but I'm still doing the chant. I like that it's not real words and nobody's trying to say anything. Terrible Ted can't burn out my tongue for making chanting sounds.

"Oooooh-wahhhhhh," she says, changing the chant a little. We follow her lead.

"Oooooh-wahhhhhh," she repeats, and so do we.

Last, she starts with "Ee-wah," and changes to "Ooh-wah" in the same breath. That is hard to do, but I give it my best.

I close my eyes like everyone else, chant with them, and feel myself relaxing deeper and deeper with each chant, letting the fear of running into Justin slip away.

"Ommmmmmm," she says, finishing the chant.

I don't know how, but we join her and all end up all ommmmming and stopping together. I open my eyes as she tells us to start thinking about creating our own chants. "Listen to the sounds in your head. Start looking for a pattern. When it comes to you, sing it quietly to yourself or in a low tone. Go ahead and try. Let it come to you. Don't force it." She turns off the recorded drum beat when a chant started by Kat begins on one side of the room. *Eenie-meenie-chi-chi. Eenie-meenie-chi-chi.*

Half the room ebbs and swells to the gentle roll of chants.

Eenie-meenie-chi-chi . Eenie-meenie-chi-chi .

A chant suddenly finds me—maybe because I realize I'm really hungry about now. I find myself wishing I ate breakfast and start a low chant: *Ooh chow-chow, ee-wow-wow. Ooh chow-chow, ee-wow-wow.*

Across the room, Kat-with-a-K continues with her chant. "Eenie-meenie chi-chi, Eenie-meenie-chi-chi," and then something magical happens.

Everyone on her side of the room starts chanting Kat's chant, and everyone on my side picks up on mine. At first, everyone is just whispering the sounds.

Eenie-meenie-chi-chi ooh chow-chow, ee-wow-wow.

Eenie-meenie-chi-chi ooh chow-chow, ee-wow-wow.

And then it builds and turns into a sort of chorus and lifts up the room, or so it feels, and sends a motion of sound back and forth across the floor, rippling the air.

Eenie-meenie-chi-chi ooh chow-chow, ee-wow-wow.

Eenie-meenie-chi-chi ooh chow-chow, ee-wow-wow.

Some voices start high and go low, like they're climbing down a ladder, and other voices start low and go high, breaking into harmony. And then, just as magically, it ends on a collective *ah-ommmmmmm.*

I just know if he was here, Mama's Jesus would have risen up at the sound of our voices, smiling with his eyes closed, or Daddy would have, for sure—only Daddy's eyes would have stayed opened. I even look to see if he's at the window, but I don't get surprised this time that he's not there. My tears aren't just because Daddy still hasn't found me. They're filling up my eyes because the chant touches something deep inside me in a way I've never been touched before. Maybe it's what the heart of calm feels like when it's not just words being said but an actual feeling surrounding you, hugging you, even—like the chant is saying everything's going to be all right.

"That was *beautiful*, ladies. Deep breaths. Now, everyone lie back on your mats and continue to breathe," the leader says quietly. A muffled thumping sound follows, and soon we're all lying flat on our backs.

"That's it. Relax. Start with your feet. Good. Feel your muscles relax. Very good. Now, let the feeling of relaxation move up to your knees.

"Relax," she whispers again. "Keep it going through you, past your stomach and your chest.

"Relax your fingers and hands, your arms and neck—your head. Relax."

The room grows quiet, like a noisy day has slipped into the quiet of night. I wake up and look around. Other girls are waking up too. Some drifted off to sleep, like me.

By the time I leave, I've nearly forgotten about Justin, RTC, and all that's happened. Emily is waiting outside the door, all smiles. All I can think about is the magic that happened in that room.

"That was a-ma-zing!" Kat-with-a-K says when she catches up to us, separating out the syllables, as they seem to like doing at this place.

"It sure was," Emily agrees. "I could hear the chanting all the way down the hall. Whose final chant was that?"

"Half-mine, half–Robe-Rage's," Kat answers. Her eyes glisten. "It was like hearing angels," she adds. "Seriously. I felt like one for real. I know I'm no angel, but do you think there are angels here on earth, Miss Emily?"

Emily's face softens. "I do believe that there are angels here on earth, Kat. We may not know they're angels, but I believe they are definitely here among us."

I make a mental note to look for angels—and add it to my list of one more thing that doesn't get noticed that I need to try to pay attention to.

"How did you like the workshop, Anna?"

"Fell asleep!" I answer, and her eyebrows shoot up.

"That's great! That means you trusted the leader enough to relax and let go."

"Or maybe you were just dog-tired," Kat says. "I know I was. I don't blame you, Robe-Rage. I fell asleep too." She breaks off from us and heads down a hall toward the common room.

"Catch me later!" she calls over her shoulder, grinning.

When we get back to the room, Emily stops short, motioning for me to do the same. She jams a hand in a pocket and pulls out her cell phone and calls security. I know that's who she calls because shortly after, two securing guards show up, and she asks them to check out my room and Kat's.

"Do I need to pull the fire alarm?" Emily asks one of them.

"There's no active fire, just the smell from a few things someone has burned. Has one of the girls been lighting fires in here?" one of the security guard asks. I look up right as his stern look settles on me.

I shake my head vigorously.

"You sure about that?"

"They were in a community activity," Emily tells him. "I do know Justin, one of our residents, was here earlier, and he's known to set fires," she adds.

The guard's right about one thing. It does smell like something has been burned. Justin said he left Kat a surprise, but what?

While we wait out in the hall, the guards go into the rooms, turning over mattresses, going through drawers, looking in cabinets, and thumbing through books. Then one of them comes out and hands something to Emily. It's the book of Emily Dickinson poems she gave to me. I freeze.

The edges of the book have been scorched. When she opens it, my poem flutters to the floor like a one-winged bird, twisting and turning before landing on a bent corner. It looks pathetic and limp.

Emily bends and picks it up and silently reads it before turning wide-eyed to me. "Anna! You wrote this?"

Before I can answer, the guard interrupts. "Wasn't just the cover of the book that was burnt, Miss Myers." He motions for her to come into the room and for us to stay out.

All that stuff about trust that Emily talked about earlier disappears. My breath comes out in short pants, and I start feeling lightheaded again.

"What's goin' on?" Kat comes up beside me, staring.

"Justin," I answer.

She turns to me, eyes round. "That nutjob was in our rooms?"

I nod.

"Doin' what?"

"Burning stuff."

Kat heads for the door to her room, but a security guard blocks her from entering.

Suddenly, I can't breathe. "Abby," I murmur.

"Who's Abby?" Kat looks over her shoulder at me, but I can't answer. I can't even move.

"Abby!" I say a little louder. The security guards and Emily come out of my room at the sound of my shouting.

The way Emily is holding Abby with two fingers wrapped around the doll's upper body is strange. At first, I'm relieved. *My doll's okay.* But when I see the melted arm dangling like a mangled worm at Abby's side, something in me snaps.

"What the—" Kat rolls her eyes toward me.

23

"AAAAABBBBYYYYYY!" I GRAB ABBY AND PULL HARD ON the burned plastic arm, only to find that it's melted to her, and when I pull at it, the plastic stretches long and thin and won't go back to its normal shape. The arm won't fit back on, and it won't come off ... it just hangs there. A growl starts somewhere deep inside me.

"Oh, man. Not again!" Kat groans, stepping toward me when a howl escapes, filling the hallways. I swing Abby like a rope and bash her against the wall. I hear a laugh coming from far away. Is it Justin, coming back to finish the job? Or is Terrible Ted laughing, because he finally found out where they stuck me?

"Anna, it's going to be okay," Emily says from far away.

I rip off a leg and hurl it down the hall at her and then pound Abby again and again against the wall.

"Easy, baby girl." The man's voice sounds far away.

Other voices close in around me, but the walls start turning and I tune everything out. Everything except the look on Kat's face. Her mouth is open, as if she's singing a high note, but she's covering it with open fingers. Her eyes are wild and disbelieving, like she's trapped in that unsure place between being scared and mortified.

Bits of sentences come out of her mouth, making her sound like me. I hear "crazy," "possessed," "twisted"—and don't like her words at all. Ben once said that seeing a monster isn't what's scary. It's seeing the person who is seeing the monster that's scary, and in that brief few seconds, looking at Kat's twisted face, I am seeing her seeing the monster.

The cold truth suddenly slams *me* up against the wall: *the monster she's seeing is me.*

24

MORE ARMS AND HANDS COME TOWARD ME. I GROWL AND snap, kick and spit, when suddenly I feel a familiar wet, cold cloth rubbing my arm and know the bee is about to sting.

Ben says we all have wild in us. He says wild is a close cousin to fear and anger. He says it comes out when we feel cornered.

"We can feel cornered by all sorts of thinks," he once told me and Sara. "It doesn't have to be a person or people who corner us. It can be emotions, or an action that traps us. And it can be ourselves cornerink ourselves."

Sara asked him, "How can someone corner herself?"

"Have you ever heard the phrase, 'She painted herself into a corner'?"

Sara and I shook our heads.

"Well, picture somebody with a bucket of paint, only the bucket is really full of excuses, and that person dips the brush into the excuses and sweeps onto the floor the excuses. Now picture that all the while she's painting, she's backink up, until a corner she has painted herself into."

I look around in a panic. I didn't make excuses. I didn't talk back. I didn't talk, period. Sometimes the wild comes out of me all by itself. I back down the hall from them, but when I turn to run, I see I have done just what Ben said the girl who painted the floor did. I backed myself into a corner. Apparently, there are more ways than one to paint yourself into a corner than excuses.

I lash out some more, kicking and growling, though it now feels like it's all happening in slow motion. The medicine they shot me up with must be starting to work.

Hands are suddenly all over me again. I smell garlic and thrash harder. It's the same smell as that bad man who burned me. I can't even look. What if it's Terrible Ted? What if he's one of the people holding me down?

"I didn't talk!" I shout. "I didn't tell them," but it comes out sounding muffled and thick.

Let me go! It's not fair that there are four of them and only one of me. Well, two of me, if The Inside Girl hasn't left me for real.

I claw at the air, trying to get them to back off.

"Give her some room!" Emily shouts, bending over me. "For all we know, she might be having a seizure!"

I snarl. All I see are faces looking down, going round and round. I kick my foot into something bulbous and squishy and hear a low gasp.

Something bubbles up inside me and boils over. I kick harder when the meds kick in. Seconds later, I'm floating away from them. Away from myself.

I see a blurred face overhead, staring down at me. I frown. She looks just like me. Even all fogged up, I figure it out. *It's not me floating up there.* It's Tig. But why does she look just like me?

"No!" I reach up. "Come back."

"Shhh," Someone whispers close to my ear. I try to wave the whisper away and thump against warm skin.

"Not safe!" I shout, but again, it comes out thick and foreign, like I'm saying, "Nah tha."

"Shhhh. It's okay. You're okay."

"Shhhhh."

* * *

But I won't shhh. And I'm not okay. I'm … I'm … I try to think of what I am when a weird kind of sleep overtakes me. Sounds are muffled. I try to make out what they are. The dull thumping could be footsteps. The higher noises sound like geese flying overhead. Why are geese flying down the hallway? Did they take me outside? I strain to hear more, but the sounds are moving away, and my arms can't stretch to catch them and pull them back.

* * *

I wake up confused and totally freaked out. *Was that really Tig?* If so, how will I find her? And Abby? Where's Abby? *Did I break her for real this time? Did Justin really burn her arm, or did I dream it? Is all this just a dream?* Can I please wake up and find out that Sara is here and everything is all right?

"Sara! Where are you?" I shout, but the airy, whistling sound that comes out of me isn't the words I hear in my head. The sound turns into a moan, the very sound a big wind makes when it's trying to push its way under a window that's opened just a crack.

I roll over onto my back. Everything's a blur. I look up into a brown sky that's closing in on me. Why is the sky brown? Did the sky and earth change places? Am I getting buried? I squeeze my eyes shut and open them again, only it's not a brown sky I'm looking into. It's a big brown face bending close to mine. It's Kat-with-a-K's dad, who's not really her dad but who she calls dad … who everyone calls dad …

"There you are! You had me a worried there for a bit. How you doin', Miss Anna?"

How'm I doing? I've turned inside out. The Inside Girl is gone. How'm I doing? I thrash my head back and forth on the pillow, searching for Tig, but she's nowhere to be seen.

The big man stands up, and a brush of air swipes my face. I breathe in and smell doughnuts, just like the bread and doughnuts Sara and I smelled when we ran past Big Eddie's bakery on our way to the Silvermans' the last time we ran away. I look again, fully expecting to see Big Eddy towering over me, but it's not Big Eddy. Everything's so out of focus—so out of reach. I open my mouth to try to talk, but my tongue is covered with sand and my breath has suddenly turned into hot, panting gusts of wind.

"Easy, baby girl. Easy." The brown man draws in a long breath and lets it out slowly, like he wants me to copy him, so I do. "They gave you a little something to help you calm down."

He grins broadly. "You've been here—what? Three, four days, and you're already a real Alice in Blunderland? Fall down that rabbit hole, did you?"

I nod, since my mouth isn't working. His big smile slips into an understanding grin.

"Been down that hole once or twice m'self," he says, nodding back at me like I just said something that he agrees with.

When he pulls up a chair, the legs scrape against the floor, making a noise like Ben Silverman used to make when he tried to get up from a chair. I wait for a smell to follow, but today there is no smell. Just a scrape.

The large man props his elbows on the bed and rolls his big brown eyes to look at the sheets holding me down, then rolls his eyes back at me.

"Did I hear right that you're a biter?"

I look away.

"Hey, hey, hey. Don't get upset. I kind of like that you put a bite to the man. I know a lot of people that wish they could bite someone. Heck, I'd bite a few people myself if I didn't think they'd throw me in the slammer."

Did he just say The Man? Mr. Government is here?

"Mean Kurt," I blurt, looking around, wondering where he is and hoping I don't see him.

The brown man laughs a belly laugh that sounds a lot like Ben Silverman's. "Girl, he done flew the coop. Quit, cold turkey."

"Chickens can't fly but a couple feet." It just comes out a full sentence, all by itself, surprising even me. Why can't I talk this well when I'm not in a daze from medicine? What am I thinking? I know exactly why. It's because Terrible Ted will find me and burn out my tongue.

He laughs an even deeper laugh that seems to just roll right out of him.

But what I said about chickens wasn't funny. It's a fact. Ben taught us that a chicken couldn't get away if it tried, short of flapping up and flying a few feet before landing and running around in circles.

"Justin!" I bolt up, but the brown man puts a gentle hand on my shoulder and presses me back down.

"He's in a cool-down room since lockdown's not available. I'm sorry to hear what happened to your doll—uh, Abby, is it?"

I nod and look around, still dazed from whatever they shot me with, but don't see her. What I do see is that I am not in my room.

"You're in the clinic," he says, reading my thoughts again. *What's with this place and reading people's minds?* "You're scheduled for your first group meeting about an hour from now, but I just wanted to come by and check up on you. I told them you might be late, or maybe you'd miss this one time."

He suddenly grins. "Boy, they didn't tell me you was a fighter, Anna-fanna- fee-fi-fo-fanna-Anna," he sings. It's a strange song but catchy. I kind of like it.

"You're lucky. You got a name that rhymes with *manna*."

I frown. Manna? Is that even a word?

"Manna in the wilderness," he says, reading my mind again and raising his eyebrows like adding the word to a sentence will make me understand it better. Sometimes that works, but right now, I don't have a clue what he's talking about.

"Manna," I say, looking around the room. This place is a wilderness. No arguing that. It's full of wild creatures.

"Manna was the miracle food the chosen people found in the wilderness when they were forced out of Egypt. But manna can also mean knowledge or wisdom." He pours a glass of water and holds it out to me.

"Wisdom," I repeat, liking the fact that my name rhymes with something smart. "Wisdom," I say again, taking the cup and gulping down the water.

"Wisdom's a powerful weapon," he murmurs, pouring more water from a pitcher on the side table into my plastic cup. "Powerful. Still thirsty?"

I shake my head. He tips his head back and holds the cup high, then pours the water like a waterfall into his mouth, swallows it in one loud gulp, and grins.

The room goes quiet like it does when more than one person is thinking at the same time.

"I've been keepin' an eye on you, girl. You been through a lot over the past couple of days. I bet it's hard to make sense of what end is up."

Only when he says it, it sounds more like "what end's zup."

My throat tightens, and I look away, fighting tears. He's right. So much has happened, except for the one and only thing I wanted to happen, and that doesn't seem fair. Sara should have been here by now, and I can't figure out what's keeping her away.

"Sometimes we're forced to make changes we don't want to make," he says quietly, setting the cup back down on the bedside table. "We don't always know if the change will be good. But if we learn from our experiences, we grow. Fact is, it comes down to one simple, truth: you got to grow where you're planted."

I look out at the maple tree. The difference between it and me is that it gets to grow in just one place. It's hard to grow when you get moved around so much. Sara might have a chance. People choose her. She might get picked by someone and get to stay in one place to grow. Maybe it wouldn't be so bad to get chosen. The thought is pushed away by the thought of what Daddy's face would look like if he heard my thoughts right now. He doesn't have to worry though. Nobody chooses Anna.

"You're an Olson. Never forget that." Daddy's voice booms in my ears.

It would be easier to remember if Daddy would just find me and remind me again. Or Sara. Or Ben. Or anybody. I don't know where Sara is. I don't know where Mama is. I do know where Daddy is—jail, but what good is knowing when I can't see them or talk to them when I'm—

25

"I'M BART, BY THE WAY," HE SAYS, PULLING MY THOUGHTS back to the white box, the brown man, the bed, the sheets that hold me down, and the "special place" that picked me: Maple View. "I saw you the other day with Kat in the cafeteria when she was stealin' your food. Just so you know, I'm the one that's going to help get you through that workbook so you can get out of here."

"Bart," I repeat.

"Yeah, it's easy to remember. It rhymes with cart, dart, mart, part, tart, and, of course, fart."

"Fart," I repeat. Like alfalfa, it can be a funny word.

"Fart," I say again and laugh so hard I wet the bed. It wasn't all that funny, but sometimes when I laugh, I start to cry or pee, whichever comes first. The room suddenly smells.

"Uh, oh." Bart's nose twitches, and he glances toward my feet.

"Hide sheets!" I blurt. Heat rushes up my neck and into my face.

"No, no. No need to hide 'em. Change 'em is more like it. Now, I'm going to go find Miss Emily or someone else to help out here. You just stay put, and I'll get us some help."

As he talks, the warm pee turns cold, and I shift so I don't have to feel it on my legs or feet.

If Sara had been here, she would have hidden the stinky sheets. But in this box they've stuffed me in, there's nowhere to hide anything—not even my thoughts.

He opens the door. "It was my fault, Miss Emily," Bart-that-rhymes-with-Fart calls out, moving quickly to the other side of the bed when Emily walks in. "I made her laugh, and she couldn't hold it."

"Well, it's great to hear that you're laughing, Anna. Rough night, huh? I'm sorry about your doll."

Emily apologizes again and again. I've never heard anyone say "I'm sorry" as much as she does. She's sorry about just about everything.

"Just so you know, Justin is in lock-down room on the boys' wing. Juvie is full, so he has to stay here in RTC. We're getting your room cleaned up. It's the cool-down on the girls' wing, because all our other rooms are full, but we won't lock you in. You should be able to go back to your room soon. Kat says to say hi."

"Hi," I say, and the Emily lady smiles.

"I'll tell her." Emily opens some cupboards and makes a *humph* sound. "Can you grab some clean rubber sheets, Bart? The clinic seems to be out."

"Can do!" I see at a glance that Bart's grinning at me, but I'm too embarrassed to look at him.

"Let's get you to the shower while Bart takes care of things here. Miss Davenport says you can be a little late to group," she adds.

"Not go?" I ask hopefully.

"I know a lot has happened since you were brought in, Anna, but you're already so far behind. Let's get you showered and get some more clean clothes."

"Sorry, Bart," I whisper as we pass each other.

"It's okay, baby girl. Accidents happen. Heck, if it wasn't for an accident, I wouldn't be here meetin' you!"

"You?" I look over at the soiled sheet and back at him.

"No, no. Different kind of accident. I have to finish up here and get a move on, but I'll come back tomorrow and tell you all about it. Sound like a plan? You got to make me one promise though."

"No pee?"

"No, no. Everybody has accidents some time or other. But look, you got to promise me you won't try and run away again. Do I have your word?"

"Word," I repeat but then frown. "Kat told you?"

"No, no. Kat didn't say anything. I read your file. It was in the clinic. Kat was there looking for Miss E, but we both figured she was called away. I took your chart to Miss Emily, though, so you don't have to worry about anyone else seeing it."

I nod. He must have read about me and Sara running away to Ben's house before the police rounded us up. I'm sad to see Bart go but glad someone so friendly will be back tomorrow.

After showering, getting some fresh clothes from the closet, and going back to the cool-down room, sleep tugs at me. I'm glad they're not locking me in again.

"That was fast! You have a half hour before group, so why don't you thumb through the workbook? Feel free to look ahead in it," Emily says, and I nod, even though I don't feel like doing anything but sleeping. I see my chart is in her hands again, just like Bart says. He's good at keeping his word.

When Emily leaves, I lie down on the bed, stare out the window, and try to push any bad thoughts out of my head. But the more I push, the more the bad thoughts shove their way right back in. *Where is Tig? Why did she leave me? How could I have let her get away? I was protecting her! I know she got out. I saw her! And why did she look just like me? Do I have a twin I don't know about?*

It was a mirage. It had to be. Like the face in the wall. I'm starting to see things. I roll on my side, feeling empty, and face the wall, when something crawling on it makes me jump. A spider!

"Every living thing has a right to live," Daddy once told us. Sara and I nodded, but Mama didn't agree.

"I draw the line at bugs," she blurted. "The only good bug is a dead one."

"Not always," Daddy had said. "Without bugs, our food supply would disappear." He scooped his hands around a spider and motioned for one of us to open the door so he could put it outside.

"I can't believe you touched that thing. Spiders have no place here," Mama argued, but Daddy said spiders keep the bug population down, especially mosquitoes and other insects that want to feast on us.

"If we didn't have bugs, we wouldn't need spiders to keep them under control," Mama argued, and on and on it went.

When Mama wasn't looking, Daddy taught us to put a cup over the spider and slide a piece of paper between the wall and the spider to get it into the cup, then to carry it outside and set it free.

Even though getting close to a spider gives me the creeps, I carefully put the plastic cup Emily said I have to save over the spider and slide a piece of paper I ripped out of my workbook between the cup and the wall. When I pull the cup and page from the wall, there's no more spider, because she's now in the cup! All I have to do is get her outside.

Getting the door to the room open is tricky, but I manage to balance the paper on the cup and hold it in one hand so I can open the door with the other. I quickly clap my hand over the paper when the door starts to swing shut, so it won't blow away. The last thing I want is a spider crawling on me. 'Specially one that's probably wondering what the heck's going on.

The halls are empty. I see shadows in the commons area. Everyone must be resting or watching TV.

I slip down what they call the east wing on tiptoes, holding my hand over the paper so it won't slip off. The only door I can find close by is marked Fire Exit. Hey, an exit is an exit. Which means it's is a way out.

When I push the door open, all moose breaks loose, as Daddy would say. The jagged sound that comes next scares me so bad that when I race outside to get away from it, I drop the cup with the spider in it. The page from my workbook flies off, looking like a cat leaping from one place to another, chasing a bug.

I hear the door click loudly behind me and try to open it but can't get it to open. I look around. It feels good to be outside. Still, I can't just stand here and when you can't just stand, you do the next best thing: Run! I'm free! *Free, free, free!*

I flap my arms, wishing I could fly. It's hard to know which way is best to go when you don't know where you are or where you're going. I barely get halfway across the parking lot when behind me people start to pile out of the building. Voices echo off the brick walls. "I saw her on camera," one of the new staff shouts. I duck behind some cars. Can't let them catch me. This is my chance—maybe my only chance—to find Sara!

I race past a mud-caked Jeep and head for the only cover I see: a giant tree. The very tree I stare at day after day outside my window. I look up to see if Tig is staring at me from the window, but it's not Tig filling the darkened space; it's Bart.

I duck.

"Don't be scared," I tell myself, like Sara used to tell me when we ran away, but I now realize we were all scared. Me, Tig, and Sara. Sara was just better at hiding it.

Soon, the whole parking lot is scrambling with grown-ups.

"She couldn't have gone far," an official voice says. "Let's spread out and search. Look in every bush and behind every tree."

"We should probably call the police," a voice I recognize as Emily's says.

"She's not a missing person for twenty-four hours," another voice says.

"What are you saying? She's twelve years old. I'm calling the police," Emily states in a "Don't argue with me" tone.

My heart beats so fast that my chest hurts. Or maybe it's the branches poking and scratching me that are doing the hurting. I head for the tree like the one under my window.

When I reach it, colorful leaves, shaped like hands, spread their wide fingers, reaching out to welcome me. I run over to it and, when I try to hide behind tree, I see that the trunk is all caved in on one side, as if someone has cut the very heart out of it.

Still, I scramble inside it and huddle down and silently sing Kat's and my chant over and over to try to fool myself into thinking I'm not scared.

Eenie-meenie-chi-chi, ohh chow-chow, ee wow-wow. Eenie-meenie-chi-chi, ohh chow-chow, ee wow-wow. I chant quietly over and over, hoping to feel calmer soon.

The tree smells earthy and woodsy. The inside walls are smooth. It hugs against me, trembling, like it's just as scared as I am. Soon, I can see red and blue and white lights flashing on the concrete walls surrounding the center and roll up into a tighter ball. But that's not all I see. I see a girl hiding in the bushes!

She presses a thin finger to her lips and looks at me with such pleading eyes that I almost have to look away. I now she's scared I might rat on her, but I know just where she's at. Sara and I hid like that behind a dumpster, hoping the police wouldn't see us. The girl pulls her head down and hides her face, but it's not her they're looking for.

All around, branches snap and the ground crunches, sounding like one giant cat munching on dry food. But it's not a cat that suddenly pokes a cold nose around the hole in the tree. It's a big dog.

I yelp. The dog howls. And my great escape plan snaps in two.

26

"GOT HER!" A POLICEMAN SHOUTS INTO A LITTLE BOX hooked onto his shoulder, and something sinks inside me. I think disappointment's pulling at me from inside out. He bends down. My jaw quivers like it does right before I'm going to bite someone.

"Come on out of there. Let's get you inside."

When I don't move, he reaches in. Big mistake.

His skin tastes different from other skin. Not salty. Not coconutty or lotiony. Not flowery. The taste is more like a penny, not that I go around tasting pennies, but I did put the one Ben gave me in my mouth once to hide it. The policeman's next moves are fast, and all I can feel is pain in my cheeks as he pinches them together hard, forcing my mouth to open. My stomach tightens. It's the same thing Terrible Ted did after he burned me and then let that hot piece of ash land on my mouth to remind me to keep it shut and not let anyone know what he did.

Blood trickles from the holes in his hand.

"Oh, Lord. I was just coming over to tell you not to reach for her," a familiar voice says. I can't look up. I know the voice, and if the tone matches the look on his face, I don't want to see it.

"I've pulled cats from trees, even rescued a bear or two, but this is the first time I've tried to get a girl out of a maple tree and got bit," the policeman says, making room for Bart to get to me.

"Anna!" Bart's voice is heavy and dark with disappointment. "You broke your promise. That hurts worse than any bite you might have sunk into me," he adds, dropping his voice even lower, before adding, "and you gave me your word."

"Words break!" I shout. Mama's words broke. Daddy's words broke. Even Sara's words broke. So why wouldn't my words break?

"What were you thinkin'?" Bart's voice is down to a wheezy whisper. He helps me out of the tree.

"Free spider," I whisper back, but he just looks at me like I'm speaking Russian, Greek, or some other foreign language.

"You put my job on the line."

I frown, wondering how I could have put a job on a line. What line? Sometimes what he says doesn't make sense, but right now, what he *means* does.

"That little stunt you pulled could get me fired, Anna."

"Fire?" I freeze up.

"Fired," he repeats, emphasizing the *d* at the end. "As in lose my job." He separates the words out for emphasis and motions for me to sit in the wheelchair he must have wheeled out with him.

"Walk!" I shout.

Bart doesn't answer. He wheels the chair behind me and pulls me back by my shoulders. It's sit or fall, so I plunk down in the chair, good and mad. But then, so is he, and he tips the chair back and starts rolling it across the stones and grass and onto the sidewalk toward the door, with purpose. I can only imagine the grim look on his face. I bounce around and look back one last time to see if the girl is still in the bushes, but if she is, nobody would know. Why couldn't she have been Sara? A sinking feeling weighs me down. I'm just fooling myself. Sara isn't coming. Nobody's coming. I swallow against that painful truth, but swallowing doesn't make the hurt go away.

"We'll need you to fill out a report," the policeman, who's out of breath from speed-walking to keep up with Bart, tells him.

I steal a glance at Bart. He nods one sharp nod at the cop, then sucks in his bottom lip. A thin, dark line marks where his lips used to be.

After he pushes the chair and me to lockdown, he turns to leave. This time maybe for good. The wall hums and clicks, and Bart turns back and maneuvers the chair to the bed, then helps me out of it, still saying nothing. He again turns to leave, this time with the chair. It's no surprise to me that I'm in lockdown for real this time.

I look around. All that's in the room is a bolted down chair and bed, if you can even call it that. More like a cot. No windows. Just a door, four walls, a ceiling and floor, and a toilet in the corner by a small sink. My eyes well up. I don't like this room. *Why can't I go to the cool-down room?*

"Cool-down? Not this time." Bart answers, reading my thoughts. He pulls a towel off the chair and drapes it over his arm.

"Sorry, Bart."

"Well, sorry doesn't always fix it, Anna. You got to learn that sometimes what you do affects other people. If I don't come by tomorrow, you'll know why," he adds, and everything in me lets go, including the pee I can no longer hold in.

Bart groans and hands me the towel before turning to leave, but then stops and turns back. He suddenly looks at me long and hard. I try to look at him but can't. His eyes have disappointment written all over them. I don't want to watch it land on me.

"Know what kind of tree you hid in was?" he says, breaking the long silence.

"Maple," I mumble. I heard the policeman say maple when he talked about getting cats and bears out of trees, and this whole place is called Maple View, so it makes sense.

"Yeah, maple."

"Rots from inside out," I mumble, remembering what Ben told us.

Bart raises his eyebrows. Surprise sparks in his eyes. "That's right. Maples rot from inside out. You want to be a maple tree that's all perfect on the outside and rotten on the inside?"

The Outside Girl cries. And *if* The Inside Girl was still inside of me, she would have curled up and died, like a withered leaf on a rotting maple tree.

27

THAT'S HOW IT FEELS ANYWAY. WHO KNOWS? MAYBE SHE didn't get out. Maybe she's still in me and really did up and die. Maybe that really was me I saw, floating out of my body. I shove the thought of Tig dying out of my head before I start rotting for real. She's probably somewhere out there as mad at me as I am at myself. Can't she see I was trying to protect her, making sure what happened to me couldn't happen to her?

It's not fair. It's just not fair.

Bart sighs and motions for me to follow him. "I'll walk you to the bathroom so you can get cleaned up, but from here on out, you need to take care of things yourself. With kids coming in and out daily, we don't have time to be chasing after clean sheets and making sure you get here, there, and everywhere. That's your responsibility. I talked with the counselor, and you're not slow in the head by any means, Anna. Don't get me wrong. You been traumatized. I get that. I don't know by what or who, and it's going to be a hard trek up that mountain, but with the right attitude and tools, it's something you can get ahold of. Something that you can control."

I don't know what mountain he's talking about, but I do know his voice is as hard as a rock. When he looks back at me, I see goodbye in his eyes, and my whole world caves in. All the crying in the world doesn't seem to be making any difference. And why should it? It's not like he really cares. He has to pretend. That's his job.

"They're assigning a new staff member to help you through the workbook, Anna," he quickly adds, handing me a tissue that he'd stuffed in his pocket. "You have to stay in lockdown twenty-four more hours, and then if you haven't done anything drastic, they'll let you return to your room.

"The new guy's name is Will. That's two staff members you've been through, and you haven't even been here for what? A week. Two weeks? Try to not bite him, okay?"

"Leave?" I blurt. I'm all out of tears but still feeling choked up.

"You chose to run away on my watch, Anna, and that reflects on me and how I do my job. Now my boss is watching *me*."

"Didn't run!"

"Run, walk, crawl—it don't matter. You left the building plain and simple."

To save the stupid spider, I want to shout, and I don't even like spiders.

"Manna," I whisper, hoping it's a magic enough word to keep him here.

Bart hangs his head and finally looks up. He takes in a deep breath, which he lets out long and slow.

"Manna is still open for business."

Even though I'm all twisted up with worry, something inside me leaps for joy. He's keeping a promise. *He* didn't break *his* word.

I start to think about the wilderness that is my life. It's looking pretty bare. No flowers. Just a red plastic cup, a toothbrush, and some clothes. Thank goodness they let me keep the books Emily loaned me.

Bart waves his big brown hand in front of my face, and I look up at him. "Some learning has to be done on our own, and in our own time. I'll come by and check on you, but I'll be written up, Anna. It's kind of like probation, so running away like you did means I won't have as much time with you. It's called consequences."

I didn't run away, I scream in my head, but all that's doing is making me madder. Still, a word he says pokes at my brain. "Pro-ba-tion." I say the word slowly, breaking it in threes like they do in this place. Isn't that what Daddy said he got after getting out of jail? Maybe this place really is a jail.

"Probation, yes. It means they'll be watching my every move."

He can't go. He just can't. Who will talk to me? Who will make everything okay?

My mind races. "Accident?" I blurt, hoping to remind him of his promise to tell me the story of how he got to be here. Surely, he can tell me one last story, can't he?

Bart's thick eyebrows rise up high over his round brown eyes. "So, is that how it is, is it? You want to hear the story of the accident now? It's a bit late for that. Don't you think?"

I don't answer, but something in the way I look makes him sigh again. He walks over to the cot and sits down on the chair beside it.

"You see this?" He pulls up his pant leg and props his leg up onto the side of my bed, only it's not a leg; it's a metal peg. I gasp and can't stop staring.

"Yeah," he says. "I don't have a leg. You know why I don't have a leg?" He narrows his eyes when he looks at me, like he's trying to see right through me.

"Maple?"

He frowns slightly, then suddenly smiles through the frown, shaking his head and standing up. "You know, Anna-fanna. For all that's going on with you, you're a smart girl, and don't you ever let anyone tell you otherwise. No, my leg didn't rot off. What happened was that I took a friend's motorcycle for a joyride and went way too fast around a curve. Next thing I know I'm sliding on concrete with the bike on top of me. When I finally stop sliding, I look over and see a leg in the middle of the street and wonder, *What's a leg doing over there?*

"Well, that was *my* leg, Anna, only it wasn't connected to me anymore. I did something stupid and lost my leg. And you know what?"

I shake my head, almost afraid to hear the "what" part of his story.

"I spent the next six months in a hospital trying to learn to walk again. Only, not on a leg but on a peg.

"Get mad?"

"Oh, I got mad all right. First, I cried like a baby. Then I got angry, and even though I didn't bite anyone, it's not like I didn't want to. And you know what the doc said?"

I shake my head.

"He said, 'What are you going to do, Bartholomew? Lie there and cry and feel sorry about losing a leg? Or learn how to make legs and help others who lose their limbs to learn to walk again?

"Long story short, you can kick and scream and bite and growl all you want to, but that doesn't solve a thing." He pauses and cocks his head to look at me. "You like words, I can tell, so here's a puzzle for you. What do you get when you take the *l* off of growl?"

I spell the letters in my head: g-r-o-w-l. "Grow," I murmur.

"That's right. Grow, because sometimes you have to quit growling and do what we talked about before and grow where you're planted, Anna. It's that simple. That's the only way to survive, especially in here.

"Now, your little running-away stunt doesn't mean you get to pass on everything you have to do to get out of here because of falling behind, and right now, you're way behind. After you get out of lockdown, they might make you double up on your schedule, just to get you caught up. Tomorrow, you'll do group, followed by Behavioral Mod, and then your workbook assignments, and then a tutor is supposed to come by and help you with your studies. You got some serious catching up to do, baby girl. No getting around it.

"If you play your cards right, though, you could be out of here by Thanksgiving."

I frown. *Thanksgiving?* No. No. He must mean *Halloween.* I have to be home for Sara's twelfth birthday. I can't miss my sister's big day. Who will make her a cake out of mashed potatoes or give her a present? Will Ben and Rachel have her on her birthday? I fight back new tears.

"Sara's birthday," I whisper, and Bart blows a stream of air, making his cheeks puff out. "Halloween," I add, my voice cracking with hope.

"It's hard to be away from family, especially on holidays. I get that. I know you want to be out in time for your sister's birthday, but I have to be totally up front with you, Anna. I doubt that's going to happen. You've barely started on the workbook, and you have at least a month of Behavioral Mod to get through."

He pauses. His expression is both far away and crinkled, like he's trying to figure something out. "I'll see if I can round up something for you to put a costume together and will come by to see you on Halloween for the party they throw here, so you don't feel left out. How's that?"

I nod, trying to look grateful that he's going to come visit me, but I'm still stuck on his other words. The ones that said I probably won't be out of here by Sara's birthday. "I likely won't see you again until Halloween," he adds, and my throat tightens. I put on a brave face, but next time I see a spider, I'm going to smash it.

"Ask Will or Emily to help you with the questions if you get stuck, and I'll help when I can get back over here."

"Okay," I whisper.

"Let's get you to the showers and over to the closet for clothes."

I'm glad the halls are empty. Deep down, I'm mad. I didn't start out planning to run away. The door closed; I couldn't get back in. Then I got scared. Everything happened so fast. Yeah, I hid in the maple tree, once I dumped the spider, but I was scared, that's all. Now I have one more thing to be mad at after Mama, Daddy, Ruth Craig, Sara for not finding me, this horrid place, and let's not forget me, and that stupid spider.

That night before going to sleep, I think about what Bart said about growing where you're planted and how this garden—this wilderness I've been planted in—is so bare and lonely and dead. Bart says I have to start doing stuff for myself. Maybe he's right, but how? Sara has always been here to do it for me.

I stare at the blank page in the journal and decide it's my time to plant the seed. But then I have to stop and think. Trees start with a seed. What's my seed going to be? I think about me and Sara and Hope, the rat we buried together, and decide my seed will be a seed of hope:

> If I had to plant a tree,
> I'd start out with a seed.
> The seed would sprout a stem of
> hope so that the tree could feed.
> My tree would grow a strong, thick
> trunk to weather every storm.
> I'd add some long, slim branches
> and lots of leaves to give it
> form. I'd feed my tree with
> different things, like patience, love,
> and hugs, and leave a real in-
> viting space for birds and bees
> and bugs. My budding tree of
> life would be a plain and simple tree
> that over all reflects the way
> I'd someday like to be.

28

EMILY IS RIGHT. THE LOCKDOWN ROOM IS MUCH WORSE that the cool-down room. Outside, the sky suddenly unzips, and rain "thunders down like a million marbles" is how Sara would tell it. I can't see the rain, but I can sure hear it.

Some people go through life adding up all the stuff they have. I go through mine clinging to whatever I have left, and right now, about all I have left is Abby. Sara and Abby have been with me "through thick and thin," as Daddy would say.

Sitting on the edge of the cot, my memory takes me back to when I got a letter from Daddy. It was the one and only letter that he'd written to me from jail. I got to the mailbox and grabbed it before Mama could see it and rip it up.

When I read it, I laughed and laughed and then cried. Daddy can be so funny. He wrote how he wished I was here and then must have reread it and saw that "here" meant jail and that by writing that, he was saying he wished I was in jail, so he crossed it out and wrote how he wished he was there, at home, with me and Sara. His letter had lines crossed off, just like when he writes a new song and decides to change different words or lines to make the song better.

In his letter, Daddy told me he was working on a new song. "You're in it, Anna. You and Sara. Not by name but by heart."

As I read Daddy's letter, I traced his words with a felt pen, because

I wanted to feel what it was like to write what he wrote, but after I wrote over them, the words turned thick, dark, and smudgy. I ended up throwing his letter away. Now I wish I had kept it, 'cause when you're ripped away from someone, even smudgy, covered-up words are better than no words at all.

Daddy wasn't the only one who wrote a letter. Mama wrote one, too, before she ran away. Sara has the letter. I didn't let on to her that I could pretty much read most of what Mama wrote. Tig taught me to read when the school stuck me in special ed. Tig would probably tell you it's her, not me, that can read, but really, Tig and I both can. Anyway, just because you're almost eleven doesn't mean you can read. Every chance she got, Sara sounded out the letters in Mama's words, trying to make sense of what she wrote, so she could maybe figure out where Mama was and why she left us.

It was hard not to just blurt out the word Sara was stumbling over in Mama's letter, but after that horrible thing that happened with Terrible Ted, talking wasn't safe, and some words could set me off without me even knowing they could do that.

Sara will figure out Mama's words soon enough. Maybe Ben can help her, and she'll see that Mama ran away thinking she was doing something good for us, giving us a chance to have a new home—a new start—something like that.

But if Mama were here right now, she'd see that her plan gets a big fat F—or would have, if life had a report card. Still, I wish she took me with her. If she had, that horrible thing I keep trying to forget wouldn't have happened.

Daddy's grade wouldn't be much better, but at least he didn't run away for good. Daddy's problem is that he just can't stop drinking. But even that didn't keep him from finding us. Daddy figured out where they put us. We always had that to look forward to, but I don't see how Daddy can find me here. And with Sara and me separated, he now has two places to find instead of just one.

I can't think about all that without feeling more awful than I already feel. The reason feelings are called feelings is because of what they do to your insides: twisting, turning, churning. One of the worst feelings is disappointment, and I've had a lot of those. One of the biggest was Sneaker, the stray cat Sara rescued that we had to leave behind. I try to tell myself she's okay out in the cold. She has to be disappointed in me and Sara for leaving her. And now I've disappointed Bart, who doesn't even know I wasn't trying to run away.

Disappointment is one of those feelings that you can give colors and shapes to. It makes my face turn red and my eyes go all twitchy. It flat burns a hole in me that won't close up. I push the thought away at the same time that I push myself up to my feet, by trying to think of what the opposite of disappointment might be.

Anticipation comes to mind. I start pacing. At first, I didn't know what *anticipation* meant, thinking it must be some kind of holding place for wishes, but one time when Daddy had to go to jail again and Mama was put in some crazy house, as Daddy called it, for trying to send me and Sara to Jesus, we were led to what might have been anticipation's door—actually, it wasn't a door. It was a window.

It happened when Sara and I got taken to our first foster home. We worried that Daddy wouldn't be able to find us. Then one day, we heard a tapping on the window, and when I turned and looked outside, my chest felt like a balloon filled up with air—probably because I had sucked in my breath and was holding it. The feeling was both scary and exciting, because even though the setting sun was behind whoever was tapping, the shape looked just like Daddy's. I got dizzy with aching to have it be true and let out my breath before I dizzied myself faint.

I sink back down on the cot. I now think anticipation must be that place between wanting and getting. Maybe it ends with a good kind of surprise that might only last a second or two, but even a flash of feeling good is better than not feeling good at all. Sara and I dashed to the window and slid it open, closing the space between us and Daddy with a zillion and one whispered questions. Daddy had already popped off the torn screen so he could hug on us.

"Shh, shh, shh!" The hair on his chin tickled my face. He didn't have whiskers before. "Didn't I tell you girls I'd find you?" We cried and cried as quietly as two happy girls could, begging him to take us home, but he said he had to go sign some papers and it might take a while. He also said to keep our secret that he had been there. He smelled of smoke, and after he left, I could smell the smoke in my hair and on my fingers, just like in the old days.

Our temporary foster parents smelled it too.

"Where did you get the cigarettes?" they demanded in "I-won't-believe-a-word-you-say" voices.

"We didn't." That part was true. Daddy was the one with the cigarettes. Not us.

"Don't lie. We can smell it on you."

I wasn't sure if they meant they could smell the smoke or a lie, but it must have been the smoke, because Sara and I never smoked a day in our lives, and we weren't lying about that.

Still, they made us say we did, because grown-ups have to have answers, even if they aren't the right ones. So, we lied and said we had smoked, keeping Daddy's secret visit safe. They believed what they wanted to hear, proving to me that they couldn't smell lies after all. They tore the room apart, looking for the cigarettes or the wrapper, and made us stay in our room to punish us both for smoking and for refusing to tell them where we got the cigarettes.

But Sara and I didn't care. For two days, we smelled each other's hair and hugged on each other, rolling around on our beds like two happy kittens, knowing Daddy would come back. Daddy's smoke went away, just like I thought he might have done when we hadn't heard from him in days.

Disappointment is hard not to wear on your face. For me anyway. This time, even Sara couldn't hide her disappointment. Looking at her was like looking in a mirror. I know she was feeling upset with Daddy, just like I was, and feeling disappointed in a parent is an even worse feeling than the feeling of disappointing him, but there was no running from it. We didn't talk about it much, but that doesn't mean we weren't thinking it and feeling it.

"It's not fair."

"Nope."

"He promised."

"Yep."

But it turns out good news can sometimes show up when you least expect it. Daddy arrived days later than he had said he would, but at least he showed up. It took about a week before we got to leave. Daddy didn't just find us; he found Mama, too, and we got to be a whole family again. It didn't last long though.

Since Daddy's a musician, it meant he had to go farther away this last time to find work. Mama by then had run away for good, and with Daddy off looking for work, me and Sara had a real scare trying to find Ben and Rachel Silverman's house.

But now a new scare has taken its place. I look around at the bare walls, fighting tears.

"Find me, Daddy. This place doesn't feel safe," I whisper.

Daddy once said the government is supposed to keep us safe. He called the government "The Man." I haven't met The Man yet. Strange, seeing how Sara and I have been dragged from one temporary foster home to another, you'd think that one of these times we would have bumped into him—The Man, I mean.

If we had, I would have told The Man that I don't feel one bit safe, except when I'm at Ben and Rachel's house. To think that Sara and I just left their house not that long ago for the-who-knows-how-many-ith times these past months. My guess is six. And now, here I am in this room with no windows.

If this is Mr. Government Man's house, he needs to know I don't feel one bit safe. I pace the floor, measuring each step, like a caged animal. The cot looks cold and uninviting, but it beats sleeping on the floor. I lie down on it, pulling the thin blanket up under my chin. The only way I can go to sleep is to stare at the wall and picture a window in it, so that I can finally give my eyes—those now closed windows to my inner self—a rest.

And then the Windows failed - and then
I could not see to see.

29

THE NEXT MORNING, THE WALL BUZZES, THE DOOR CLICKS, and Emily pokes her head in.

"Good morning, Anna. There was trouble on the floor last night, so we're going to need the room. We're letting you out of lockdown early. Go get some breakfast, then work on your workbook in your room after. I'll check in with you later. Grab your sheets and get started." She looks around. "Where's your red cup?"

I point toward the chair and slip out of bed, fully dressed. I grab the sheets and blanket and follow her out of the room and down the hall.

Behind us, another girl is being taken, kicking and screaming, to lockdown. I get just a quick look at her and realize it's the girl who was hiding in the shrubs. She glares at me like I'm the reason she got caught.

"Breakfast is almost over, so grab what you want and take it back to your room."

"Kat?"

"Kat's already left for school. She'll be back in time for group this afternoon." She heads down one hallway, and I turn into the laundry room and stick the sheet in the washing machine, making sure to tuck it under all the other sheets already in the washer so no one will figure out it's mine, and then I head for the cafeteria.

Some staff members and residents, as they call us, are already cleaning up the cafeteria, but I find a tray with yogurt, fruit, a blueberry muffin, and some orange juice and take that back to my room with me. I force myself not to look for Sara. I know in my heart of hearts she's not here and that looking for her and proving that to myself will only make me feel worse. Better to pretend she is.

Back in my room, I look over and see Abby on the bed, her mangled arm reminding me of what Justin did to her and what Terrible Ted did to me. I pick her up, wanting to tell her how sorry I am for what happened with Justin and for me always ripping her apart. *Can I be just as bad as Justin? Am I evil?* I look her over. For all the pounding on the walls, she doesn't even look hurt. Except for her arm, that is. Some hurts are hard to see. I prop Abby into a sitting position on the table across from me, so it doesn't feel like I have to eat alone. But it's hard to eat with someone staring at you who you've been mean to. I turn and look out the window at the tree and birds, glad to have a window to look out of again, but I can still feel Abby staring at me.

Look, I finally tell her through my thoughts, *I don't know why I do all that stuff to you. It's like this volcano builds up inside me, and you're so easy to grab onto and swing and hit things with. It's not your fault that you ended up being made a doll and I got born a person.* Abby probably wishes I was never born.

It's weird to think about not being born when you have already been born. Sometimes I say to myself, "What if you weren't here?" Right now, that thought is coming at me head-on. But not being here would mean that I never got born, which means I couldn't have had the thought of not being here.

Ben said I wouldn't have been born if it hadn't been for Daddy and Mama getting together. "No other two people could have made you."

If Mama and Daddy had never met—if one little thing had changed their lives where maybe Daddy didn't play at that lounge or Mama didn't party that night and need a ride home—I wouldn't be here.

You'd like that, would you? I say to Abby in my thoughts again.

She just sits and stares, her expression never changing. I stab at the yogurt with a spoon and keep talking to her in my head. *You could get away from me you, know.*

I try to get myself to shut up. Am I really going to tell the only thing I have left how to ditch me?

It wouldn't be all that hard, I continue. *Just fall on the floor, under a chair or the bed. Someone would find you over time and would give you to someone else.*

I look away, fighting back another wave of tears that seems to start in my throat. Picturing my own doll wanting to get away from me makes me feel even worse. She didn't pick me. Daddy picked her for me. I bet if it had been her choice, she would have wanted anyone but me to have her.

I should have left you in the car. Sara would have taken good care of you.

I can't even look at her and feel the hot tears on my cheeks before I even know I'm full-out crying. She sits up so tall and straight, with her mangled, burned arm hanging down to the table like a twisted brown cord. I prop my elbows on the table, fingers fisted into two tight balls, with my thumbs pressed firmly against my mouth, and stare at her.

They want me to use what they call "I-messages," so here's one for you. "I am sorry, Abby." It comes out a full sentence—and out loud.

But that's all I manage to get out and slip back to talking to her silently. *I am sooo so sorry for being mean. It wasn't about you. I don't know why I took it out on you. Ben says we're sometimes meanest to the people we love the most.*

It feels like I've been talking to her for a whole hour, but the clock says it's only been about ten minutes.

"I am sorry, Abby," I say out loud again, sounding like Miss Emily, who's always sorry about something.

Right after I say I'm sorry, Abby falls over, freaking me out, like I've done so much damage she can't even sit up by herself anymore.

Friends don't beat up friends, and Abby is more than just a friend to me. It clearly means only one thing: I suck at being a friend. I stare at her unblinking face, wondering how many other dolls out there are hiding behind their owners, getting beat up and pulled apart.

My stomach twist to knots. I can't eat. I set Abby back in a sitting position and pull out my journal to write another entry, not because I want to write but because I want to make some money and get out of this place. Emily did say writing would help me. Plus, it gets me points.

Today's question in the workbook is: "Tell us why you think you are here and think about where you would want to go."

I'm here because our caseworker tricked me, I say, but I don't write that. And anyway, it wasn't all the caseworker's fault. If I weren't so unlikable, she could have kept me with Sara and put me in the foster home that Sara went to. Maybe even let us stay with the Silvermans. The thought that I could be the reason we couldn't stay with them is almost too much to bear.

The crayon shakes, but still I write:

I
am
a grain
of sand
caught in
the gums of
an alligator.
It makes her mad
to have grit in her
teeth, but her tongue
is too big to get rid of
me. *Snap!*
Oh, no!
I break free and
join the sea,
but now
all alone,
I can't
find
me

I put the poem in the shape of a gator and even think about taking out the word teeth, because it might remind them that I'm a biter. But I leave it in because it's the alligator, in this case, that's the biter. Not me. As for telling them something about me, there's really nothing to tell. Not anything I want them to know anyway. Am I happy? No. Am I mad? Yes. Am I feeling trapped? Yes. Do I have a voice? No. What's left to tell?

My poem doesn't actually answer the question from the workbook, but it doesn't *not* answer it either. It does show that I'm here because I got caught between Where I Was and Where I'm Going. I figure they'll all know what that feels like, so what more is there to tell? I wait to see if Emily, or Bart, or anyone is coming to make sure I get to group, but when nobody shows up, I pack up my stuff and head down the hall.

I've never been in group before, so I don't know what to expect. I do know that if they ask me to say anything, I'm going to keep my mouth shut. What if Terrible Ted found a way to get in? No way am I going to give him a chance to bust me for talking and burn my tongue out. No way.

30

I GET TO THE DOOR AND JUST STAND THERE. I KNOW I SHOULD go in and sit, but I suddenly feel like something I can't see is keeping me out. Some girls and a guy I recognize as Thomas from the cafeteria are already in the room, which has a circle of chairs in the middle and a few bookcases around the sides. A window looks out onto a grassy area that has some picnic tables like the ones I can see from my window.

"Hi!" a woman's voice calls out. "Anna, right?"

I nod.

"Come in, come in. I'm Miss Davenport. I lead group sessions here at Maple View. Pick any empty chair.

"Group, this is Anna. She's new to Maple View, so be sure to talk to her outside of group and make her feel welcome." After a deafening silence, she clears her throat. "Hello?"

"Hi, Anna," the group says all together, including Kat-with-a-K, whose expression matches her tone. She looks at me and rolls her eyes. I don't guess she wants to be here either.

"You can sit here." Miss Davenport pats an empty chair beside the Thomas boy. So much for choosing.

"Okay. Let's get started. Since Anna is new, let's go around and say our names and one thing about ourselves we'd like to share. Kat, why don't you start?"

"Well, you already said my name, so one thing about myself? I get out of here in three weeks and will be home for Halloween."

"You hope," another girl pipes up.

"I don't hope; I know," Kat snaps, shaking her head in that weird thing she does and leaving her mouth open after saying *know*, like no other words are left in her mouth to spew. Wait. She gets to go home in three weeks, and I'm stuck here for another six, if I get everything done? Who's going to be in her room after she leaves? What if it's runaway girl who already hates me?

"Good, Kat. Danny, you want to go next?"

"Like she said, she already said my name, and in case you haven't guessed, I like to win." Her eyes narrow when she says win, leaving little room for arguing. I never heard of a girl named Danny before.

"I'm Jo-Jo," a lanky girl sitting next to Danny blurts. "I got a call from my mom today."

Her news makes Miss Davenport frown. "So, did she have a baby girl?"

"Yeah, but it was born dead."

The one named Danny scoffs. "If it's dead, it didn't get born."

"It's not still in her, so what else would you call it?" Kat challenges.

"Dead, that's what," the Thomas boy answers.

31

I JOLT UP STRAIGHT IN MY CHAIR, SUCKING IN AIR, AND LOOK around at the others. Kat looks at me and rolls her eyes again, this time in a big, exaggerated arch. She tips her head back against her neck and shakes it like she's saying no to the ceiling. I look back at Jo-Jo. How can they all be so mean? This girl's baby sister died! I think about Sara maybe dying, and tears jam up my vision.

"Jo-Jo," Miss Davenport says, in a tone people use when they're warning you about something. "Do you want to rethink what you said and maybe share something else?"

"You're such a liar," Danny cuts in. "Your mom is only five months along if she's even having a baby. I bet she's just fat. How is anyone going to even believe you when all you ever do is lie, lie, lie?"

"I didn't lie when I said you were a loser," the one called Jo-Jo answers. Thomas laughs.

"Okay, ladies." Miss Davenport opens her folder. For some reason, that gets everyone, even Kat, to sit back in their seats and stay quiet. It must be some kind of secret code.

"Go ahead, Anna. Did you want to share something?"

"Pass," I blurt, and she nods.

"Okay then. Clair ran away, so she won't—" she starts to say when Danny interrupts her.

"I saw them hauling her in. She tried to run away again. She's in lockdown."

"She only had a week left too," Jo-Jo adds. "She's so stupid for running with just a week left."

"Jo-Jo," Miss Davenport scolds, frowning. "Clair is not stupid. What she did might not have been very wise, but she is not stupid."

"Just sayin'." Jo-Jo shrugs.

I sit mum. They must not know what I did, only I wasn't trying to run away. But if they do know, they're not saying anything. And that's weird, since they seem to know everything and everybody.

"I think, given the tension in the room, instead of going over your first question, we'll break from routine and do a project. Let's everyone gather at the table. Bring your chairs."

A long table at the side of the room has colored paper, tape, colored crayons, and poster boards. I drag my chair to a spot and sit.

Danny picks up a crayon, grimaces at it, and tosses it back onto the table. "What are we? Preschoolers?"

"Today, each of us will make a goal map," Miss Davenport says, ignoring her.

"A what?" Danny throws her head back and groans.

"You heard me," Miss Davenport chirps. "You'll see different cut-out shapes of paper in all different colors. Choose two circles—one for the beginning of your map and one for the end. Then choose where you want your first circle to be taped."

Jo-Jo slaps her circle right in the middle of the poster board. "Mine's starting right in the middle. That way, I'm close to the edges, and it won't take me long to get anywhere."

"Are you sure?" Miss Davenport asks. "In this pile are other shapes that might represent challenges you face on your journey from where you are to where you want to be, so feel free to use those on your maps as well. Okay, team? You have forty-five minutes left. Go ahead and start your maps! Feel free to share with those around you what the shapes you have chosen represent."

Taking a deep breath, I reach for a blue circle to start my map, unsure of how this is going to go or why it even matters. Unlike Jo-Jo, I stick my circle in a corner of the poster board and tape it down.

"You can trace where you've already been," Miss Davenport offers, "or let the first circle represent where you are now. Today. At this moment."

As the minutes unfold, shapes, lines, colors, words, and pictures start to fill our maps. I glance around. We all have the same materials to work with, but no two maps look alike.

My map has lots of starts and stops, but Kat-with-a-K's map has squiggly lines that go all over the board with nothing stopping them.

When we finish, Miss Davenport has us line our maps up on the wall beside the table, so we can see that while we all have a starting and stopping point, everyone's journey is different.

"Okay, we have time for one of you to share your journey with us. Who wants to share?"

At first, no one says anything or makes a move to talk, but then Jo-Jo breaks the silence.

"Oh, fine. I'll share so we can get this over with. My map starts in the middle, because sometimes I feel like I'm in the middle of a space and everything's moving around me."

She points to the squiggly lines all around the middle, making it look like she's drawn the sun. "This here is a block on the line to show where I am now, which is at this place. I don't have to go very far to get here, but I have a long way to go after I get out."

She points to a series of triangles, squares, rectangles, and bars that make up a kind of neighborhood around her center circle. "My challenge," she says, staring at her map, "is that I got to leap over these buildings here and somehow get out of this hood, only I don't see how. It's not like I'm a bird and can just fly outta here."

I study her worried face, and for a second, I see Emily Dickinson, even though I don't even know what Emily Dickinson looks like. But I don't have to, it turns out, to see her in Jo-Jo. Or even to see *me* in Jo-Jo, even though we don't look one bit alike.

I look around and see the others seeing themselves in her too. It only lasts a few seconds, but it does make Jo-Jo and her map seem more real.

"The reason I had you all draw your maps today was to show us how different we are and how alike we are," Miss Davenport says after thanking Jo-Jo for sharing.

"Look over here," she adds, and we all look to Miss Davenport's poster. "What just happened in group today is that we have found a common denominator between our self"—she draws a circle—"and our neighbor's self." She draws another circle, only she lets the middle of the circles overlap.

"This area right here?" She colors in the middle section where the two circles have crossed. "This is the common denominator. And while each of our maps have similarities—our journeys are so different. I'd be willing to bet that if each of you shared your journey with someone next to you, you'd discover a common denominator.

"That common denominator can be a starting point for a lot of things. Can you think of some?"

"Hating," Danny blurts, and all eyes shoot to Miss Davenport.

"Can you say more on that, Danny?"

"Hating is like that detour on the map you take when there's no other place to go, like when somebody does something to you that gets you so mad you turn on them like a raging fire, hating what they did, what they said, what they stand for ..."

Miss Davenport nods but stays quiet, then says, "Have any of you felt the kind of rage Danny is talking about?"

Silence circles us like a pattern on our maps. Finally, Kat pipes up. "Come on, you guys. You know you have felt that kind of burning rage."

I jolt at the word *burning*. I wish they would stop saying it and pull my arm tight against my side.

"How about you, Anna?" Miss Davenport says quietly. "You've drawn into yourself like you need to protect someone. Did someone do something to you that filled you with rage?"

I drop my head down so my eyes don't give me away. Fear is hard to hide, and there is no way I'm going to talk about or show them my arm.

Miss Davenport doesn't leave me in agony too long. "What about some other common denominators that can fill that inner circle?"

"Connecting," Kat adds, and Miss Davenport smiles, nodding.

"Dreams," I manage to say, and again Miss Davenport nods.

"Food," Thomas blurts, and they all laugh, but Miss Davenport hushes them. "Thomas makes a good point. Diet does play into how we behave. Any others?"

"Healing, too, I guess," Jo-Jo says.

"Yes. Healing. Connecting. Dreams. Food. Even hating. Wow. You're all amazing. Let's stop there, but discussion about what you discovered or about your maps doesn't have to stop here. When you next journal, talk about your challenges and how you might overcome them. Talk about things you might have in common and your hopes and dreams. Any last thoughts before you go?"

"I had a dream about the ocean last night," Jo-Jo says.

"Sounds like Anna's word *dreams* triggered something," Miss Davenport comments, smiling at me. "Want to share your dream, Jo-Jo?"

"I was maybe five, and I was visiting my gramma in Los Angeles who lives not too far from a beach."

"You have a grandmother?" Danny interrupts, but she's not asking the question like she really wants an answer.

"Everyone has a grandmother, stupid. They might not know who she is, but that doesn't mean they don't have one."

"Ladies." Miss Davenport steps between them. "Common denominator," she reminds us. "Jo-Jo. What else happened in your dream?"

"Well, not that I feel like saying anything more, but Grams took me to the beach, and the sand burned the bottom of my feet like I was walking on fire, and I screamed until she carried me down to the water, so I could stick my feet in the ocean.

"Grams put me down on the cold, wet sand right after a wave whipped on by us. I clung to her leg like it was a tree and watched that same wave whip back around on the sand and head straight for me. There was no gettin' away, and that wave smacked against me and sucked the sand right out from under my feet, rippin' me from Grams's leg, like I was no more'n a toothpick. Grams ran out and caught me before I sucked up too much water. I thought for sure I was a goner. Though it was just a dream and all, I got taught good and fast that my life could change just like that."

"Like it takes a stupid dream to learn that lesson," Danny snaps. "Forget the ocean. Just walk out the door."

32

Miss Davenport blocks the door and asks us all to sit on the floor. "Let's take a few minutes and talk about this," she says, waiting for Danny to sit, but Danny remains standing.

Jo-Jo snaps her fingers and points to the floor, but only a whiff of sound comes out. I can't get my fingers to snap either. Ben says you have to press your thumb hard against your third finger, then slide your thumb across your finger to make the snapping noise. It kind of hurts.

I stare at Jo-Jo stunned, really, by how intense her dream was and how we could see it all unfold, like we were watching her being torn from her grandma in a movie. I could even hear the waves crashing in my head, which is strange—hearing something that's not even close to where you are, as clear as if you're right there on the beach itself. And I could hear the screech of the seagulls, and she didn't even talk about seagulls.

"Now, leaving out all the 'stupids' and 'idiots,' let's talk about dreams for a minute. How are your dreams different from other kids out there?" She points out a window. "Anyone?"

Her question throws me. I haven't thought about people dreaming differently. I mean, their dreams would be all different, but I don't think that's what Miss Davenport is talking about.

"I think what you be meaning to say is that in here, we dream dreams about being trapped or wanting to get away from something," Kat says, " like Jo-Jo trying to hold on to her gramma's leg and all, but maybe kids out there, maybe they be dreamin' 'bout how they is going to be famous ath-a-letes or movie stars or somethin' like that, cuz they can afford them kind of dreams. They not dreamin' of gettin' shot or beat up or left to die in some dark alley."

Thomas nods and drops his head to his chest.

You could hear a feather hit the floor in the silence that follows. But you know what? Kat-with-a-K is right. We do dream differently here. And here doesn't have to be just in RTC; it's wherever we're planted.

"So, would you go so far as to say fear fuels your dreams?" Miss Davenport asks.

"Definitely," Jo-Jo says immediately, and who can blame her? Her baby sister was born dead, and dream or no dream, the ocean practically swallowed her alive. Who knows if she would have survived if that wave had swept her out to sea?

"Does the fear make you respect things more?" Miss Davenport's eyes do the roaming thing again. I look down.

"It do me," Jo-Jo answers. "I mean, there's no way I'm gonna think I can outsmart a thing as big and powerful as the ocean."

"The ocean can make us feel small, can't it?" Miss Davenport agrees. "Let's talk about power for a minute. What makes you feel powerful? A better word might be empowered."

"Getting away with something," Jo-Jo says, then laughs. I glance over at her, surprised that she would even admit to something like that.

"Keep going with that, Jo-Jo. What about getting away with something makes you feel powerful?" Miss Davenport makes a motion with four of her fingers, like she's asking Jo-Jo to scoot forward, but it turns out, she just wants her to talk more. We're all now standing in a circle in the middle of the room, making our own island.

"It makes me feel like I outsmarted someone, and maybe that's not right, but it feels good."

I feel my head nodding. Funny how when you nod, your head moves, but whatever you're looking at stays in place.

"I see that speaks to you as well, Anna. Want to share?" Miss Davenport's eyes finally come to rest on me, and my shoulders scrunch up to my ears. Heat creeps up my neck and is quick to turn my face a burning-hot red. I feel caught off guard, even though there was no getting away from being called on.

"Not really," I mumble.

Miss Davenport smiles. "That's perfectly okay." She glances at her watch. "You're free to head back to your rooms or to the commons area before going to your next activity.

"Thanks for participating, everyone. Anna, we're glad to have you with us."

I glance back at the others, who are all nodding, until Miss Davenport turns her back. Then they all start making faces and gestures at one another and me that even I know would cost them points if they were caught. Was anything they said even true? Is that how to get out of this place faster? Just make stuff up?

While I walk, I note different kids doing different things. Some are watching TV in the commons area. Others are at tables doing their homework from school or their workbooks from here. Others are curled up on couches, sleeping or pretending to sleep. I spot Justin and drop my head down quickly, hoping he didn't see me. I don't even have to look at him to know he's smirking. *He's out of cool-down already? How can that be?* He walks across the hall toward the office, and I glance through the office window and freeze.

Terrible Ted is talking with the front office staff lady. I plaster my back against the wall, arms spread out like a cross, and try to make myself as flat as possible, hoping the frame around the doorway can hide me from him. I peek around the wall and see that another staff pats Justin down, then opens the door to the front office for him to enter. Terrible Ted grabs him by the back of the neck and shakes his head violently, like he's trying to separate it from Justin's neck. Terrible Ted's smile is pure evil, like he's just waiting for Justin's head to roll away on the floor. The office lady tries to say something to him, but his glare turns her to ice.

His slicked back hair drops in oily strands on his forehead as he shakes Justin, and I shrink down deeper into myself, feeling a wave of worry for Justin. I mean, what is Terrible Ted to him, and why is he taking Justin? Is Justin a foster kid too?

The thought never entered my mind before, but now, looking at the two of them, watching Justin wilt and watching Terrible Ted, who looks just like the devil in overalls, bully him, is almost too much to take in. Especially when I'm so terrified myself that Terrible Ted might see me and know where he can find me next time he feels like burning someone.

When Justin looks up, I duck back against the wall, hitting my head and wincing at the pain, but when I next turn and look, a bigger pain attacks me. He sees me. I try to look away but can't. He tries to straighten up and make himself tall, but he's not fooling me. He's scared too. Terrible Ted turns his evil face toward the glass.

Right then and there, my feet turn to concrete.

33

EVIL OR NOT, SOMETHING ABOUT TERRIBLE TED FILLS A ROOM. Ben would say he has "big energy," but it's pure evil energy. I know because I was held down by that evil energy. I slowly slide my back down until my butt reaches the floor and wrap my arms up over my head.

"Please don't let him in here," I whisper out loud, squeezing my eyes tight, like my not seeing him is going to somehow make a difference.

"Robe-Rage!"

I hear fast footsteps approaching from down the hallway but don't have to turn around to know who's coming.

"Did you check the schedule? Where're you headed and why you hunched down like that?

"B-Mod," I answer, just as she glides in beside me and bends down.

"Been there. Don't do that," she says, slightly out of breath, grinning. "Wha'd'ju think of group? Pretty lame, huh? Has B-Mod assigned you to any ther-a-py yet?"

"Is he still there?" It's hard to believe that not only am I talking out loud, but I'm making enough sense for Kat-with-a-K to understand what I'm saying.

"He? He who? Oh, you mean Justin? Naw, he's just leavin' with his uncle. By the looks of that dude, I bet he'll wish juvey wasn't full when his uncle gets done with him."

"That's his uncle? Are they gone?"

"Yeah. Man, Justin's got you totally freaked, don't he!"

I stand up slowly, stare at her, and nod, even though Justin isn't what has me freaked.

"B-Mod," Emily calls from across the room.

Kat returns my stare, then laughs. "Oh, right. This is your first one. Well, be ready. They're gonna make you a plan, and you might not like it, but you know what I say, right?"

"No."

"Fake it till you make it!" she exclaims, doing that head-shake thing, like her saying is the most obvious answer in the world.

I glance back at the office window, don't see Terrible Ted returning to snatch me, then think on her words for a second and nod. Kat's saying starts to make sense. Her words aren't something Miss Davenport would have smiled about, but around here, when grown-ups aren't close by, you can pretty much think and do and say whatever you want.

"Fake it," I repeat, and she nods.

"You got to, girl. Fakin' is jus' part of life. Whatever it takes to get through the day, right?"

I nod, faking like she might be right. And who knows? Maybe she is.

* * *

I try it out and fake it through three more weeks, getting used to the schedule, to new people coming in and out—some madder than wasps like Sara would've been, others more scared than I am, or was, when they first stuck me in here—doing lessons with my tutors on math, science, and English. I've already got some tokens built up, but I had to give almost half of them back for chipping out the wall in cool-down.

Halloween decorations start popping up, and talk is all up and down the halls about how both Jo-Jo and the one named Clair have disappeared from the center. Kat says they probably ran away for good.

"They'll be on the streets in another way, if they's not careful," she warns.

But all I can wonder is how did they get out without setting off alarms? After lunch, I go outside with Kat and search the ground for holes they could have crawled through or rocks they could have climbed up on to get over the wall, but the yard's pretty clear of all that. So, it must have been an inside job. Maybe they slipped out when visitors came in. I don't see any other way.

"It's not like the first time they both've took off," Kat says, reading my mind. "And you is not the only one havin' thoughts of excapin'."

"Who says I—" but then I stop. There's no arguing. She busted me. I was and am thinking about that very thing every day. So, in between group, B-Mod, recreation, community workshops tutoring, and trying to get the stupid workbook done, something else happens. I get a routine going—a "usual," as Miss Emily called it way back when—and find that getting up and doing things just like the day before feels kind of comfortable. It's a new kind of new normal. Get up. Shower. Get dressed. Eat. Follow whatever schedule I'm on. Do the workbook. Eat some more. Do rec or rehab. Eat dinner. Go to my room. Write in my journal. Get in my jammies and sleep. It sure beats having to eat paper towels, like Sara and I ate after Mama and Daddy left and all the food ran out.

Then do it all again the next day, and the next, not that anyone is counting.

I catch sight of Bart way down the hall, waving and grinning. He's carrying Halloween decorations. "I'll have your costume stuff soon!" he calls out.

I grin and wave back. Like I say, Halloween isn't my favorite holiday, because crawling through creepy webs and having monsters and ghosts jump out at me isn't my idea of fun.

What keeps me going, though, is the thought that one of the ghosts could be Sara sneaking in. She's great at tricking people. I look around at the other kids walking up and down the hallways, wondering if any of them can be trusted to watch out for her and not give her away if they see her. Maybe Kat could be. She might be able to keep my secret and get Sara over to me if she sneaks in in costume.

I catch Emily's eye, and she does this exaggerated point toward the offices in front.

I nod. "I know!" I call out. "B-Mod!" She nods, gives me the thumbs-up sign, and returns to talking on her cell phone.

34

B-Mod has me nervous even before I reach the room. The last visit I had with the short, round woman with a soft, doughy face and steel-gray hair wasn't all peaches and cream, as Rachel used to say.

"Hello, Anna," she whispers, covering the phone with the hand that's not holding it to her ear. Her slight accent is different from Rachel and Ben's, not as heavy. "'Scuse me for a moment," she says, turning back to the phone call. "Zauzet sam," she says into the phone, or at least that's what it sounds like.

"I am busy," she whispers to me.

Oh, good. No more hour of questions. "S-sorry," I stammer, turning to leave.

"No, no!" She quickly covers the phone. "That was Croatian, my native language. I speak it to someone else. Not too busy for Anna. Come. Sit. Please." She motions for me to sit in a chair in a glass cubicle, then walks around the desk that looks like it's also made of glass and takes the other chair opposite me before quickly finishing up her phone call. Behind her is a big glass wall. It looks like a giant mirror.

She hangs up and smiles. "Sorry for the confusion. You remember I am Dr. Kitanovski. I am going to work with you for the next few weeks on—" She pauses, opens up a file, and runs her finger down it till she sees what she must have been looking for. "Ah, yes. Controlling temper. How does that sound?" She looks up from the folder.

When I don't answer, she turns her head and looks where I am staring. "Oh, the window? Yes. It is one way a mirror, one way a window," she explains, and I nod stiffly. Bart already told me that people can sit behind that window and see us, but we can't see them.

"The university in town sometimes sends students over to observe. But there is nobody observing today," she adds quickly, and I breathe a sigh of relief. "I see here in your folder that you have many times moved around. Tell me, how did all that moving make you feel?"

For some reason, I flash on Jo-Jo's story in group about the ocean tearing at the sand around her feet and that sinking feeling she must have felt trying to hold on to her grandma. I could even feel what she must have felt like, curling her toes in the sand, trying to grip it and not let go, but then the waves rush past and wash all the grip away, sweeping her out to sea.

I rock faster in a chair that's not even a rocking chair and almost tip over.

The doctor nods. "Off balance. Is that what you feel?"

I shrug.

"That is okay that you feel that way. I want to help you to get back in balance," she adds, sliding a plastic bottle of water closer to me. "For you."

For the next hour, we talk—well, she talks. I scribble. She gives me these sheets of paper and a pencil and tells me to just scribble every which way all over them, so I do. It seems a bit lame, but I like not having to care about saying anything, or drawing anything, or even staying on the page. I scribble this way and that, upside down, sideways, and when the page is full, I stop, and she gives me another blank page, only this time, she presses something on her cell phone, and music starts to play.

"What music do you like?"

When she says music, Daddy pops into my head, and tears spring to my eyes. I grab the water bottle, take a swig, and swallow hard to keep the tears away, but I think she sees them.

"Country," I answer, keeping time to the music with my fingers on the hand that's not holding the pencil. I hum to the music. The scribbles aren't so dark and messy this time. I pass her the second scribbled paper when I'm done. She takes it and slides one more blank paper across the desk toward me, then clicks on her phone again and plays orchestra music.

I never heard the piece that's playing before but start humming along with it, just like I hummed to the country tunes I did know. I look up and catch the look of surprise on her face. "You know this piece?"

"No."

"I read in your file you had a special gift for being able to hum a song you have never heard before, but seeing it and hearing it? That is amazing."

It's true. I can sing along to music I've never heard before. I don't know why or how, I just can. But I'm not the singer in the family. Daddy is. And Sara. She got the "singing jeans," or so Daddy would say.

By now, I'm growing tired of scribbling. The doctor lady adds my last paper to the others, shuffles them, then pulls one of the scribbled drawings out from the middle and plants it right in front of me.

"Now, for today's session, look at your drawing, Anna, and name things you see in it. You can turn the paper this way, that way." She rolls her hands in front of her like she'd driving a car, and speaks slowly, like Rachel used to, I guess so I can understand her words better, but hearing is not my problem. Talking is.

I play along and turn the paper, first one way then another. At first, all I see are my scribbles. But then something kind of magical happens and shapes start to appear, just like they did that night in cool-down room when I gouged out the walls.

I try to shake that thought. Trying to set what I thought was a cat-girl free cost me almost four poems, and if you count them at five bucks each, that's twenty bucks. A wasted taxi drive is what I call it. But it's not a taxi I see in my scribbles.

"You see something! I can tell by the sparkle in your eyes. What is it you see, Anna?

"Tell you what," she says when I don't answer, and pushes a box of colored pencils toward me. "Why don't you pick a color and fill in any spaces you want to fill."

"Abby," I say, picking up a black pencil and coloring in spaces. Bart said he thought my doll had been brought here, but so far, I haven't seen her.

"Abby. That's your doll, right? Is that what you see in the drawing?"

"Want Abby," I answer. No, I don't see her in the scribbles. I don't even want to. I want to see her for real. I want my doll back. She's the only thing I have left from my real home.

The doctor lady reaches under the desk and pulls Abby into view. The doll's hair, which has never looked worse, falls down over her face, and her melted armpit and dangling arm make my own arm—the one Terrible Ted burned—start to hurt. I stiffen and freak out when it feels like I'm turning stiff like Abby again. Only this time, Abby and I are joined together in a way I wouldn't wish on anyone. We both have burned arms.

I flash on Justin. Does Terrible Ted beat him? My face heats up just thinking about what Terrible Ted did to me and what he might be doing to Justin, and panic grabs at me like that ocean wave grabbed at Jo-Jo's feet. The doctor lady puts Abby back in her lap and stares first at me, then at my drawing.

"Very nice, Anna! Now, look and tell me what you see in your drawing."

"Cats," I tell her. "And dogs."

Her eyebrows shoot up. "Good, Anna. Now say the whole sentence. 'I see cats and dogs.'" She pronounces each word evenly.

"Cats and dogs," I answer, just as evenly.

"Cats and dogs, yes. Now use the I-message and say, 'I see cats and dogs.'"

Why keep saying it? We both can see them. What difference does it make how I say it?

"Try again, Anna. Say the whole sentence. I teach you I-messages so you can say how you feel. Try. Say, 'I see cats and dogs,' and if you do, I give you Abby."

She pulls Abby up from her lap, and I jump up and reach across the table to grab her, but when I do, she pulls Abby out of reach again. "I give her to you, but first you must say, 'I see cats and dogs,'" she repeats, over and over.

"Abby!" I shout. I grab for her again.

"What you want me to do? Use your I-messages, Anna. Say, 'I want Abby.'"

"Abby!" I shout, half-sitting, half-standing, trying to get to her. What does she think I want her to do? Give me my doll! That's what. "Abby!" I shout again.

She sets Abby back in her lap and leans back in her chair. "Okay, Anna. Let's try something else. I won't give you Abby just yet, but I will give her to you if you say just one complete I-message. It does not have to be a long sentence. It can be as short as three words. 'I am mad!' Use your I-messages.' Say, 'I am mad!'"

"Mad!" I shout.

"I am mad," she repeats.

"Mad!" I scream, jumping up from the table and gripping the edge so I don't topple over.

"Say the whole sentence, Anna. 'I am mad.'"

It's not like I didn't give her enough chances to give me my doll back. But she just wouldn't do it. I sweep my arm across her desk, sending papers, pencils, folders, and books crashing to the floor. The books barely miss my foot, and before I can pull it back, hands appear out of nowhere and are all over me, grabbing my arms, shoulders, legs, and feet. I growl, thrashing every which way, trying to get them to let me go.

Someone has me from behind, holding me in a tight hug, with my arms pinned to my side. I fight, kicking and screaming, but someone else grips my legs. A different someone has wheeled over a wheelchair, and I'm lifted up and shaped to fit onto it. Straps wrap around the arms of the chair, pinning mine down, and another strap holds down my legs so I can't kick.

Another bee sting leaves me limp on the outside but still fighting on the inside. Before they wheel me out, I hear Dr. Kitanovski telling someone that my stay must be lengthened.

"Six months," Dr. Kitanovski tells someone. "I'll write up order."

What order? Who's giving orders? Is she the judge? Am I in court? Did they trick me? What's happening?

The lids on my eyes flip open and closed, and my mind freezes as they wheel me down the hall. I can't move arms or legs or anything. I'm now stiff as Abby again. My one arm dangles over the side of the chair. Whoever's pushing the chair tips it back, and my eyes close. Suddenly, I'm in one of Emily Dickinson's poems. *And then the Windows failed /And then I could not see to see.*

That little anger burst costs me two days in lockdown and twenty-five points. At this rate, I'll never get out of here.

35

As the last days before Halloween unfold, new secrets are revealed. For one, I find out that Jo-Jo has been in RTC at least as many times as I have been in temporary foster homes. It turns out Danny was right. Jo-Jo made up the whole story about the dead baby. Jo-Jo's mom wasn't even pregnant.

Miss Davenport makes us all write a paragraph about lying, even though it wasn't us who lied; it was Jo-Jo, and she ran away. Why do we have to write about lying when she's not even here anymore? I write that she should learn to write down her lies and make a story out of them instead of trying to trick us. Ben says stories are either fiction or nonfiction and that fiction means not real. At least if she wrote fiction, Jo-Jo would have a place to put her made-up stories, and maybe everyone would stop calling her a liar.

But Jo-Jo isn't my worry right now, and neither is writing about lying. Sara is my worry. Halloween sneaks up on me like one of the ghosts hanging in the hallway, and if it's Halloween, that means it's also Sara's birthday, and I have no way to wish her a happy day. Certainly, a happier day than I had at B-Mod.

I don't even want to think about it. I wanted to ask Dr. Kitanovski if we couldn't at least call Sara on her birthday, so I could let her know I remembered it, but then all that I-message misery happened.

At the next B-Mod meeting, we played the stupid scribble game again, and she *still* wouldn't give me Abby. I almost got put back in the cool-down room, but when I started shouting, "I am mad," over and over like a crazy person, Dr. Kitanovski looked at me, "proud as whiskers" as Daddy would say, like I'd done something amazing.

This place is nuts.

Some good news is that Dr. Kitanovski finally decides the stupid picture game isn't working after all and that we should try something different. She says she's going to look into equine therapy, whatever that is. But hey, if it's not scribbling on paper or shouting stupid I-messages, count me in.

The bad part of the day is that Dr. Kitanovski still won't give me Abby. "Let us fix her," the doctor said, like a doll could scribble on paper and shout, "I am mad."

Nuts, I tell you. It's the day before Halloween, which I call Devil's Day, since the night before Halloween is Devil's Night.

The good part of the day is that Bart is on his way over to bring me stuff to put together a costume, not that I'm even close to being in a partying mood. I would be if Sara was here.

Angry as I still am over not getting Abby back, I can't help but laugh when I see Bart. He's got a patch over one eye and funny, poufy pants that come down to his knees. His peg leg is uncovered for all to see, and he's wearing a cape and carrying a yardstick for a sword, since this place has an antiweapon policy (which Justin either didn't get or didn't care about).

"Ready to party, matey?" Bart says, lowering his voice. "It's right here in my bag of loot!"

He pulls a bag out of a bigger bag and hands it to me. "Well, go on. Open it."

I peer into the bag and frown and grin at the same time. It's a costume of sorts.

I pull out a smaller-sized pair of poufy, black pants that look a lot like his, only the legs are long. Also in the bag is a white shirt, cut ragged on the edges, a thin black vest, a red bandana, I think he called it, to tie around my head, a wide black belt with a big plastic buckle shaped to look like a skull, and these soft-sided, black, fake leather, knee-high boots.

"For me?"

Bart grins. "Yes, for you. It's a stowaway costume. You can be a stowaway on my imaginary ship!"

"Stow-a-way," I murmur, wishing it could all come true and I could stow-a-way out of here.

"You did good for the most part this past month, Anna-fanna-fe-fi-fo-fanna-Anna. You had little rough patches here and there, but I can't help but notice you earned some points and even some money. And," he adds, "you're keeping up in your journal!

"It'll all come together," Bart says, reading my silence. "Ready to get group and B-Mod out of the way so you can join in on the Halloween party? Don't be lookin' all surprised, Anna. Your last session didn't exactly earn you a lot of points."

"I guess," I mumble. Still, I don't see why I have to go on Halloween.

"Guess? I see that look in your eyes. You don't just guess; you know! Don't freak out, but some people might be coming by to observe."

"On Halloween?" But what I'm really thinking is, *On Sara's birthday?*

"You know, you're probably right. The university might have rescheduled observations because of Halloween, but it's not an official holiday, and around here, it's just another day. Nothing to get worked up about. The doc just wants to check on you after your last … well, let's just call it an incident … to make sure you're okay. And she might even have a little something for you."

"Abby?" I say, relieved he didn't say that they stuck her in a donation box, or worse, threw her away.

"I'm not saying anything more. Hurry and get cleaned up. I'll be back in five to check on you and see if the costume fits before we meet the others for the party."

After Bart leaves, I hurry to the bathroom and shower, then throw on underwear, jeans, a sweatshirt, socks, and shoes. I place the costume Bart brought over on the bed to change into later.

The wall hums and buzzes, and the door pops open.

Bart grins, sizing me up. "Ready?"

"Ready," I answer, not feeling one bit ready.

"I brought something for your soiled sheets," Bart says, holding out a bag.

"No need," I tell him, feeling a slow grin curl my lips.

But I'm not the only one grinning. "Whoa, girl. They're dry? Now, that's what I'm talking about! You just earned yourself some more moolah, baby girl!" Bart's laugh rolls down the hall ahead of us.

"Moolah," I say, liking his word for money.

When we get to the door, he pauses. "As you know, we get new residents coming in and old ones going out every day, so you never know who's going to be in group today."

I hesitate, looking down the hall, but Bart points the other way. "Group first. Then B-Mod, then—" He starts singing a yo-ho-ho-ho pirate party song and dances down the hallway, goofy as all get-out. I guess even grown-ups have to act like kids sometimes.

When I reach group, I cross the room, keeping my head down. I'm sure they all heard about my meltdown in B-Mod and how I ended up in cool-down, but nobody knows it started when I saw Terrible Ted in the window. I find an empty seat and sit. Beside me, I see a pair of red shoes and realize Kat-with-a-K is there.

"Hey." She scoots her chair over to give me room.

"Hey," I answer back. "Great shoes," I whisper, staring at her feet.

"That be kick-ass shoes," she whispers back, grinning, and I bite my lower lip and glance up at the new lady to see if she heard Kat say the swear word, but clearly she didn't. She wouldn't be grinning at us if she did.

"Welcome, Anna. I'm Jamie, your new group leader."

I look back at Kat, eyebrows raised, but she just shrugs.

"Let's go around the circle and introduce ourselves."

I take a deep breath and try not to roll my eyes. It's easy to lose points in group for "copping an attitude" is how they call it.

"Clair."

I stare across the circle, recognizing the girl I saw in the bushes the day I let the spider out. She looks back, grinning slightly.

"Jay Dee."

"Kelly."

"Kat."

"Thomas."

"Anna," I mumble. Practically all new faces.

"Justin Time," a boy's voice says, and I stiffen. *Justin is back?* I glance over to the chair on the other side of the Jamie lady, and Justin smirks, then says softly, "Uncle Ted says hi."

I look away, sinking deep down in my chair. *Did Terrible Ted come inside? Is he here?*

I can't breathe and don't dare look up.

"Stick to Justin, Justin. I know your last name isn't Time," leader Jamie says. "Okay then. I understand you all did a lesson for this week's workbook assignment. Kat. Let's start with you. The first topic on page twelve is 'Solving a Problem: Describe a time something didn't go your way.' Why don't you read what you wrote and how you handled it?"

Kat opens her workbook to page 12 like she's batting flies from each page. "That be easy," she says, when she finally gets to the right page. "I wrote about gettin' busted for stealin' a sweater. It was a Saturday, and I woke up so cold that my old sweatshirt wasn't doin' nothin' to keep me warm. Keesha, my stepmom, wasn't home, and my dad, he ain't never home, so I took off to Bargain Central to find me something warmer to wear.

"The store was almost empty, so I went over to the coats and sweaters and took one off a hanger and hung my sorry ass—uh, I mean my sorry sweatshirt—"

"Go on," leader Jamie urges but not without giving her the stink eye.

"Well, I hung my sorry sweatshirt on the hanger, tradin' it for the sweater, but when I walked out, security was all over my a—uh, well, you know, saying how I stole the stupid sweater and how shoplifting's a crime and all."

I steal a quick look around the circle. I know what it feels like to get busted. I got busted when I hid in the tree, but getting busted for stealing in a store? How is she going to explain her way out of that one?

"So, what did you write in your journal about what might have been a better way than stealing to handle the situation?" the Jamie lady asks.

"Well, first off, mainly just to conversate, I technically 'borrowed' the sweater. I didn't steal nothin', because I was gonna return it when the weather got warmer," Kat answers, but clearly by the look on the Jamie lady's face, it's not the answer she's looking for.

"Is it a store you went to or a library?"

"What your sayin's a gimme, Miss Jamie. The store don't have no books, just clothes and whatnot, and I wasn't wantin' to borrow a book. I needed a sweater to keep me warm, not a book tellin' me how to keep warm."

"So, let's put it to the group. Is there a difference between borrowing and stealing, and if so, what is it?" Miss Jamie looks around the circle.

Clair pipes up. "Easy. If you steal, it means you aren't gonna bring it back."

"'Zackly. But I *was* gonna bring it back," Kat snaps, doing that head-shaking thing she does, "so like I was jus' sayin', that makes it bor-ro-wing." She breaks the word up.

I look over at Kelly and then at Clair. For the first time, I see how much Clair and Kelly look alike, making me wonder if they're sisters. The thought sends a heated chill through me. *Why do they get to be together when I don't get to be with Sara? We're sisters. So, what are they saying? Some sisters get to be together and others have to be split up? How fair is that?*

"How would you have handled it, Clair?"

"For starters," Clair says, stretching her short legs straight out in front of her like she's making a bridge or something. "I would have picked out something a whole lot better than a sweater to steal. I mean, if you're gonna get busted nine times outta ten, why not get something cool, like a coat or something?"

"Jay Dee?"

"Beats me."

"Saying 'pass' will do," the Jamie lady reminds him.

"Thomas?"

"Pass."

"Justin."

"I'm with Clair." He lifts a foot off the floor and bumps it against one of hers. I look over right when she sends him this secretive look and smiles. What's with that?

While Miss Jamie goes around the circle asking others what they would have done, my mind races. Why *can't* there be stores that are like libraries where you could borrow and return stuff?

36

"ANNA?"

"Pass."

If I had answered, it would probably have been to say that what's not yours is not yours, but then I remember the rainmaker, a thick tree branch filled with seeds that made a shivering sound like rain when you tipped it back and forth, and how I kind of took that from Pablo when Sara and I stayed at the MacMillans' house, and how he took it back. The MacMillans were temporary foster parents. He ended up giving it to me before they moved out of the country. It would have been nice to have the rainmaker here. I wonder what ever happened to it.

"Okay, well what are some other things Kat could have done besides steal the sweater?"

"Borrowed," Kat corrects coldly.

"Freeze her ass off," Jay Dee answers. "It's not like she's the only one that has had to live with being cold." The one called Kelly fist-bumps her.

"Swearing has cost you five points, Jay Dee. Pull out your notebooks, everyone, and write a paragraph or two on stealing. Anna, I'll get you a paper and pencil."

"I didn't swear," Jay Dee counters. "Ass is just another word for—well, ass."

A snicker passes through the group, but Miss Jamie isn't laughing. "And you just docked yourself ten more points."

"Oh, man. That sucks."

"Does this count toward our journal?" Kat asks.

"If you take it seriously, it can. If not, it's just a group exercise."

"Does spelling count?" Kelly calls out, waiting for the answer.

"Do your best," Miss Jamie tells her. "Here you go, Anna."

I hesitate before taking the paper and pencil. We were never given pencils before because they could be used as knives to stab someone. The new lady clearly doesn't know the rules.

"Hey, I need a pencil too," Justin blurts, and the whole group chimes in. Next thing we know, she's handing out pencils like candy.

I reluctantly stare at the paper. I say reluctantly because I don't have a clue what to write. Tig would have rattled off something cool for me to say. How unfair of her to leave me. Without her here to help, I decide to pretend I'm Emily Dickinson and write what she might have written if she'd found herself stuck in group. It's hard to write under pressure.

> Branding
> Letters
> Brand Me and
> Rob Me of
> My True Identity,
> But the Mark is on Him
> Not Me.
> The Mark's on him,
> And his Mark is Cruelty.

I think back on me and Sara and how much I relied on her to get us through all the mess and to stand up for us. I had to since Terrible Ted threatened to burn my tongue out if I talked. But words have a lot of power. People say them, and then you have to decide if you believe them. Not all words are true. Lies are words, and they aren't true.

Anyone can tell a lie. How can I know if my words or anyone's words are true? I still hear Terrible Ted in my head: "You tell anyone 'bout this, and I'll burn that tongue right out of your mouth."

Suddenly, I can't breathe any more of this tense air filling the room and jump up.

"Out!" I shout, waving my arms and spinning toward the door. I need to get outside. Get in the sun. Get some air.

"Anna. Calm down," the Jamie lady calls out.

"I want out!" I shout again, turning in bigger circles. "Out! Out!"

As I pull away, I hear words following me. "Out of her mind." "Lunatic." "Crazy." "Freakazoid."

It's like someone has pulled a string in me, and I spin and spin as everything around me blurs. I want out of the room, away from Justin, away from the memory of Terrible Ted, away from all of them. I want to turn inside out and hide inside myself where it's warm and safe—where nobody can get to me. But I feel empty, like Abby must feel. What's happening? Who am I? It's like I don't even know.

"Deep breaths," Jamie says, close to my right ear. I draw my shoulder up, trying to cover it, and swing my arm up but don't hit anything but air.

"Give her some space," the Jamie lady says to the group. I know it's to them, because her voice has turned away from me and drifts across the room.

"Writing is a journey, and sometimes when we write about personal things, it triggers something in us that might bring up some unpleasant memories. I'm sure that's what has happened here with Anna, but it's nothing to make fun of. Go back to your rooms or to your next activity."

I hear feet shuffling by my head, and unless they're suddenly walking on air, I realize I must be down on the floor. I don't remember falling. Did I fall? I open my eyes and see Justin standing over me. He reaches down, like he wants to help me up, and his sleeve inches up on his arms.

Then I see them.

The burn marks.

He's covered with them.

I look in his eyes, frowning. He stands up suddenly, his face reddening, and tugs on his sleeves to hide what his uncle has done to him.

I pull at the neck of my sweatshirt and slip my bare arm out the top, raising it over my head, and he sees the burns. We look at each other, saying nothing. While I slip my arm back under the sweatshirt and into the sleeve, he turns and heads for the door.

I hear Bart's deep voice. Next thing I know, I'm in the hard wheelchair and everything starts bumping back into focus.

"What just happened here, baby girl? You fall down that hole again?"

Bart knows what happened because he's in the knowing place. It's that I-get-it space that says to someone that even though you can't have had the exact experience they just had, since you aren't them, you still know what it's like. When you're in that knowing space, nobody even has to say anything.

"Let's get you to therapy and maybe get you to feeling better. It might seem that what just happened there was a bad thing, but I'm proud of you, Anna." He whirls the chair around so I can see him better. "It might not seem like it, but that what happened back there was progress! It's like you didn't take a tiny step toward getting out of here, you took a giant leap!"

"Leap," I repeat, feeling my tongue flick against the roof of my mouth.

"Yeah, a giant leap," he says again, wheeling me to the door of the therapy room. "That's two giant leaps in one day. Dry sheets. And using your I-messages!"

His voice oozes with pride, but I'm not feeling too proud right now. I hate what Terrible Ted has turned me into. And I'm shocked at what he's done to Justin.

Before taking me into B-Mod, Bart explains in a low voice to Dr. Kitanovski what just happened in group, and she looks at me intensely, as if she's trying to read my thoughts.

I look away and wait.

"Maybe we should hold off today?" Bart suggests, but Dr. Kitanovski shakes her head. "Better strike while the iron's hot," she whispers.

Bart squats down, favoring his real leg, whispers that he'll see me later, and leaves.

"Can we talk about what happened in group, Anna?" Dr. Kitanovski asks, rounding her desk and reaching toward me, like she's going to help me to transfer to a regular chair. But I don't need help and sit in the other chair before her hands get too close and I do something that will keep me here longer.

After a few seconds or so, she circles back around her desk and sits down slowly.

"I see you have your journal entry with you, Anna. May I read what you wrote in group that perhaps triggered a memory?"

I look down at the paper in my lap. Sometimes sharing what I write leaves me feeling exposed. I wonder what Ben would say if he heard that. But I don't have to wonder too long, because I suddenly hear his voice in my head, like he's right here beside me. He once told us, "Sharink our words can expose our inside self. To be willink to do that takes a lot of courage and trust."

This trust thing that keeps coming up eats at me, or maybe it's that mouse I wrote about in my poem nibbling away at the trust. I'm about to tell the Ben in my thoughts that I don't know what trust is when I stop myself, because I actually *do* know what trust is. Trust is Ben. Trust is Rachel. They're the most trustworthy people Sara and I know.

Ben and Rachel showed me and Sara what trusting people look, sound, and act like, and right now I miss Ben and Rachel so much. Trust is what a soft blanket feels like, and right now, I could use a soft blanket. I could also use my doll, since she's all the family I have left.

"Abby," I mumble.

"You wrote about Abby? May I see?"

"Not Abby!" I shout.

"Okay, not Abby. I tell you what. How about I let you hold Abby and you share what you wrote in group?"

Dr. Kitanovski leans back and pulls Abby out from under her desk. My mouth drops open at the sight of her. Abby's hair is totally, and I do mean totally, refashioned. Her clothes are trim and clean: jeans, red shoes, and a white shirt. This is Kat-with-a-K's doing. It has her name written all over it, from the red shoes all the way up to the new do.

"Abby," Dr. Kitanovski says, turning the doll toward her. "What is making Anna so afraid to talk in complete sentences and has her wetting the bed?"

"Didn't wet bed!" I shout, raising my arms up to hide my face. *Really?* Does she have to say everything I do wrong for anyone who might be behind that stupid one-way glass to hear? And why is she talking to me through my doll when I'm right here in front of her? Did I suddenly turn invisible? Actually, turning invisible wouldn't be such a bad thing right now.

"Who is Anna afraid of?" she asks, not even picking up on how upset I am. Clearly, she didn't attend the how-to-read-thoughts class like Bart and Emily and Ben.

"Is it her daddy?"

"No!" I drop my arms down and bolt from the chair.

"Is it another relative?" She keeps twisting Abby's head back and forth, back and forth, like Abby is saying no for me.

"Stop!" What if she guesses? What if she says, "Is it Terrible Ted?" and he's hiding behind the one-way glass? What if he thinks I told her? Only, I didn't tell.

"She guessed," I shout at the two-way window.

That's not the same thing as telling! He can't burn out my tongue because someone guesses his name. He can't. It's not fair. *I didn't tell.* I kept his stupid, awful secret. He can't burn out my tongue. He just can't!

"Stop!"

"Is it—"

"Stop! Stop! Stop!"

I drop back down on the chair, putting my head to the desk to hide my face, not caring if my snot and tears are messing up the desktop. She has to stop. I know he's up there behind the window. I just know he is.

She reaches across the desk and rests her hand on my arm, and I jerk away, pushing my chair back.

"Don't touch me!"

"Good, Anna. Say it again."

"Don't touch me!" I shout.

"I won't touch you," she says evenly, standing and leaning toward me over the desk. "I will respect your space. Did you hear what you just said, Anna? You said, 'Don't touch me,' and I bet that sentence has been burning inside you for a very, very long time. Who is it that you really don't want to touch you, Anna?"

"Give … me … Abby." I say each word slowly and evenly and smack my journal entry on her desk when I say Abby's name.

To my shock, she hands me my doll! But something in me snaps. What if it's too late? What if Terrible Ted is on his way down the hall right now to get me? What if he really did see me that day and now he's in some stupid costume and nobody here—not even me—recognizes that someone a million times worse than Justin and his stupid lighter is right here, waiting to grab me and burn my tongue out?

I hurl Abby across the room at the strange mirror and hear her clatter when she hits it and falls to the floor. "Go away!" I shout. "Get away from me!" My throat is raw from screaming. I know the sound of thundering feet, and it's no surprise when a crowd of staff people push through the doorway. I also know that once they all squeeze in here, they'll morph into one giant octopus that will put its hands all over me to hold me down, and then the bee will come by to sting me. I know all of this because I'm in the knowing place. I'm not stupid.

Which is why, this time, I don't spin. I don't get dizzy and pass out. I don't growl and thrash and lash out or scream. For once, I don't even freeze. This time—

I bolt.

37

SWINGING, DUCKING, AND SQUIRMING, I WRIGGLE PAST them and head straight for cool-down. I know that's where they'll stick me since lockdown is already taken. At least in cool-down, I can be locked in and Terrible Ted can't get to me.

The door to the room is open, so nobody has been put in it yet. I race in and slam the door, for once happy to hear the loud click of the lock, and flop on the bed, mad at myself for hurling Abby and leaving her out there all by herself. Didn't I promise to protect her? *Why am I so mean to her?* I hate this place. I hate being stuck here. I hate not being able to leave. I hate my life.

I hate myself.

Someone knocks on the door, and I start breathing so hard I'm panting. I can't live like this. The wall hums, and the buzzer buzzes.

I jump up and look for something, anything to fight with, but all that's around is a book on the bed. I grab it and whip it up in the air, fully poised to hurl at whoever comes through the door.

"Hey, there you are." Bart smiles, but it's a forced smile that finally settles somewhere between sorry and pity. He doesn't even flinch at seeing me ready to throw the book at him.

"Not a good book to be hurling at someone," he says calmly, and I put my arm down, setting the book on the bed.

He gives me that pity-sorry look again.

I used to think sorry and pity were the same thing, but they aren't. "Sorry" you can wear like pants, or a shirt, or a sad face. But pity? Pity is like blistered skin. It burns when anything even comes close to touching it.

"We still got a lot of learning to do, Anna." He starts on a story, but my thoughts are still on Terrible Ted. I should tell Bart. Bart would know what to do. Bart would keep him away. But what about when I get out of here? Who's going to keep him away then?

"His brave actions were the birth of something new," Bart says, like he's come to the end of his story.

"Birth," I repeat. Bart doesn't know it, but he's just reminded me that it's Sara's birthday. How could I have forgotten? *Did someone make her a cake? Did she have fun or get to do anything special?* Bart digs in his pocket and hands me a tissue.

"Looks like I lost you again, baby girl, but then, that was a long lesson I just gave you about a society of brave people."

I swallow my tears and turn my attention back to Bart. "So-sigh-ety."

"Society. Yeah. That's like a group of people that stick together." He hands me a power bar, and I peel off the wrapper.

"Like glue," I add, shivering.

Bart grins. "Yeah, like glue. You got it, Anna. History is all the stories that glue us together." Bart sighs, then takes off his coat and drapes it over me. The warmth of it feels safe and takes the shivers away. I finish the last of the power bar and turn my attention back to him.

"And just like those brave people in history, you got some deciding to do. Some kids in here, they can't help themselves. Something is missing, and they're lost beyond lost. But you? You got a good heart and a good head, and you got soul, but you trap that innocent girl way down deep inside you. Don't you think it's time to let her out?"

I catch my breath. He knows about Tig? "She got away," I say. Tears spill down my cheeks and quickly turn cold.

Bart's eyebrows slowly rise as he stops to think. "No, no. She didn't get away. She's still here. Matter of fact, she's sitting right in front of me. Don't you see? That girl you trapped inside you is you, Anna. Always has been. Always will be. Only you needed to set her free.

"Now, you can stay here in this place and fight, and bite, and scream, and torture yourself and everyone around you, or you can kick it into gear and learn something. You can grow. Manna is a place to grow—to discover—to find yourself. Are you up to the challenge?"

I nod.

"We're breakin' new ground, Anna-fanna, like a seed sprouting through concrete. Ever see where a tiny flower pushes up through the cracks in the sidewalk?"

"New ground," I repeat, nodding.

A slow smile spreads across Bart's face, and he pushes himself up from the chair to leave. "The world is an exciting place, Anna, and is filled with so many, many things to learn about. When we learn, it's like we're planting our own Tree of Knowledge, or a Tree of Life."

"Poet-Tree," I murmur, breaking the word in two, and his eyebrows shoot up before a laugh escapes him.

"Poet-Tree. Yes! I like that," he says, lifting his coat off me. "Did you know that the Tree of Life, or Poet-Tree, as you called it, appears in many, many societies around the world?"

I shake my head, already missing the warmth of his coat.

Bart continues his story. "The Mayan Tree of Life, for instance, is a cross that signifies north, south, east, and west, which represents the source of all beginning. The Babylonian Tree of Life had magic fruit on it! Coiling snakes guarded the tree to make sure that only the gods got to eat the magic fruit!"

I'm not sure what Mayans are or the Babble-whatever he said was, but it turns out they weren't the only ones with a Tree of Life.

"Now, the Chinese Tree of Life is a peach tree that produces fruit every three thousand years! And it provides immortality to the one that eats the fruit!"

"What's im—immor—"

"Immortality? That means living forever," Bart explains. "And let's not leave out the Tree of Life in the Hebrew legend of the Garden of Eden—an apple tree that represents good and evil."

I nod. Ben read us a story about Adam and Eve and the garden they lived in.

"Ever cut an apple sideways?" Bart asks.

I shake my head.

"I'll be right back."

He isn't kidding. He's back in the room in under a minute. I know, because I count one-one thousand, two-one thousand, all the way up to forty-three one thousand before he returns.

"Look here," he says, holding up what looks like a whole apple, until I see the line across the middle where he has cut it. "Ready?"

I nod, not knowing what to expect but hoping the surprise isn't a worm—or worse, half a worm.

"What do you see?"

He turns the halves out toward me.

"Stars!" I grin. Who knew apples had stars hidden in them?

"That's right. Stars. Like I say, the world is an exciting place, filled with so many things to learn about. Sometimes we search and search for something, and it turns out we had it in us all the time, like this apple and these stars.

"We got to—"

"Grow where we're planted," I murmur.

Bart grins. "Yes! There will be times when you'll want to give up, but when that happens, just think of me with my one leg, or that maple tree lookin' so fine and strong when it's rottin' out from the belly, and keep on going. Deal?"

I look down at Bart's pant leg, knowing a fake leg is hidden under it, but Bart doesn't let not having a leg stop him from doing things that need to get done.

"Deal."

"Okay then. Come down to the cafeteria for the party," he says, starting to leave, then stops. "I don't guess they'll hold tonight against you. I'll have a talk with Miss Emily and see what the plan is. When I go, I'll leave the door unlocked so you can get out. It will lock on the outside when you close it, so be sure to bring everything you're going to bring to the party."

I'm not feeling like partying. But staying here by myself doesn't sound one bit fun either.

"Oh, man! I totally forgot. I brought you something." Bart reaches over his shoulder and pulls Abby out of a backpack and hands her to me.

I hug her and hold her out, but something about her is different. She still has the new look Kat gave her, but she also has something else: *two good arms.*

I stare at Bart. "You made Abby new arms?" I say each word like it's an I-message, and Bart grins, but the smile doesn't last long. He looks down.

I look back at Abby. She looks so good! So complete. So whole!

"I made the one to replace the one that got melted," Bart says quietly, rolling his eyes up to stare at the doll. "The other—" He stops, like he's trying to find the right words, and looks out the window. "The other is the original."

It takes a minute for his words to sink in. *Original?*

The word hangs like a dangling spider between us. "But I don't—" My mouth twitches uncontrollably. I can barely breathe. "Sara was *here*?"

Bart stares at the floor.

My voice cracks. "But why—*why didn't …*"

He looks up, his face broken with worry lines. "Because you lost it, Anna. Dr. Kitanovski was trying to get you to share what you wrote and to use your I-messages like it says to do in your workbook, and she was going to give you back Abby *and* let you see Sara, but you lost it."

I barely hear him.

"Sara was behind the glass?" I say, gasping for air.

Bart's chin drops to his chest. He turns to a brown blur. All that time I was screaming at Dr. Kitanovski, I was sure that Terrible Ted was behind the one-way mirror, waiting to grab me, when it was really Sara who was there?

They should have told me. I would have acted better. I would have acted any way they wanted me to act so I could have seen her, talked to her, wished her a happy birthday. Showed her my room and maybe even introduced her to Kat-with-a-K.

What if I could have gone home with her?

"Not fair!" I shout. "Not fair!" I scream again, sounding just like Sara sounded when she yelled at our caseworker about having me stuck in this place.

"What's not fair," Bart says in a calming voice, "is what you're doing to that blameless girl trapped inside of you.

"What's not fair," he says a little stronger, "is you fighting me and everyone here tooth and nail—the very people who are trying to help you. What's not fair," he continues, and I press my hands tight against my ears, but I can still hear him, "is that you don't trust the strong, good-hearted, loving girl that you are. That's what's not fair."

"Okay! Okay! Anna's not fair! I get it!"

"Yes, Anna's not fair—to Anna," he adds emphatically. "Why not give Anna a chance? Why not be fair to Anna?"

"Go away."

Bart hesitates a moment, sighs a deep, long sigh, and then turns to leave.

When he's gone, I fall on the bed, wanting more than ever to turn into Abby—something stiff and plastic and empty that can't get hurt. But I don't turn into anyone because there's no one left to turn in to.

Sara was behind the glass.

Coming to see me was probably her birthday present. Only what Sara saw was me kicking and screaming and throwing Abby at the glass.

I cry and cry until no more tears will come, all the while searching for something, *anything*, to hold onto. Then I remember how Ben always told me and Sara that if ever things got so low that you don't think they can get any worse, to remember that the sun can break through a storm cloud and bring about a better, brighter day. I try to think of something, *anything*, that can make this day not hurt so bad.

Then it comes to me. Sara left me something: Abby's arm. She knew that clue alone would be enough for me to know she'd been here and that she hadn't forgotten me.

I heave air out and in, out and in, until my head feels dizzy. Yes. Sara was here. No, I didn't know it. Yes, that sucks. No, I can't breathe.

Sun, where are you?

I try to think of what Emily Dickinson might say if she were here.

She found you. She hasn't forgotten you. Your sister loves you suddenly pops into my head in a voice that's different from mine. Is it Emily's?

Right now, Emily's words, or whoever's words they are, keep me from giving up.

She found me. Sara found me.

Emily opens the door—not Emily Dickinson, but the Emily that works here.

"I just heard."

Nothing more needs to be said, and we both just stare out the window at the maple tree, she by the table and me from the bed. My eyes are puffy and so sore from crying. Finally, she comes over to the bed and sits down beside me.

"I talked with Dr. Kitanovski, and there's a new therapy program she feels might be a good fit for you. I know she briefly mentioned it to you, but I wanted to talk to you about it and see if it's something you might want to try."

She looks at me with such sadness in her eyes.

I nod.

They broke me. I can't fight her or any of them anymore. I've been shattered into a million pieces. What if I can't be put back together again? What then?

"It's called equine therapy," Emily continues. "Equine is another name for horses. I don't know if you heard, but Will quit last night, and Bart has been reassigned to this wing. After the holiday, he'll drive you to a horse ranch not far from here three days a week, where you'll work with one of the horses.

"There's a nice trainer over there, and she'll teach you about the horses and help you pick one that you want to work with. Does that sound like something you might want to try? It will get you out of here, and you'll get to work with animals.

"Horses don't talk back," she adds, like she's trying to sweeten the pot, as Daddy would say. She forces a smile.

I try to make my lips curl up into a smile, too, but even I know it isn't working.

What I want to do is cry, but no more tears will come. I end up just making those sniffs that show up between crying. I'm both surprised and not surprised that Will quit. It's not just residents, as they call us, coming and going. It's staff too.

"Dr. Kitanovski also feels that you need to stay with us a little longer than forty days to get this all figured out. She's recommending that you stay six months until you feel safe and are able to successfully communicate."

"I heard," I murmur. It's my new sentence. But I'm also hearing for the first time, even though I've been here over a month, that people here do care about me. It's not just a job for the Emilys and Barts. I also see that I built up all this fear of Terrible Ted based on something that wasn't even true. He wasn't behind the glass. Sara was. And if I think I am afraid just because of seeing him, think how Justin must feel being related to him. Why couldn't Terrible Ted run away instead of Mama and Daddy? They were messed up, but they weren't burning us.

Maybe I could have told Bart. Even should have that day that I almost did, and maybe Justin wouldn't have gotten more burns.

I look at Emily, and while a great urge is there to tell all, I can't do it yet. But I want to. Maybe wanting to is a good place to start.

And just like that, the jail with feathers just gets its wings clipped. No flying out of this place anytime soon, but I can't think that much about it. Not today. Today is my day to think about my sister.

38

AFTER EMILY LEAVES, I HUNCH OVER A PLATE OF MEATLOAF and mashed potatoes and peas, and remember the assignment for this week's journal is to focus on the very thing I try not to focus on, but if I don't do it, I can't get the tokens, and I can't advance through the program to get out of here.

Bart once said, "You can try to avoid the thing that haunts you the most in life, but you will find it becomes your shadow, and it's hard to shake a shadow."

I grab a crayon and for once don't try to get Tig to write it. Don't try pretending that I'm Emily Dickinson writing it. Don't try to write about something else and pretend it's the same thing. I just stare at the blank journal page and shiver as I say the prompt we were given: "What about trust scares you the most?"

Ben once told me and Sara that if we "line up our head with our heart, our feet will follow."

At the time, I wasn't sure what he was trying to say, but now that I'm older, I think I am starting to get it.

Ben was saying that if your brain is saying one thing, and your heart is saying another, your feet will not know what way to go. It's like sending mixed messages.

The brain is about thinking. The heart is about feeling, and we think they are different, but they are also a lot alike.

Ben also said, "If you don't like what you are thinking, change your thoughts."

Bart says that if you ask ten people what trust is, you'll get ten different answers, but the answer that counts is the answer you give yourself.

So, I ask myself, this time, and not the blank page, "What about trust scares me the most?" and the first thing that pops into my head is that it always seems to fall under things that get broken. I decide to write a poem for my journal:

The Token

If I had a token
for all things broken,
a rich girl I would be.

The list would start
with a broken heart
and promises made to me.

Through sad goodbyes
and broken ties—
trusting "unconditionally"

Snapped in two
because (who knew)
Trust needs to start—with me.

Ben talked to me and Sara about trusting ourselves and what he called our instincts, but it isn't till right now that I realize my trust has always been in other people, not me. He said trust came with that long word, *unconditionally*, which might be the longest word I know and maybe the hardest to understand.

The closest I can come to understanding it is that unconditionally might mean "no matter what," but that feels dangerous to me. I mean, is Justin supposed to love Terrible Ted unconditionally, no matter what? That can't be the final meaning. It must have to do with not hurting someone, which puts it on them to be trustworthy enough to not go around hurting others.

But then what about me? I hurt other people when I bite. No wonder I can't be loved. But Ben also said that we should do nice things and want good things for other people without expecting something in return. I didn't know what he meant back then, and it's still hard to know, but it has me thinking how Emily and Bart have done a lot for me, but what have I done for them?

A new thought makes me smile. I rip out two blank pages of my journal and write Bart on one and Emily on the other. I try to think about what each of them might really like. I know Bart probably would like to have his leg back, but that's not going to happen. And Emily seems to like books, just like me, but I can't just go buy her a book. An idea starts to take shape, and in my head, I hear Bart's voice say, "Sleep on it." And I do.

Or try to anyway, but that's not what happens.

39

THE NIGHTMARE IS UNEXPECTED. I MEAN, I WENT TO SLEEP on a happy thought, and then a spider shows up, wraps me in a sticky cocoon of thread, and won't let me out till I solve a crazy riddle:

"What is the thing that opens a door but isn't a key, an ax, or shoulder, or knee, but when used, it is said, can set you free?"

The real nightmare part is that I gave her the right answer—yes, me, Anna Olson, came up with the answer "Truth," and that awful spider gave credit to a dumb horsefly that actually thought it was a horse and not a fly.

When I open my eyes, I'm wrapped in white. Panic grips every fiber, and with what little room I have all wound up in that spider's web, I kick and claw and bite at the trappings around me.

For a second, I flash on Daddy calling it "the cocoon of death" when a fly gets caught. Is that what this is? Am I dying?

"Whoa! Whoa! Whoa, Anna-fanna-fee-fi-fo-fanna-Anna. What's got you all in a twist?" a familiar voice smelling of hot chocolate says. "Look at you all tangled up in the sheets."

Bart pulls, and my face pops through. "And what did you do to your pillow?" He holds it up, and stuffing falls out of the torn side. "Take a bad trip?" he offers.

I nod. "Giant spider," I answer.

"Oh, her."

"You know her?" I stare at him.

"Oh, everybody here knows Her Royal Scariness. She's a mean ol' thing. Big, long-legged, hairy … Does that sound like her?"

I nod.

"Were you the fly she caught?"

I shake my head. "Miss Right got away."

"Miss Right, huh? That be the fly?"

"Horsefly."

His big brown eyes study me. "I see. Not just any fly but a *horsefly.* Interesting.

"Well, did you know that each thing that shows up in those nightmare escapades you go on is really you?" Bart looks at me, eyebrows raised.

"Even the spider?"

"Yep, even the spider. She caught you and wrapped you up so you couldn't get out, right?"

I nod. *I'm the wicked spider?* My heart beats faster than I can think.

"Are you, maybe, still locking something up inside you that wants to get out?" Bart's eyebrows rise even higher over his big, round brown eyes.

I look at him, afraid to even move. *Tig already got out.* But would I have let her out if she hadn't gotten out all by herself? I turn away, not wanting to hear the answer to my own question.

"Something maybe that's not just the girl you been holdin' back? Something you're maybe afraid to talk about?"

I sink deeper into the sheets. He's getting dangerously close to the thing I can't talk about—inches, maybe—from the truth.

"Just something to think about." Bart puts a paper bag on the table. "We all hold stuff in, Anna. Sometimes that stuff is anger, because we're so mad at something or someone, and we don't rightly know what do to with that boiling feeling inside us. And some other times, it's a part of ourselves we keep tucked away safe, so nobody can hurt it—hurt us."

I swallow against a growing lump in my throat and try not to cry.

The quiet in the room suddenly feels loud and uncomfortable. Bart takes a deep breath. "Well, I came to tell you how sorry I am you missed the party last night and to give you something before we take off to the new equine therapy they've ordered for you. But maybe you need to rest up after that nightmare."

I sit up as best as a person can who's wrapped up in a sheet and push away thoughts of giant spiders and webs and flies, plus any thoughts of how *I* can be the giant spider *and* the sticky web and the horsefly. How can I be three things at once?

I suddenly realize that the trip I went on in that bad dream is kind of what my world feels like: one big unsolved riddle.

"You have another something for me?" I turn my thoughts back to Bart and the plastic bag he's holding and am quick to remember the last present he brought me. *Where is Abby anyway?*

Bart does that mind reading thing again. "If you're worried about Abby, she's right here." He reaches over to grab her, hands her to me, then holds out the bag he brought in. It has a caterpillar pictured on it. I stare at the picture.

"You know, Anna. To become the butterfly, you gotta let the caterpillar go. It's a strange thing in life, but to move forward, you gotta let go of anything that's holding you back. Let go. Then and only then can you spread your wings and fly."

Let go?

But that would mean letting go of Sara. And what about Mama and Daddy? They let go of us, and look where that got them. Daddy's in jail. Mama's nowhere to be found. Sara's in a foster home. And I'm stuck in a crazy house. And who knows what their real plans are for me?

"Spread wings and fly," I repeat, like any of that is possible.

"You travel pretty light, Anna-fanna," Bart says, stretching the bag toward me. "They said this is the only stuff you came in with. They were supposed to put it in your dresser when they got you settled in, but it got mixed in with other stuff. So here you go."

I open the bag and peek in. At first it looks empty. But then I see something shiny at the bottom.

I dig down and pull out a penny and stare at it. When I put two and two together, something inside me breaks.

"THERE YOU GO AGAIN, BABY GIRL. ALL THIS FUSS OVER a coin? That must be some penny." Bart folds up the bag and sticks it in a cupboard before turning back to the bed. "Doesn't make much cents," he adds and then chuckles to himself.

"What's so funny?" I sniff and wipe my nose on the sheets. Bart hands me a tissue.

"One penny doesn't make much cents. Four or five pennies—those make more cents."

I smell the penny. It's shiny but smells old. "Oh. Not sense, but cents. I get it!" What's funny is how so many words can sound the same and mean something so very different. No wonder people get confused. But I'm not in the mood for any more riddles.

"I think I just figured something out. You want to hear my theory?"

"Theory?"

"Yeah, theory. It's something someone makes up to explain something nobody understands."

I nod. "Makes sense." It's the sort of sense Sara always had. I hold up the penny.

He laughs. "So, my theory is that *you* don't trust the one person you can trust, and that's what's holding you back."

"Ben?" He's wrong there. I've always trusted Ben.

"No, Anna. Not Ben. You. You've never trusted you. You let other people make decisions for you, but at some point, you must decide what makes Anna tick. What does Anna want? And then take the steps to make that happen."

Did he read my token poem? It doesn't really matter. What matters is how do you trust yourself when you don't trust yourself?

"The key is to start small," Bart says, doing that mind reading thing. Make a list, maybe, of things you know you can trust yourself to do.

"Get up on time. Do your morning routine. Get breakfast. Go to workshops. Then get to the more important stuff like getting your writing done, promising only what you can realistically do, and being honest to yourself and others when you make a mistake. That's what I do anyway."

"Not trustworthy," I blurt.

Bart smiles, but then his face turns serious. "Are you sure about that?"

I thought I was sure, but after he asks me if I'm sure, I'm not so sure.

Bart looks back at my hand. "Are you going to tell me about that penny? Or is it a secret?"

"It's Ben's penny," I say, remembering the day Ben gave me and Sara the first two pennies he got when he came over to America.

"Ben again, huh? I got to meet this Ben. He sounds like a pretty fly dude."

"Fly."

"Yeah, fly, which is what we have to do if we're going to get you to equine therapy on time. Ready? I got my jeep outside all ready to roll."

The only "outside" I have had in this place is the grassy area out in the side yard, under my window where Kat and I sometimes eat our lunches, so the thought of getting out of here motivates me to get a move on. "I'll hurry," I tell him, slipping out of bed.

Bart grins. "Okay then. Be back in ten."

"Ten," I agree, and he leaves.

41

TEN MINUTES TURNS INTO AN HOUR LATER. WHEN BART and I walk toward the jeep, excitement twists and turns through me, because this could finally be my ticket out of RTC. Well, maybe not my ticket, but right now it's my transportation, and I can't wait until Bart pulls out onto the street and I can look back at RTC and picture it all behind me. Sara found me once, and she might again, but maybe I could be the one finding her.

I take in a deep breath of the crisp, clear air and let it out slowly, happy at the thought of maybe finding Sara, happy to be free, if even for just a few hours, happy that Bart was able to talk his boss into taking Will's place and bringing me to horse therapy, and, well, just plain happy.

Ben always used to say that people spend a lot of time searching for happiness. "If you have faith, happiness will find you." I wonder if faith is something you have already inside of you, or if it has to find you too.

Bart backs the jeep out of the parking space but only after he's sure I have my seat belt fastened. I get to sit up front with him. He grins over at me. I think he's happy to get out of the residential treatment center too.

"Ever been by horses?" Bart asks, changing gears.

"In stories," I answer, flashing on Ben's story of the Trojan horse.

And then there was that time Emily, or Miss Emily as Bart calls her, talked about proverbs and looking a gift horse in the mouth.

Bart grins. "Everybody likes a good horse story." He turns on the turn signal. I look around, but nothing looks familiar.

"Teeth," I blurt, and Bart glances at me, eyebrows raised, as he rounds another corner. I'm still thinking about Emily's saying, "Don't look a gift horse in the mouth," but when I open my mouth to say something, all that comes out is teeth.

"Sure, baby girl, horses have teeth. But they also got something else called 'horse sense.' Know what horse sense is?"

I shake my head.

"Horse sense is sometimes called common sense or good judgment. A horse faced with a decision generally makes a good one."

"Like Sara," I say, thinking how Sara, even though she's a human and not a horse, has good horse sense. I wonder how she ended up with it and I didn't. Is horse sense another thing that finds you? Sara has never been around horses that I know of. Maybe that's why the doctor wants me to go hang with them, so I can get some horse sense too. And maybe if I get some horse sense, I can see Sara again. I start to relax about going to this ranch. What was it called again?

"The Nevada Equine Ranch," Bart says, giving me the answer after reading my thoughts again, "has rescue horses."

I know rescue means to save someone. "Who'd they save?"

"Well, that's the funny part. The horses didn't save someone. Someone saved the horses. The Wild Horse Federation rounded them up so they wouldn't starve in the desert. They were taken to a ranch and tamed and fostered out; some got adopted, and a few of them were kept by the ranch owner and trained to be therapy horses."

Horses get fostered out and adopted? I raise my eyebrows just thinking about what he said. If that's true, then horses and I do have something in common. None of the temporary foster families Sara and I went to had horses.

"You'll be working with a therapy horse," Bart adds.

"Therapy." My tongue doesn't have to do much work to say the word, leaving most of the work to my lips. "Therapy," I say again. But I'm wondering how a horse who doesn't talk can help someone like me, who also doesn't talk. It will be an awfully quiet therapy session.

Suddenly I bolt upright in the seat. "Oh, no!"

"What?" Bart looks over and frowns.

"I forgot."

"Forgot what?"

"Kat. She leaves today." How stupid of me not to have gone to the Halloween party. Kat told me she was leaving the day after Halloween. That's today.

"Go back."

Bart's frown deepens. "We can't go back now, Anna. Your therapy starts in just a few minutes. Maybe Kat will still be there when we get back."

I fall back against the seat, wondering if I'll ever get to see Kat again.

"Kids come and go," Bart says, sighing. "You learn not to get too attached. The sad part is she could well be back in RTC if things go sour for her."

I look out the window, hoping things don't go sour for Kat. It turns out that the horse ranch isn't that far from Maple View. I see it long before we get there, because on my side of the road, a big pasture appears like one of those mirages Ben told us about, only this pasture is real, and on it are real horses. In the distance, I can see buildings and fenced-off areas where other horses are standing.

"There's the stable over there," Bart says, pointing out the front window. He flicks on his turn signal, and my heart starts beating a little faster. It's funny how turn signals can mean one thing to someone driving the car and something completely different to someone being taken to a place that they are unfamiliar with.

"Nervous?" Bart says, stealing my thoughts again.

"A little."

He pulls up to a fence and puts the jeep in a different gear, then turns off the engine and pulls on the parking brake. It makes a long zipper-like sound, like someone zipping up a thick jacket. "Ready?"

I shrug and push the door open, unsure of what ready for horse therapy would feel like.

"Hello!" a voice shouts, and we both look to see a woman wildly waving a cowboy hat at us. Seeing the hat makes me think of Daddy. I know it probably sounds dumb, but I look around to see if he somehow got word that I was going to be here and maybe snuck in. But then I remember something else Ben once said. He said that if people put want before need, they'll find themselves in a hole that's impossible to get out of. I look down as we walk across the dirt toward the lady with the cowboy hat. It's hard not to want, want, want. I want lots of things. Want can sometimes feel like a need. I want Daddy, but I also need him. I want Mama to come home, but I also need her.

"You want me to stick around?" Bart suddenly asks, and I hesitate.

Yes, I want him to stay, but do I need him to? Probably not. I feel myself slipping down the dark hole of decisions. Want. Need. Want. Need.

I start to say yes when the lady with the cowboy hat yanks me up from the hole and dangles me in the air. Not really, but her words make it feel that way. "Sorry—Bart, is it? But only Anna goes in with the horses. And me, of course. You can hole out in your jeep if you like and wait, but therapy is just with her and the horse and me.

"I'm Bunny Sue, by the way. I run the ranch here." She sticks a dirt-stained hand out toward me.

I look up at Bart. He reaches his hand over to hers and shakes it. My nose starts twitching and itching, and a smell I have never smelled before forces my face to crinkle up. I bury my nose under my sweatshirt.

"Manure," she says, grinning. "Also known as dung and horse poop. You'll get used to it. You city kids probly never smelt the likes of it before. Right, missy?"

I stare at her and don't say anything.

"Well, no matter. Like I say, you'll get used to it, and if not, just breathe through your mouth. That way you don't have to smell nothing."

I try her idea, but it's hard to do, and anyway, when I swallow, it's like I'm eating the manure. I can taste it. Already I don't like this place.

"I'll wait in the car, baby girl. See you soon. Be nice to the horses."

The one called Bunny Sue laughs. "Oh, she'll be fine."

I look over at her. She doesn't look like a bunny.

"You're thinkin' about my name, aren't cha?" She tilts her head and looks down at me, like she just busted me for something. I have got to work on making my thoughts not being so easy to read.

"Not really," I lie.

"My name's really Bonnie Sue, but my grandbaby? She says it like bunny, so that's what everyone calls me now. Bunny Sue."

I nod. It makes sense in its own way, I guess. She leads me over toward a fenced-in area where three horses are standing.

"First thing you learn about is these gates. You see how you slide this bar over and push to open the gate? That's so the horse can't push against it from the inside and run you right over. This here's the hook. After we go in …" She steps inside the fenced-in area and motions for me to follow. "You can't stand out there and second-guess, Anna, or them horses will make the decision for you."

It must be that horse sense Bart was talking about earlier. I nod and follow her in. "Like I was sayin', after you go in, you slide the bar back like this, and then put the hook through the hole to latch it. Got it?"

I nod.

"Well, let's see. You go on out and come back in."

I stare at her for a second, feeling myself start to freeze up, but I decide to try this horse sense they keep talking about and reach for the hook.

"That's it. Now slide—yes, yes. You got it. Now, remember—pull from inside, push from outside, or the horses will run you over."

I pull the gate open and slip out. Close it. Slide the bar and hook it through the hole.

Bunny Sue grins. Her hair is the color of the dried straw I see all over the ground.

"That there's hay," she says, reading my thoughts again. I turn my head away and pretend to look at something else. "Okay, well, get on back in here so you can meet the horses."

I open the gate and slip back in, planting myself behind her as she starts toward the horses.

"Normally, they'd walk over to greet us, but they must have picked up on you being nervous. This here is Concho," she says, reaching up, putting one arm under his neck and rubbing his forehead with her right hand. He's our oldest horse and keeps all the girls in line. Don't you, Conch, you ol' buzzard, you. Say hi to Anna."

The horse snorts and nods his head a couple times, like he really can understand her. He's magnificent. Big, strong, and scary but also cool in a don't-get-too-close-but-I-admire-you kind of way. While Bunny Sue tells me about Concho, another horse comes up from behind and nudges me in the back. I jump, and she draws back, startled.

"Try not to make sudden moves around the horses. They're monocular. Do you know what that means?"

I shake my head, edging away from the horse that nudged me, but she follows me and nudges me again.

"Get away!" I snap, and she draws back again and even shakes her head, like she's telling me, "No!"

"Look at me, Anna," Bunny Sue instructs, and I do, but I'm very aware that the pesky horse is right behind me, because I can feel her hot breath on my neck. I draw up my shoulders and shake my head, so my hair will cover my skin.

"Put your hands like this." She presses her hands together like she's saying a prayer, and I match what she's doing.

"Good. Now do this." She presses her hands up to her face, still pressed together, and places them between her eyes, like she's parting her face in two."

I do what she does, though it all seems a little weird.

"Now open the side of your hands that's by your face, just to the inside of each eye and hold it?"

Again, I do what she does, but I have to turn my head, because my hands are blocking my sight.

"No, no. Don't turn your head."

"I can't see!"

"That's right. You can't see straight in front of you, but can you see out the sides?"

I nod. On my right side, I can see the pesky horse has come up beside me and is staring at me with one giant blue eye. Wait? The horse has blue eyes? Concho didn't. His eyes were brown.

"Monocular means that the horse cannot see like we see out of two eyes but sees out of each eye separately." She raises her hands up by her own eyes and points one finger left, one finger right. "So since they can't see right in front of them, it's important not to startle them."

The pesky horse nudges me again, and I pull away.

"Over there is Molly. She's our newest Appaloosa and has just finished training. What horse do you think you'd like to work with?"

"Concho," I answer. He's big and tough, and riding him would make me feel big and tough too.

Bunny Sue smiles, not at me but at the pesky horse. "You sure about that? I think," she says, still smiling, "that someone else has chosen you. Meet Sapphire."

At the word *fire*, I break the rule and jump, startling all three horses, and they draw back and make whinnying noises.

"When they whinny like that, it means they're alarmed," Bunny Sue warns. "Can you turn and let Sapphire know you didn't mean her no harm?"

No way am I going to do anything with a horse that has fire in her name. I freeze and stare at the ground. For the second time, I want to get out of this place.

BUNNY SUE MOTIONS FOR THE HORSES TO ALL BACK UP AND goes over to the fence, where she picks up a long leash, or what looks like a leash anyway.

"Let's take Sapphire out of the corral and walk her over to the arena."

Corral? Arena? New words to me, but I have nowhere to go but with Bunny Sue and Pesky, so I shuffle along behind.

"Stay up here with me beside the horse. You don't want to get behind them. They kick."

"Yeah, well, I bite," I want to say, but I stay quiet. She wraps the leash around the horse's head and ears and hands the long part to me.

"You can take the reins and lead her."

Okay, so a horse's leash must be called *reins*. I walk ahead and pull on the rein, but the horse pulls back, almost knocking me off balance.

"Come *on*!" I growl, yanking on the rein, and she backs up and shakes her head at me again, pulling me back a few steps. I pull a little harder, but she rears her head up and almost flips me. I hate this horse.

Bunny Sue comes up beside me and makes this clicking noise out of the side of her mouth, and the horse suddenly tips her ears forward and starts to walk. I look over at her one blue eye staring at me and narrow mine, so she can see who's boss. She stretches her nose out and nudges my shoulder, this time knocking me off balance. I stumble forward but then right myself.

When we get to the arena, Bunny Sue has me lead her over to a post and tie the reins around it. "You don't want to make it too tight, and there's no need to tie a knot. Just loop it around the post and stick the reins through here." She shows me while Pesky stands and watches. The horse could probably figure out how to get away easily, after watching how we tied her, but she doesn't make a move to leave and just waits and watches us.

Bunny Sue ducks under the reins and comes over to my side of the horse. "Over here are the brushes. Grab the one with the long prongs and let's start by brushing her mane," she says, walking over to a shelf holding a bucket, a roll of paper towels, and another bucket, but I can't see what's in that one.

"Main what?" I ask, reaching for the same kind of brush that she pulled out of the bucket.

"No, different mane. This is the horse's mane." She grabs the hair draped over the horse's neck, then runs the brush through it.

"Take it nice and slow, because it might have some tangles."

I follow her lead, brushing through the tangled mess until finally it gets smooth. Pesky rubs her head against my shoulder. At first, I start to pull away but then just stand there, like she does, and take it.

"Now let's take the brush that has the shorter bristles and brush her sides and flank."

"Flank?" My lip curls, and my tongue flicks against the back of my front teeth when I say the word.

"Flank. Yes. That's back here by her hips. Again, remember, you want to brush *with* the direction her hair grows, not against it, and there's a ticklish spot at the flank that might make her move back, so stay beside her. If you do have to walk behind her, give yourself plenty of space so she can't kick you."

When the brush passes over her flank, her muscles ripple. It must feel good. I try brushing my arm, but the teeth on the brush hurt, and I yelp.

"Horses have thicker hides than humans," Bunny Sue says, smiling, but I don't see anything to smile about.

"Okay, now let's give her a little treat. This bucket here has carrots. We do the small ones because a lot of kids come through the ranch for therapy and we don't want to overfeed the horses. Want to give her a carrot?"

I shrug and nod at the same time. Before passing one to me, she lays one on the palm of her hand and puts her fingers together. "You want to give it to her like this. Her nose is soft and might tickle when she grabs the carrot, but try not to pull away, and keep your hand arched and stiff so she can grab the carrot."

She does it once to show me, then hands me a carrot. I balance it on my hand, like she showed me, and squeeze my fingers together. When the horse muzzles my hand, though, I freak out and pull it back, dropping the carrot in the dirt.

"You can try again," Bunny Sue says. "Don't worry. She'll find the carrot."

Gross. Eating carrots off the dirt? The carrot was covered in it. *Don't they have any taste buds?* I dig my hand in the bucket and grab a pile of carrots, thinking, if nothing else, it will keep her nose and teeth far from my hand.

"Ah, ah. Just one, remember," Bunny Sue reminds me, and I angrily drop the carrots back in the bucket, short of one. I take a deep breath and look the horse in the eye, squinting, so she can see I mean business with a look that says, "Okay. Are we going to do this?"

She pulls her head up and down twice, like she's answering my thought.

"Really?" I say, stretching out my hand toward her nose. I take my other hand and grip around my wrist to help keep my carrot hand steady. She stretches her neck toward my hand, pulls her fleshy lips back, exposing some very big teeth, and takes the carrot.

I laugh and pat her neck, then pull back.

"Very good, Anna. Sapphire likes you. I can tell."

While Bunny Sue is talking, Sapphire reaches out her nose and sniffs my arm, then drops her head so her nose is even with my hand, and just like that, she bites my little finger.

"Ow!" I shout, pulling my hand back. Tears spring into action, blurring my vision. How dare she make me trust her, then bite me. But an even worse thought pulls at me. Didn't Mean Kurt say, "You bite us, we bite back?" Is this what he meant? That they'd send me to some horse ranch so I could get bitten?

"Did she bite you? Let me see, Anna."

I back away from the horse and hold out my shaking hand. "Oh, I see. She bit your little finger. That's cuz it smelled and looked like a carrot. When you grabbed all those carrots, you put the smell of carrot all over your hand, and she don't know the difference between your finger and a carrot."

I glare at the horse. I bet she knew. I don't know how, but she probably figured out I was a biter, and this was her way of getting back.

My finger burns, but when I look again, no skin is broken. It's just a little red. My thoughts dart back to Dr. McMillan, our last foster dad, and how his hand bled when I bit him. And the staff at Maple Leaf and the policeman. It must have hurt when I sank my teeth into them. I had no idea biting hurt so bad. I was just trying to keep them away.

I stare at Sapphire, who's one big blur. Was she just trying to keep me away? Maybe Bunny Sue is wrong. Maybe the horse doesn't like me. "Join the crowd!" I want to shout at her.

Bunny Sue pats me on the shoulder and says she's going to go get a small Band-Aid. "You think you'll be okay for a few minutes with Sapphire, or do I need to call someone to come over here?"

"We're okay," I mumble.

"Over there is Lester shoveling manure. If you need help, call him." She waves at the one called Lester and points to me. He nods. When she leaves, I take a paper towel from the roll on the shelf and pour some water from a nearby water bottle onto it, then wash the dirt off my hand. Sapphire watches and inches closer to me. I don't back away this time, and she lays her head against my chest, like she's trying to listen to my heart.

I pull my arm under her neck, like I saw Bunny Sue do earlier, and pat her long nose with my free hand.

"It's okay," I whisper. "I bite too." She lifts her head and nods, and I grin.

"It's not like you chose your name," I whisper. "You couldn't know I'm afraid of fire." Her ears prick forward at the word *fire*, like she knows just what I'm talking about.

She takes a deep breath and lets it out hard and fast, making a sputtering noise with her lips, and I laugh. "I can do that too, you know." And I sputter back at her.

She pulls back, not like she's trying to get away from me but like she wants to get away from the pole.

"Go back?"

She nods, and I pull her reins free. "Okay, let's go back." As I lead her out of the arena and toward the corral, she keeps an even step with me.

"I see you two have made up," Bunny Sue says, coming up from behind. "Here's a Band-Aid." She hands me a little one, but I wave it away. "I'm okay."

We all three walk in silence. "You did a great job with Sapphire today, Anna. Would you like to come back next time and ride her?"

I nod.

"What was the best part of today's time with Sapphire?"

"The arena."

"Ah, you liked brushing her and talking with her at the arena?"

"Yes."

"I think that's when you two got closer," Bunny Sue says, smiling at the two of us like we're her kids or something.

"When I talk to her," I whisper, staring at the dirt passing under us as we walked, "she hears me."

I turn and stare at Sapphire, suddenly realizing something: Terrible Ted didn't take my voice away like I thought. He just scared me into thinking that he did. All this time, I could talk, but I was too scared of what he would do to me.

"Will you practice talking in sentences to the mirror in your bathroom each day? And maybe even to someone at the center you think could be a friend?"

"Kat-with-a-K," I murmur, but then I remember she's probably already gone.

"Kat, sure, if she's friendly to you. And Bart. Bart is a friend. Practice with Bart. Doctor K signed you up for a month of therapy. Do you want to come back and work with Sapphire again? Or a different horse?"

"Sapphire's good." By now we've reached the gate, and I slide the bar, push it open, and turn to give Sapphire a hug. She gives me a look that I hope is happy and nuzzles my back, like she wants me to go in with her.

"I have to go, Saf, but I'll be back. I promise."

I say the words that once got broken when they were said to me, but I was not going to break my promise to Sapphire.

She walks past me and into the corral, and the other horses trot over to greet her.

When the gate is locked behind us, Bunny Sue turns toward me. "It was nice meetin' ya, Anna. I look forward to seeing ya soon."

"You too," I answer, looking past her at a figure coming slowly toward us. He's a million miles away, but I can see his smile all the way from here.

"You can go," Bunny Sue says, and I take off, sprinting toward Bart, waving my arms wildly. In that stretch between Sapphire and Bart, I feel something I haven't ever felt before. I think it's what free must feel like.

"I did it!" I shout when Bart's deep laugh reaches me. "I talked! I talked to a horse."

"Listen to you and how great you sound. Did you talk horse sense?" Bart asks, wrapping an arm around my shoulder and leading us to the jeep.

I laugh. "Yeah. Maybe a little."

On the drive back, I think about all the things Sapphire taught me, and not one word came out of that horse's mouth. I'll have to tell Emily I didn't have to look that horse in the mouth, and her teeth were just fine. I nurse my little finger, rubbing it gently.

"She bit me," I blurt, and Bart's eyebrows arch up.

"Bunny Sue or the horse?"

"The horse!" I laugh, punching his arm. "Sapphire thought my finger was a carrot."

Both Bart and I laugh.

"I don't want to bite anymore. It hurts."

Bart takes in a deep breath and lets it out, all the while grinning. "I think that horse taught you more in half an hour than any of us could have taught you at the center in a month."

"She's manna," I whisper.

"Manna in the wilderness," Bart agrees quietly, and we both look out over the desert. Even though the ground is brown and fall is in the air, I notice all the lingering wildflowers scattered here, there, and everywhere, adding patches of bright color to the earth.

"You hungry?" Bart glances over at me.

"Starvin' Marvin," I answer, quoting Kat-with-a-K.

Bart's laugh can probably be heard clear down to Sapphire's corral. "Well, then, let's eat."

He pulls into a fast-food place and gets us both hamburgers, fries, and a shake. His is vanilla, mine chocolate.

"Sometimes there's nothin' like a good, unhealthy shake," he says, grinning.

I slurp a response, and we both laugh again.

Maybe life can have some good times and not be all bad.

43

THAT NIGHT WHEN I'M BACK IN MY ROOM, I CAN HEAR KAT moving around quietly in hers, but I don't call out to her. She's packing, still hoping to leave before they lock down RTC for the night. I'm glad she hasn't left yet, but I know she's feeling eager to go. For now, I flop down on the floor beside my bed and crack open my journal. I haven't taken a shower, so I still smell like hay and horse stuff. I decide to write Sapphire a poem:

> I feel your breath upon my skin
> and stroke your flowing mane.
> I can't wait to brush your flanks
> and see you once again.
> We'll walk and talk and maybe even
> trot the twists and bends
> so you can see the brand-new me
> and we can be best friends.

Kat sneaks in and scares the bejabbers out of me. I yelp, scaring us both, and then we laugh, all embarrassed—at least I am for being so jumpy.

"Whatcha writin'? And what's that awful sme-eeh-ell?"

I show her the poem, and she grins when she finishes it.

"So, I take it what I'm smellin' is that horse?"

I nod and reach for Abby, then pull my arm back and just hold my hands together.

"You don't have to hide you want to hug on your doll. We all have things we do to keep us real."

"You have a doll?" The words just spill out.

"No, but—" She withdraws a bit before sitting on the floor beside me, picking fuzz off her jeans. "I do got my own dee-vices to keep me connected with what's real and all."

I'm not sure what dee-vices are, but something about the way she drops her voice to a deep whisper makes me think she doesn't share this with just anyone. I almost stop breathing so I can hear her.

"Okay, don't tell no one, but I name my pillows," she whispers.

"You what?"

She nods and grins. "Uh huh. You heard me. It's what keeps me from, you know, losing it. 'Specially at night when you got no one around but yourself for company, or when people forget they's supposed to pick you up."

I look up at her and nod, knowing just what she means. Kat's always so happy, so together. Then it hits me. Maybe she's like Sara—someone who hides stuff she's feeling behind a smile or a laugh, so no one can mess with her and make her even more unsure of everything. Wasn't she the one who said, "Fakin' is jus' part of life?"

"Naming my pillows helps me keep things close when people around me disappear. It helps me get to sleep," she adds, and I nod again.

I know the wretched feeling that loneliness brings. It's that empty space you know you can't fill, so you give dolls or things like your pillows names to try to make the space seem less empty. Kind of like me pretending Sara's here when she's not.

"So? What are their names?" I whisper.

"See there! I knew you could talk," she says in a normal talking voice, freaking me out. But I'm just as surprised as she is that I'm talking in complete sentences. Maybe this horse sense therapy is doing some good after all.

"Why you not talkin' in group and stuff? Why you pretendin' to be slow?"

"Not pretending!"

"So, you sayin' you is slow?"

"No! Just—"

"Jus' what? Say it. Jus' …"

"Scared!" I yelp-whisper, fighting back tears. Surely, she knows what feeling scared feels like.

"Who you scared of?"

I look around, not that anyone is in the room, but just saying his name makes me look. "Ted."

"He your daddy?"

"No!"

"Uncle?"

"No!" I whisper even louder.

"So, who's this Ted guy anyway?"

"A TFD," I whisper, looking away, "which stands for temporary foster dad."

A long silence follows. "Okay, so, no namin' your pillow Ted," she says, and we both laugh. "Why you name your doll Abby?"

I shrug. I don't actually remember naming Abby. Maybe Daddy did before he gave her to me, probably after a song he liked or something.

"The names of your pillows?" I say, hoping to bring her back to her secret.

"Oh, yeah—well, when I was just a kid, I named them things like Fluffy and Foo-Foo and Stiff."

"Stiff?" I grin. That doesn't sound like a pillow name to me.

Kat laughs. "Yeah, I had one pillow so hard it could practically stand up on end and walk away. When it ripped one day, I found out that the stuffing was bamboo or somethin' and musta got wet and turned all stiff. But now I name my pillows things like Pearl, and Violet, and Blue—ones I can wrap my head around."

I like her pillow names.

"So, how 'bout you? What names'd you give yours?"

What would I name my pillow? "Probably Hope," I whisper. She doesn't have to know that Hope is a dead rat or that thing with feathers that Emily Dickinson writes about.

"Hope? Yeah, okay. That be a cool name. I bet you'll be a famous poetry lady someday the way you already crankin' them out like you do. Too bad you can't write yourself out of this place."

"Maybe I can," I answer. "Why do you think I'm writing all these poems? They're going to be my ticket out of here. My taxi ride. My hope with wings. I'm not quite sure how, but that's the plan."

"Listen to you! You go, girl! Puttin' a plan together."

I had no idea having a plan could feel so good—or loosen my tongue so much. So many words spewed out, I'm almost out of breath.

"Well, we better be gettin' some sleep. Tomorrow's Token Friday, and we trade the tokens in for cash. I been savin' mine. Just seventeen hours"—she peers over at a clock on the wall—"and forty-three minutes till I'm free." She grins. "Make that forty-two, not that anyone's countin'." She pushes herself up from the floor and is still grinning when she looks down at me.

"But aren't you—"

"Outta here? Yeah, I thought so, too, but Daddy never showed up, surprise, surprise, and my auntie Clarissa called and said she can't come till tomorra afternoon."

"She'll be here," I tell her, even though I don't know whether her auntie will or not, but I want to make her feel better.

"That be right. I know it too. Okay then. Night, Anna. Night, Abby. Night, Hope."

"Night Kat, Pearl, Violet, and Blue," I answer, grinning.

"An' Chartreuse, an' Rosie, an' let's not forget Daff-o-dil. I got lots of pillows, girl." Her voice trails off into her room.

I jump on the bed and grab Abby and my pillow. "Hope tomorrow's a good day," I whisper, sinking under the covers. I still can smell a hint of hay and horses, but I don't care. I kind of like it.

I can't wait to go back to the ranch, but it turns out I'll have to wait a whole week. I try to picture what Sapphire's doing. Does she sleep standing up? Lying down? Are the other horses with her? I press my arm against my nose and breathe in the smell of hay, and for the first time in I don't know how long, I fall asleep smiling.

44

WHEN I WAKE UP, I RACE TO THE CAFETERIA, BUT KAT'S not anywhere.

"Where's Kat?" I ask Emily when she stops by.

"And here I thought you were going to tell me how therapy went with the horses," Emily answers, rubbing her nose with her fingers.

"It went great! Where's Kat?"

"Her aunt came for her early this morning. She went into your room to say goodbye, but you were sleeping so soundly, she didn't want to wake you. I know you're disappointed, Anna, but when kids find out they can leave, they don't generally stick around. Would you stick around for her if it were your time to go?"

She had a point. I shake my head. No way. I would find the fastest way to the closest door. Still, I thought I was going to see her at least one more time. "Will I ever see her again?"

"Probably not. But there's a saying, 'Don't cry for not having more time with someone, but smile for the times you had together,' or something like that."

I nod, even though her saying doesn't make me feel better about not seeing Kat right now. I'm sad and a bit mad, now that I'll be back to not knowing anyone I want to hang with.

"Did she say anything?"

Emily's face brightens. "Actually, she did say something a bit odd, but maybe you can decipher it. She said to tell you—here, wait. I wrote it down." She unfolds a piece of paper and recites:

> "The answer is clear: It's hidden in Hope.
> And will give you the answers you need to cope.

"Your poetry must have rubbed off on her," she adds. "Oh, and don't forget it's Token Friday and to bring your tokens to the office for cash."

I nod, frowning, not over what Emily is saying but over Kat's message, which I repeat over and over in my head, wondering what the heck she was trying to tell me. One thing is clear: she left me something and wants me to find it. But what? And where is it?

"So, tell me about the ranch. Was it fun? Did you get a good horse? You look and sound wonderful!" she says, making the word wonderful sound big, round, and important. "Though you could stand a shower."

I laugh. Emily is right. I stink, but for once, I don't care. "It was fun. And Sapphire was a great horse. I'm going back next week."

Emily just stares at me, wide-eyed, like an elephant just walked out of the room or something. "Well, well, well! Welcome back, Anna Olson. Listen to you! Talking like your old self again. Group starts in a few minutes, so better clean up and meet everyone there." She crinkles up her nose.

I grin. "Hay and manure," I say, and Emily laughs.

"Yes, definitely manure. I'll check back with you later."

I shut the door after her and start tearing into my room. Kat had to have left me something. She had to have! I check the drawers, the bathroom cabinets, the table, under the table, under the chairs, and even Abby, to see if she wrote or hid something on her.

Nothing.

I open my journal, and a folded page falls out. When I open it, I see a list of words:

Violet
Daffodil
Blue
Hope

Pillows! She's talking about pillows! I race into her room, but all her pillows are gone. I race back into my room and whirl around to the front of the bed, ripping through my blankets and sheets to get to my pillow buried in them.

I shake it. Nothing. Is she just messing with me? An old anger starts to build in me, but when I grab my pillow to hurl it across the room, I hear something crinkle.

Ripping off the pillowcase, I find it. A piece of paper. She left me another note! But when I unfold it, all that's written on it is a phone number. Under the phone number, she drew a big red heart.

My breathing stops.

I look around the room, hoping she has also left me a phone. Did she leave me *her* number? Does this mean I'll get to call her and maybe see her again after all? Will she get her auntie to come and get me too?

I look around some more. No phone.

I stick the note with the phone number in between the pages of my journal and strip off my clothes to take a hot shower. Somehow, someway, I will have to get hold of a phone and call her.

In the shower, I let all the dirt and manure smell wash off of me. The only thing I don't wash is my hair. While scrubbing, I think, *What would Sara do to get a phone?* But a new thought slips in: *What would Sapphire do?*

I picture myself at the ranch talking to Sapphire. "What would you do, Sapphire? You can't talk. You don't have a phone. But you have a phone number."

I grin, picturing Sapphire nuzzling me, and then in my imagination, she pulls her fleshy lips back and says, "I would use horse sense."

"Great, but what would you do?" I would persist.

"I would ask you," she says, and at first, I'm mad in a frustrated kind of way, but then I laugh. So, I change the scene in my head and have Sapphire coming to me, saying, "I have a number but no phone. What do I do?"

The first thought that comes to me is, *Find a person with a phone! Then ask if you can borrow it.*

Sapphire says, "Good thinking, Anna."

I pull on clean clothes, bag the stinky ones—grinning, because the bag doesn't contain stinky pee-soaked sheets, not my pee anyway—head for the laundry room to drop it all off, then run to the front office to get my tokens for the week, all before going to group.

When I round the doorway to group, I freeze. I stare at the usual circle of chairs, but only one person is sitting in the circle.

Justin.

45

"LOOKS LIKE IT'S JUST US SO FAR," HE SAYS, CROSSING HIS arms.

I look toward the door for Miss Davenport.

"She's not here," he says, pulling out a cell phone.

I stare at it. Then squeeze my eyes shut, picturing the phone number Kat wrote on the note, then open them again. "Can I maybe use your phone?"

Justin's grin deepens. "Depends," he answers, and I draw back, just like Sapphire drew back on me when I said or did something that upset her.

"On what?"

"I was hopin' you could maybe tell Danny how much I like her," he says quietly, and a slow, uneasy silence slips between us. We're looking at each other, and it feels like all kinds of secrets are passing between us when he breaks the silence.

"Sorry about burning your doll," he adds, looking away. "I thought it was that Kat girl's. I have nothing against you."

"What do you have against Kat?"

He shrugs. "She just talks so much. Plus, she's a pretty easy target," he admits, glancing at me before quickly looking away again. But then he looks back and says, "Listen, I don't know why my uncle burned you, and I don't want to know, but I think you should hear it from me that I told the shrink about him and what he does—you know—to kids."

"You told Dr. Kitanovski?" My heart starts beating so fast I can hardly keep my breath quiet. I force myself to take deep breathes. "Do your parents know what he does?"

"What parents? Why do you think he picks me up when they let me out of here?"

Did his parents run away from him, too, like Mama ran from us?

"I'm not trying to make out like we're suddenly friends or anything. I mean, I'm seventeen, and you're … what? Twelve?" He doesn't wait for an answer. "I just thought you should know that he's finally locked up now and probably will be for a long time for all the stuff he did. The cop that talked to me said he wouldn't be getting out any time soon."

"Thanks for letting me know," I say, hoping he isn't making the whole thing up. I test him. "But if your uncle is locked up and you don't have parents, who's going to pick you up?"

He shrugs. "I'm almost old enough to be on my own. I can fake it until I am, but getting out of here with no one picking me up means I'll be running away."

I nod. Faking it seems to be the key message to learn about life around here. He probably has more in common with Kat than he realizes.

"And in case you're wondering, no, I didn't say your name to anyone. So, you're not involved. I did tell the shrink someone here got hurt by him, but I didn't say who. If he did it to you like he did it to me, I know he threatened to burn out your tongue if you talked. Thing is I'm old enough now that he doesn't scare me anymore. So even if he does get out, he'll come looking for me and no one else. And then I'll pay him back for everything he did."

I look at him and this time don't look away. I think about Ben talking about how to love someone unconditionally, and maybe this is what he was talking about. Just five minutes ago, I would never have put love and Justin in a sentence, and him telling me all this? It means he feels he can trust me. Anna No-Middle-Name Olson. Not Tig. Not Sara. Me.

"Thanks for letting me say all that. I've been holding in about Uncle Ted for years, but when I saw the burns on your arm and how scared you were when you saw him through the window that day, I knew he was the one that burned you."

Tears spill down my face, but I don't move to wipe them away.

"Sorry you had to live with that for so long," I murmur, looking away. I take a deep breath, wondering how many other kids are hiding what was done to them out of fear.

"Hey, you're talking pretty good today. What changed?"

"Horse sense," I tell him, grinning.

"I won't even ask," he says, before suddenly holding up the phone. "By the way, this thing is fake. I just keep it so I look like I have something everybody wants on our wing."

I try not to look too surprised or disappointed. How would I call Kat now?

"Thank you," I whisper.

He shifts in his chair. "For what?"

"For turning in Terrible Ted. And for being brave. And for—knowing. You're the only one who does—and who probably ever will. I owe you."

"Yeah, well—" He looks more and more uncomfortable, until he finally says, "Look, you won't owe me anything if you can put in a good word about me to Danny."

My mouth opens, but no words come out. Finally, I manage to say, "I thought you liked Clair."

"Nah. Clair's your age. I like Danny, even though she treats me like crap."

"I can try, Justin, but I don't know her all that well."

Justin starts to stand. "One of us better go see why nobody's here."

"I'll go." I jump up and start moving toward the door. "I saw Emily on my way here, heading for the clinic. Maybe she's still there."

I reach the clinic right as Bart walks out its door. "Hey, baby girl. You sick?"

I shake my head. "Do you have a phone I can use?"

When he blocks me, his look hardens. "Now, why d'you suddenly need a phone? Who would you be calling?"

"Kat. She told me her phone number if I wanted to call her."

"Not allowed. Sorry, baby girl. We can't stop residents from giving out their number, but we also can't give you a phone to call her. Kids around here make things up, not that you do, but some kids would tell us someone said they could call, when they just wanted to find out the person's number to harass them."

I nod and stand rooted to the spot, but Bart doesn't leave. "Aren't you supposed to be in group?" He looks down the hall past me.

I nod. "Nobody's there but Justin."

"The group leader's not there?" Bart pulls out his phone. "Emily, where's the group leader? Anna and Justin are the only ones in group."

"I'll be right there," I hear Emily say before they hang up, and it tells me she's not in the clinic.

"Okay, Emily's on her way. You can wait here if you don't want to be in there alone with Justin, and I'll go to the office and see what's going on."

I nod, waiting for him to leave, and then I see it. The phone on the wall that the other residents who have phone privileges use to call home. Why didn't I think of that earlier? I don't need Justin's phone. I don't need anyone's phone.

I look around. The halls are empty. I slip quietly toward the phone and lift the receiver, quietly keying in the phone number, but who answers is not who I expect.

"Maple View front desk. How may I direct your call?"

I hang up and drop against the wall. *She gave me Maple View's number?* Is this her idea of a joke? If it is, it's a cruel joke to play on someone when you can leave and they can't.

Some kid I don't recognize rounds the corner.

"You done using the phone?" she snaps, and I nod. Everyone's strung so tight in this place.

She lifts off the receiver, and I see her press a seven before dialing in her number. Maybe that's the secret code. Dial seven first. She gets a busy signal, shouts out a swear word, and slams down the receiver.

"Do you know what room group's in?" she shouts, but I know it's really the phone she's mad at.

"One-oh-two," I answer, pointing down the hall.

When she leaves, I grab the phone and press the number seven on the pad. A new buzzing sound comes through the phone, and I press in the phone number Kat left for me.

When it rings, my heart pounds like it's moved up to my throat.

"Hello?" a voice answers; it sounds like a little kid.

"Hi, is Kat there?"

"Who?"

"Kat," I repeat.

"Cats can't talk," the young voice says.

"Not a real cat," I say, trying not to sound too impatient, "the girl named Kat. Kat-with-a-K."

Dead silence. "Kat-with-a-K doesn't live here."

My shoulders droop. "Oh. Well, thanks, anyway."

"You can talk to me if you want," he says, but I shake my head, even though he can't see me through the phone. "Or Sara, but she's not home right now."

My heart stops, or maybe just my breathing. "Wait! Did you say Sara lives there?" I can barely get the words out.

"Yeah, you know her?"

I see Bart round the corner and turn my back quickly. "Got to go," I whisper hoarsely. "I'll call back."

"Okay. But what's your name, so I can tell Sara?"

I hang up without answering, before Bart can see me talking on the phone.

"Anna. Why aren't you walking toward group?"

"I thought you said to wait here for Emily. And anyway, this girl was lost, and I was helping her find a room." That part isn't a total lie. I slip past him.

"Oh, by the way, I double-checked at the office, and I was right.

You can't call Kat. Sorry, baby girl. It's the center's policy, and we can't break the rules. She should have known better."

"It's okay," I say, walking backward to talk with him. I see him frown slightly, look back at the phone on the wall, and turn back toward me, but I whirl around before we can make eye contact.

46

When I get to group, Emily is explaining that Jamie will no longer be running group sessions or even coming to the center.

"Another one bites the dust," Justin sings under his breath. Nobody looks that surprised. Staff comes and goes almost as often as the residents going in and out. Personally, I think it was the pencils that got her busted. I wonder if someone got stabbed.

I look around to see who all is here. Danny is back and looks at me, but her expression is blank and weird, like she has zoned out. I wonder if they had to give her one of those bee-sting shots. I move over next to her in case I get a chance to say something good about Justin, so I can make good on my promise to him.

Another girl is the one I just saw in the hall trying to use the phone, and I have no clue who the third girl is.

"Tina?" Emily asks, looking at that last girl. She couldn't be over nine and curls up in her chair, kind of like I did on my first day here.

She shakes her head. Emily doesn't even ask Danny or Justin but instead makes an announcement. "We have a special guest joining us today from our downtown library."

"Could the day get any better?" Justin says dryly, and I grin at him. He grins back and looks away. I suddenly wonder if everyone has been misreading him, like they've misread me.

"Look, he's come all the way across town to spend time with you, so I want each of you to show him some respect. Remember, your efforts will be rewarded in points."

Before she can say more, Bart taps on the door. "Miss Emily, your guest is here."

When Ben walks in, my heart leaps with the kind of surprise and joy that real birthdays must feel like, and tears are quick to sting my eyes. It's like experiencing two things at once that are totally opposite: joy and sadness. I'm not sad to see Ben, not by a long shot, but all these emotions crash together inside me. They have more room, now that Tig is no longer inside me. "Ben!"

Everyone at group stares first at me, then at Ben. Even Emily stares.

Ben's eyebrows raise up in complete surprise, and a smile breaks his face. "Anna! Well, well, I didn't know such a nice surprise was waitink for me."

I jump up and rush into his big, loving hug.

"Well, this *is* a surprise. And, Anna, since you know Ben, our guest speaker, why don't you introduce him."

I hold Ben's bear-sized hand, and he squeezes it, pressing it to his heart. "This is my friend Ben Silverman, who was my sister, Sara's, and my temporary foster dad."

"Hello, everyone. I am part of a new program we are startink between the library and Maple View Center. If you like, I will come once a week to read and tell stories."

"Read to us? What are we, three?" Justin blurts, and Miss Emily opens her folder and writes something down.

"I count four," Ben answers, "but we can be any number. Today, I have brought a poem to share for us to talk about. It is by poet Rudyard Kipling. I brought only a small part of the poem, and I thought we could write our own after I read. It is called 'If' and like this goes:

If you can make one heap of all your winninks
And risk it on one turn of pitch-and-toss,

And lose, and start again at your beginninks
And never breathe a word about your loss;
If you can force your heart and nerve and sinew
To serve your turn long after they are gone,
And so hold on when there is nothink in you
Except the Will which says to them: 'Hold on!'"

Ben reads the poem twice, then hands out crayons and asks us to open our journals. For those who didn't bring their journals, he hands them a piece of blank paper.

"So, what you think about this poem?"

"Lame," Justin answers, and Ben surprises me by nodding.

"What part is most lame, Justin?"

"The whole thing. The words are lame. The message is lame. The dude clearly doesn't know what he's talking about."

Again, Ben surprises me and nods.

"And that is why it is important that you young people write and talk about what is important to you. Let's write our own 'If' poems. No worries about spellink or how you say punctuatink. Just from the heart write your 'If' poem and then we will share."

I grin and squeeze Ben's hand. It's *so* good to have him here, sitting next to me, and to hear his voice. I swear, if Sapphire had a voice, that's what I would want it to sound like, even if she is a girl. He gives my hand a little kiss and then lets it go and points to my journal. I open to a blank page, and words crowd my thoughts, making it hard to keep up with them to write them all down, especially writing with a crayon. I write:

If

If words were made of paper, I would fold them little wings
to fly about this great big world and talk of many things.
If wishes were all flowers, I'd plant and watch them grow
and show the world it's really true: we do reap what we sow.

If I could measure out in deeds what work has to be done
to make this world a better place, I'd start with number one:

1. Listen to the horses.
2. Listen to the rain.
3. Listen to your beating heart
   even when it beats in pain.
4. Listen to the hungry child;
   don't turn your back and claim
   that you are not responsible
   or that you are not to blame.
5. Listen to your thoughts and fears.
6. Listen to the wind.
7. When all else fails and you feel lost,
   get up and try again.

I put the crayon down and look around. Justin's looking at me again, and not like he wants to set my hair on fire. I smile faintly in his direction, wondering if he can read my thoughts, and he gives me a quick thumbs-up before anyone else can see.

Ben looks over at me, winks, and whispers, "Who is this girl who so well writes and talks?"

I grin. "Me!" I whisper back.

Tina is reading her poem to herself, mouthing the words.

"Okay, it looks like everyone has finished, at least for now," Miss Emily says, loud enough to wake Danny from her little nap.

"Let's go around and share, starting with you, Justin. What did you write?"

Justin sits up and clears his throat, turning toward Danny like she's his only audience:

Racing with the wind
Scorching fields of trees and life
Setting fury free.

Danny does this slow nod, and a small smile finally finds her lips, like he's written the poem about her or something. Justin returns the smile, so maybe he did write it about her after all.

"Ah, a haiku," Ben says, grinning at Justin. "Very good!"

"A high who?" Justin frowns.

"Haiku," he repeats. "Japanese poetry. Did you know you were writink haiku?"

"Can't say that I did," Justin says, and I swear I see his cheeks turn a little red.

Ben smiles. "Then you have done a remarkable think. Haiku is five syllables in line one, seven syllables in line two, and five syllables in line three. It is a powerful poem you have written."

"Thank you, uh, Ben." It's the first time I've ever heard Justin thank anyone, and I know now that he has felt the magic of Ben's gentle ways.

"Danny?" Emily pulls everyone's attention away from Justin.

Danny slumps forward and reads in a flat, bored voice:

If roses are red and signify love
And violets are blue and signify passion
And sugar is sweet, like love's 'sposed to be,
Then why's *your* love so doggone rotten?

She slumps back into her seat, looks back at Justin, and gives him that tiny smile.

I hold my breath for a second before getting enough courage to lean toward her and whisper, "He really likes you, you know. He told me."

"He told you?" she whispers back, and I nod.

"Why do you think love is rotten?" Ben asks, looking kindly at her.

Danny shrugs. "I guess because the first three things are pretty solid. Everyone accepts them and makes them red or blue or sweet, but love? Love's not that solid."

"I see. Who it is you want to love you? Can you say?"

She shakes her head and closes back down. Justin leans forward on his chair and moves his foot closer to hers. Danny leans her foot toward his. I smile inside, knowing Justin knows I kept my promise.

Ben interrupts the moment quietly. "There is a poet, Ella Wheeler Wilcox, who once wrote. In it she says:

> We flatter those we scarcely know,
> We please the fleetink guest,
> And deal full many a thoughtless blow,
> To those who love us best.

"What do you think she was meanink?"

"We're mean to people who like us but nice to people who don't," Danny blurts.

"Is this you think true?"

"I do. Isn't that why the four of us are sitting in this room with you?" Justin looks across the circle at Ben, who smiles, raises his hand in the air, and gives Justin an awkward thumbs-up. I have never seen Ben give anyone a thumbs-up before. Ben turns his hand toward himself, like he's trying to see what a thumbs-up looks like, and we all grin.

"Tina, we only have a few minutes left. Do you and Anna want to share what you wrote?" Miss Emily asks.

Tina shakes her head and curls up tighter in the chair.

I glance at Ben, thinking about the last poem he read, but mostly I'm thinking about Abby and how mean I've been to her all this time. I've "dealt her many a thoughtless blow," that's for sure. I do love her. I know she's only a doll, but she's real to me. It's like maybe she's part of me, like Bart says dreams are. Ben would say, "Then Anna is being mean not just to Abby but to Anna."

"You want to share?" Ben gives me a little nod, eyebrows raised, like he's hoping I'll read. I was going to pass, but Ben, I can tell, wants me to be brave and share. So, I do.

When I'm done, I glance at Ben, whose eyes glisten. "Thank you,

Anna, for sharink such a wonderful poem, and all of you who took time to share your time and precious poems with me."

"Thank you, Mr. Silverman, for spending time with us. Can we plan on your being here next week?" Miss Emily asks.

"Yes. This I would not miss."

I grin inside and out. Could the day get any better!

"Okay, good job, everyone. Go back to your rooms or to the commons area. Those of you going to school off-site, your bus will be here in half an hour."

I hold back and wait for Ben.

"No school?"

I shake my head. "They teach me here."

"What is this that I hear about horses?" Ben says, looking up and down the hall, like one might show up there.

"I go to horse therapy," I explain.

"Horse therapy? What is this horse therapy?"

"I get to spend time with a horse named Sapphire."

"Tell me about this Sapphire."

I laugh. "At first, I didn't like her because she was so pesky, bumping me on the back with her nose and nudging me in the arm. But we got to be good friends, even though she bit me." The words suddenly come easily for me.

"Sapphire bit you?

"Yes, but she didn't mean to. We got over it and became friends."

"I can see that." Ben gives me a hug. "I have not seen this Anna before. Where was she hidink?"

I watch the splatters on the floor slip past. Not *where* but *from who* was she hiding, I want to say, I but stay quiet.

"Have you seen Sara?" I ask when we get to my room.

Ben puts his arm around me again and gives my shoulders a squeeze. "Yes. I have seen Sara."

"Is she okay?" I press, hoping she didn't tell him how I acted when she was here.

"I see her every week," Ben says, and I fight back tears. It's not fair that Sara gets to see Ben and I don't. My stomach tightens.

"Ah, ah. Feed good thoughts, Anna. Starve jealous ones. Sara comes with her new mother to the library to learn to read."

"New mother? Wait. Sara was—" I can't even say the word.

47

"GETTING ADOPTED," BEN SAYS FOR ME. "YES. A VERY nice family will adopt her. They have a young son, Kevin, who she says is pretty pesky, like your new horse friend, but she is in a good home, Sara is."

I smile through the tears. "I talked with him today."

"Who?"

Inside the room, I motion toward a chair by the window for Ben to sit on.

"Kevin. I didn't know his name, but we talked for a bit on the phone. I was trying to call Kat, a girl here that left me a phone number. I thought it was her number, but it turns out she left me Sara's number."

"And how did she know Sara's number?"

I look away. I haven't had time to think about that, but what occurs to me now is that Kat probably "borrowed" my chart, found the number, and left it for me before she got out of here. But did I really want to share that with Ben?

"I don't need to know," Ben answers, taking me off the hook. "But I think you should by the rules follow so you don't get marks taken off your chart. Do you want me to give Sara a message?"

New tears spring to my eyes. What could I have Ben say to her that would be enough? "Are you teaching her to read?" I ask.

Ben smiles. "I am, but all this time I am thinkink you both could not read, and then I learn how Anna can read! Why you hide this from everyone?"

I shrug. Some things are too hard to explain in such a short amount of time.

"How 'bout I tell Sara how smart and strong her sister is, and what beautiful poems she writes? How 'bout I tell her you have Sapphire, and also how much your sister you miss. Would that be good?"

I nod, sniffing loudly. Ben and I sit together and stare out the window at the birds in the dying maple. "How's Rachel?" I ask, swallowing hard.

"Rachel, she is fine. She misses you and talks about you all the time to the neighbor lady."

"Miss Thistleberry?"

"Yes, that one. I will tell Rachel I saw you and will see you next week. I will ask if they will let me call you, but if not, we can visit after your group meeting next time." He pauses, thinking, then asks, "Can I maybe give Sara your poem that she can learn to read with?"

I nod and hand him the "If" poem. If I had known he was seeing her, I could have written a poem all for her. But this will have to do.

When he leaves, every sound outside the window and even those in the room scream in my ears. The air coming from the vents, the hallway sounds, the cars, the TV down the hall. I grab a pillow, hold it over my face, pressing hard, and scream. The muffled cry joins all the other noises. I curl up on the bed and rock and rock and rock.

I want to go home. I want to be with my sister. Only I don't have a home. And my sister has a new one. Where does that leave me?

My answer comes quickly this time and sounds a lot like Bart talking in my thoughts: *Grow where you are planted.*

Some homes aren't actual places but are what you make of the place you're in.

My body is a home. It was a home for Tig, but she escaped. Bart says he thinks that she didn't escape but that I turned inside out and the real me broke through.

I never thought about The Inside Girl being me, but maybe she was. Maybe I was just trying to protect myself. Crazy, right? But maybe it's true.

I lie on my bed, trying to picture Sara in her new home. If they're going to adopt her, they'll probably change her last name. Will Ben tell them I have her number? Will the new family change their number so I won't be able to find her?

That night, in my thoughts, I have lots of people to thank and be hopeful for. I thank Kat for leaving me Sara's number. I hope her dad magically reappears in her life and that he's nice to her, like Ben is to me.

I hope Justin doesn't start any more fires, scaring people and keeping them away from him, and that he finds something else to be excited about that doesn't destroy things. Like maybe getting to know Danny better. I also hope Abby forgives me for being so mean to her all this time.

So many, many things to be hopeful for and about.

Hope is a thing with feathers.

Emily Dickinson was so right. She saw things other people couldn't see. Maybe that's what poetry is: a window to things that not everyone has seen before. Not clearly anyway.

Emily let me see through her window, and maybe her hope with wings is what led me to Sapphire. What if Sapphire has hidden wings, will someday grow a single horn, and is really a special kind of flying unicorn? Wouldn't that be something? A horse with angel wings.

I also smile at finally knowing what I can give Emily for all she has done to help me. It will take a bit of doing, but I will rewrite all my poems into a blank book and will write a special poem just for Miss Emily.

Now all I have to do is think of something for Bart. But what?

What if …

48

BUNNY SUE SEEMS HAPPY TO SEE US. "HOW'S LIFE BEEN treatin' ya, Anna?"

"Good enough," I answer, and she grins and then waves at Bart, who's heading back to his jeep.

"Good enough works," Bunny Sue agrees, leading me to where Sapphire is waiting. Today, she's in her stall, finishing up her hay.

"You want to try ridin' today?" Bunny Sue asks, and I nod vigorously. "Go ahead and put the lead on her and bring her out here. Remember not to stand behind her. I'll go get the saddle."

I reach up and put the lead around her mouth and up over her ears and click my tongue. Sapphire seems happy to see me too.

"How you been?" I whisper, and she perks her ears forward. "I get to ride you today, if that's okay by you."

She pulls on the lead and nods, making me laugh out loud.

"I got Sara's number," I whisper, and she looks at me out of her big blue eye with what I'm sure is complete surprise.

"I know. I'm surprised too. Kat got me her number." I don't even want to think about how she got it or the chances she took that could have cost her tokens and all her points. I suddenly flash on Bart talking about going to the clinic and seeing my chart there and giving it back to Miss Emily, and how Kat had been there too. That had to be when she got it. It just had to be.

Sapphire blows out of her mouth and makes her lips do that tremble thing. I laugh again, and she doesn't even pull back.

"Over here, Anna," Bunny Sue calls, and I lead Sapphire over to a platform that has steps on the side. After she secures the saddle onto Sapphire's back, she reaches for the lead and points me to the stairs.

"One day soon, you'll be saddling her up all by yourself. But for now, climb up to the platform and straddle the saddle."

"Straddle the saddle," I repeat, liking her words.

"This here's the horn," she says, reaching up and grabbing the knob on the front of the saddle. "You can hold onto it if she gets a bit frisky." She hands me the reins and adjusts the stirrups to fit the length of my legs.

"Look over the side so you can see her mouth."

I lean, being careful not to lean too far and fall off.

"See how the reins are nice and loosey-goosey around her lips?"

I nod.

"Pull back on them gently."

I do as she says and pull back on the reins, and Sapphire pulls her head back and takes a step back as well.

"See how that makes her pull back?"

"Yeah."

"Okay, now draw the reins to your right."

When I do, Sapphire turns and starts to walk to the right.

"Now to the left!" Bunny Sue calls out, and sure enough, Sapphire turns and starts walking to the left. "If you nudge her sides gently and click your tongue, keeping the reins straight, she'll go forward. Don't nudge too hard or she'll go into a trot or canter, or even a gallop. Let's keep it to a clip today, and we can build up to them other things. Deal?"

"Deal," I say, eager to ride.

"Okay then. Go on ahead and take her into the arena and circle it."

The thrill of being up high, walking around the arena with Sapphire, is something I've never felt before, and I lean forward and pat her neck.

"You're a good girl," I coo. She nods, making me laugh openly again.

I gently pull the reins to the left and turn her around to head back, where Bunny Sue is waiting with the brush bucket.

When we get to the platform, I slip off and climb down the stairs, eager to lead Sapphire to the brushes. Bunny Sue pats my back, telling me what a good job I've done, but really, I didn't do anything. Sapphire did all the work. Hooked on the fence rail by the bucket of carrots is a set of horseshoes I have not seen before.

Bunny Sue catches me eyeing them. "I had Sapphire reshod," she explains, "meaning I had a new set of horseshoes put on her and thought you might want one or two of her old ones here. They're good luck, or so people say."

"I'd love them!" I gasp, surprised at how heavy they are. "I now know just what I want to give Bart. I'll save one horseshoe for me and give him the other for good luck. We all need good luck!"

"What a thoughtful girl you are, Anna. I bet he'll love that. Hey, I have to go up to the ranch house to take a call on the house phone. Are you okay brushing her down?"

While she's talking, I grab a carrot from the carrot bucket and lay it on my hand for Sapphire to snack on—the carrot, not my hand this time.

"We're fine," I assure her, watching Bunny Sue test the lead to make sure it's properly tethered to the pole. "We'll be right here when you get back."

"I'll leave my cell in case you need to call me. Just push this button here to reach me."

I stare at the phone.

"What? You ain't never used a cell phone?" Now she's the one staring. She shifts her weight to a more relaxed stance. "That's okay. Everybody's got to start somewhere."

She shows me how to press the button to activate it. "Easy peasy, right?"

I nod, anxious for her to go to her call.

"See Lester back over there shoveling up manure?"

I follow where she is pointing and nod. Lester waves, and we both wave back. "He'll be over here in a minute to see how you're doing, but if you need help, just holler, and he'll be here lickety-split."

I nod and grin. I like being treated like an adult.

"Okay then, get to brushing! If you like, take her back to the corral after. Just remember to fasten the fence proper."

I nod, grinning. When she's gone, I look at Sapphire, who's looking at me. "You know what I'm thinking, don't you, girl?"

She nods, and I grin. My heart starts beating too fast to count.

I pet Sapphire's nose with my free hand, all the while gripping the phone. "Should I call her?"

Sapphire doesn't nod this time, and that makes me breathe a little harder. I want her to be with me on this. But she doesn't shake her head either. It's like she's trying to tell me that the decision is mine.

I look over at Lester, who's busy shoveling, and back at Sapphire. "Let's just do it," I say and press the button at the bottom of the phone. It lights up. I press the button picture that looks like a tic-tac-toe board, and the numbers one through nine and zero pop up.

Then I take a deep breath, hook my arm under Sapphire's neck, and hug her to me. She nuzzles my shoulder, calming my shaking hands.

Slowly and carefully, I punch in the number Kat left for me, which I memorized and said over and over to myself all these weeks.

The phone rings. I look wide-eyed at Sapphire, whose ears prick forward. She reaches out and nudges me, like she did that very first day we met.

The ringing stops, and there's a pause. Suddenly my stomach lurches, and I feel like I'm going to puke. Sapphire turns and breathes hot air on my cheek.

"Hello?" Sara's voice sounds strong. Confident. Just like Ben said she was.

"Hello?" she says again.

I look at Sapphire in panic, but she presses her head against my chest, urging me on. I can feel her hot breath now on my arm.

"Sara?" I can barely get her name out. The phone goes dead, and at first, I think I'm too late. Maybe she thinks no one's on the other end and hangs up, but then I hear short, quick breaths and know the connection's not dead. She's just crying.

"Anna?" Her voice is tight. "Is that really you?"

"It's me," I answer, burying my face in Sapphire's mane. She steps closer to me.

"How are you?" Her question opens a whole wave of emotions.

"Good enough," I answer, gently brushing Sapphire's back so I don't hurt her invisible wings.

"I just came home from seeing Ben!" Sara gushes. "I love your poem, Anna. It's crazy good!"

If only, I think, then close the thought. *Grow where you're planted,* Bart's voice booms inside my head. And even though I'm rooted to the dirt, standing beside the best horse in the world I could ever hope to have as a friend—just hearing her say she loves my poem lifts me up so high I can almost see what's possible.

"Can you talk?" Sara whispers anxiously.

"I can!" I answer openly, because not only do I have time to talk, but I have my voice back, and while I can't make him disappear, Terrible Ted and anyone like him will never *ever* take my voice away again.

As we talk, I lead Sapphire slowly back toward the corral, hugging her every few steps. Poet Emily flashes in my mind. She's right. Hope *is* a thing with feathers. But even more than that, if I shade my eyes from the bright sun, I can see Hope soaring higher than the highest clouds on broad, feathered wings.

CPSIA information can be obtained
at www.ICGtesting.com
Printed in the USA
BVHW040830060722
641427BV00006B/51